NANNY DISPUTE

A NANNY / SINGLE DAD ROMANTIC SUSPENSE

SHANDI BOYES

COPYRIGHT

Editing: Crossbones Editing

Editing: Courtney Umphress

Proofreading: Lindsi La Bar

Cover: SSB Covers and Design

Cover Image: Wander Aguiar

ALSO BY SHANDI BOYES

Denotes Standalone Books

Perception Series

Saving Noah *

Fighting Jacob *

Taming Nick *

Redeeming Slater *

Saving Emily

Wrapped Up with Rise Up

Enigma

Enigma

Unraveling an Enigma

Enigma The Mystery Unmasked

Enigma: The Final Chapter

Beneath The Secrets

Beneath The Sheets

Spy Thy Neighbor *

The Opposite Effect *

I Married a Mob Boss *

Second Shot *

The Way We Are

The Way We Were

Sugar and Spice *

Lady In Waiting

Man in Queue

Couple on Hold

Enigma: The Wedding

Silent Vigilante

Hushed Guardian

Quiet Protector

Enigma: An Isaac Retelling

Twisted Lies *

Bound Series

Chains

Links

Bound

Restrain

The Misfits *

Russian Mob Chronicles

Nikolai: A Mafia Prince Romance

Nikolai: Taking Back What's Mine

Nikolai: What's Left of Me

Nikolai: Mine to Protect

Asher: My Russian Revenge *

Nikolai: Through the Devil's Eyes

Trey *

The Italian Cartel

Dimitri

Roxanne

Reign

Mafia Ties (Novella)

Maddox

Demi

Ox

Rocco *

Clover *

Smith *

RomCom Standalones

Just Playin' *

Ain't Happenin' *

The Drop Zone *

Very Unlikely *

False Start *

Short Stories - Newsletter Downloads

Christmas Trio *

Falling For A Stranger *

One Night Only Series

Hotshot Boss *

Hotshot Neighbor *

The Bobrov Bratva Series

Wicked Intentions *

Sinful Intentions *

Devious Intentions *

Deadly Intentions *

Coming Soon

Nanny Dispute *

Protecting Nicole (November 23)

WANT TO STAY IN TOUCH?

Facebook: facebook.com/authorshandi

Instagram: instagram.com/authorshandi

Email: authorshandi@gmail.com

Reader's Group: bit.ly/ShandiBookBabes

Website: authorshandi.com

Newsletter: subscribepage.com/AuthorShandi

TikTok:https://www.tiktok.com/@authorshandiboyes

1

BRODIE

"Desk duty."

As I thump the steering wheel of my truck with my fist, Lucy's glistening eyes lift to mine. I grin at her before making out my angry bump is merely me grooving along to the latest pop group coming out of Ravenshoe.

My last assignment before eighteen months of rehab after being injured on the job gifted me more "cool creds" with my daughter than I am used to. It gave me direct access to the number one band in the country and saw Lucy looking at me with more value than most single fathers get.

When Lucy's attention returns to the Spotify app on my phone, I direct my focus back to Thane, my once brother-in-law and now regular sounding board. "Sixteen years I've given them, and they put me on f'ing desk duty. The movement of my arm is back to full capacity. There's not even a twinge of pain when I rotate it."

I grind through my lie while circling my left shoulder to back up my claim like Thane isn't on speakerphone. I got shot in the line of duty. My torso absorbed and disregarded the bullets like a pro, but an intern's bad patch-up of the exit wounds has been the biggest obstacle to my recovery.

Occasionally, I still get stuck removing my undershirt, and although rehab has drastically improved the range of movement in my upper body, I face issues any time I lift my left arm above my head.

I didn't tell the director that, yet I'm still scheduled for desk duty three weeks from Monday.

"I told you, man, all the money is in the private security sector now anyway." I *pfft* at Thane when he says, "I'm sure Million-Dollar Marcus would give you a position quicker than a backhanded clit slap."

I glare at the dashboard of my truck when Lucy asks, "What's a clit slap?"

With his maturity as low as his IQ, Thane starts to explain, "A clit slap is when Uncle Thane's girlfriends don't—"

"Is the name of Uncle Thane's new cat," I interrupt before he can scar my daughter more than losing her mother when she was only six months old.

For the first time in months, the shimmer in Lucy's eyes is from something more than sadness. "You got a cat?" She bounds out of her seat to get up close and personal with the speaker booming out her favorite uncle's voice. Their bond makes me feel like shit that I tried to block Caroline's family from having direct access to Lucy five years ago, but I was grieving and not in the right headspace to realize she is as much theirs as she is mine.

We all make mistakes.

Lucy takes Thane's wheezy laugh as confirmation he got a new pet. Thane is my late wife's youngest brother. He is twenty-five, lives the life of a bachelor even while shacked up at his parents' mega mansion, and is clueless on how an almost six-year-old's brain works.

He often puts me in a pickle.

Today isn't any different.

"Can we come pet it?" Lucy's eyes are on me, pleading and begging. "Please, Daddy. I want to see Uncle Thane's cat. I bet he's pretty and furry, and his breath smells like tuna! The last time I saw a cat was when Ms. Fiona brought hers for a visit. It didn't like me. It scratched my arm." After lifting the sleeve of her long-sleeved shirt to display the imaginary scratches, her nose screws up in disgust. "And it pooped in the garden. Well, not *in* the garden. On the footpath. You trod on it and walked poop throughout the house, and Ms. Fiona wouldn't clean it up. She said if you'd looked where you were walking, you would have seen the poop." With a sigh, she folds her arms over her chest and huffs. "She was bossy and mean and—"

"The reason we're getting a new nanny." My comment sours her mood in an instant.

We got lucky in the four years following the death of my wife, but with Ms. Mitchell moving to West Virginia to assist in the raising of her grandbabies, we've gone through more nanny placements than I have occupational therapists in the past six months.

I'd like to blame the "intolerable working conditions" on Lucy, but that would be as blatantly dishonest as saying my shoulder no longer hurts.

I'm not the most tolerable person in the world in general, but when I'm being weaned off the pain medication responsible for my ability to dress without sobbing like a baby and forced to face the possibility of a desk job for the remainder of my career, "intolerable ass" is a deserving title.

Ms. Mitchell didn't put up with my crap. She was stern and raised Lucy with values Caroline would be pleased about. We've been lost without her, and as much as the nanny placement officer assures us she can be replaced, she will forever be irreplaceable to Lucy because she doesn't want a nanny.

She wants a mother.

Ms. Mitchell was too old for the title, but her stories about her children and their occasional visits gave Lucy the family she craved. Her impressive baking skills stamped her place in my daughter's heart.

Lucy can be bought with chocolate chip cookies. I've used this knowledge to my advantage numerous times in the past month as we've sought a new in-house caregiver.

Since we depleted our local agency of unknowing victims, the agency extended its search horizon. They assure me Ms. Seabourn will be the perfect addition to the team. It hasn't been the best start, though. She was meant to arrive before my meeting this morning but missed her train.

Her new arrival time is 4 p.m.—which clicked over almost an hour ago.

"Shit." I apologize to Lucy for my potty mouth, toss her my wallet so she can remove my penalty for the swear jar in her room, then throw the gearstick into reverse so I can back out of our driveway instead of fully entering it.

"You forgot your new nanny again, didn't you?" Thane asks, barking out a humored laugh.

I wring the steering wheel. "My meeting ran over, and since I was frustrated with the result, I drove straight home."

As I dismount the curb, Lucy asks, "Who's that?"

When I follow the direction of her gaze, my throat dries. Long, lean legs, a sweltering midsection unhidden by low-riding cut-off jean shorts and a midriff top, with tits that belong on the glossy pages of the magazines I'm sure Thane still hides under his mattress.

My words are as hot as the blood roaring through my veins. "Jesus Christ, I've never seen such a fantastic pair of—"

"Swans!" Thane interrupts, snapping me out of the trance the stranger's body placed on me. "Such nice swans."

As Lucy flattens her face to the window to search for said swans, I yank out the cord responsible for my wife rolling in her grave. I never acted so disturbing while we dated, and I chased her for months before she agreed to go out with me.

"Killjoy," Thane mumbles when the dashcam stops broadcasting the image of a blonde galloping down the front three steps of my home. Like every Baywatch long-range beach shot, she is slow-moving and extremely bouncy.

When I return my truck to the driveway, the mystery blonde most likely selling Girl Scout cookies holds her hand up to shelter her flawless face from the low-hanging sun but doesn't creep further down the footpath.

I place my truck in park and switch off the engine. "Watch Lucy for me."

"It would be easier to babysit if you turned the dashcam back on." Thane almost has me over the fence until he adds, "I can keep one eye on Lucy and one on the blonde who'll keep me company for my next seven showers."

While grinding my back molars together, I remove my seat belt, crank open my door, then slip out of my truck. I don't brace my gun while approaching the stranger trespassing on private property. She barely weighs one twenty, so a weapon won't be needed to take her down, but I keep my tone stern to ensure she understands my dislike of unwanted visitors. "Can I help you?"

I hate myself even more for my initial response when her voice comes out as sweet and feminine as her unaged face. At a guess, I'd say she is late teens/early twenties, making me over seventeen years her senior. I should not have responded the way I did. It officially makes me a dirty old man.

"I think it is the other way around. I'm here to help you." She smiles at my confusion while meeting me halfway down the footpath. "I'm Henley." When she thrusts out her hand in offer, the curves peeking out from beneath her midriff top become impossible to ignore. Her body is on display for the world to see, but I should still not be looking, even more so when she finalizes her introduction. "Henley Seabourn."

I cock a brow. Surprise is all over my face. "Our new nanny?" When she nods, sending waves of glossy locks toppling down her shoulders, I shake my head. "Nope. No. This is *not* happening." Disgust morphs onto her face as I ask, "Are you even old enough to work in this state?"

"I'm twenty-two."

Great. She is as young as I expected.

"And have plenty of experience—"

"Not enough for this role," I interrupt, my tone curt. "I asked for a *mature* nanny."

I wave my hand at her stomach, which has nothing to do with her experience. It merely announces why we can't work together.

I've not had the urge to stare at anyone's midsection since Caroline passed, but I'm an eye strain away from retinal detachment with how much effort it takes to keep my eyes off Henley's stomach.

"*This* isn't what I asked for."

"Wow," Henley bites back, her smile not heralding the sternness of her expression. "Sexist *and* age discriminating." She doesn't give me a chance to respond. Her dressing down commences immediately. "The Age Discrimination in Employment Act of 1967 protects employees under forty"—my mouth gapes—"which I assume you're begrudgingly approaching even while hoping it will excuse your poor attitude"—she smiles at my narrowed glare before poking me in the chest—"from being discriminated against based on age. You have been through every nanny the agency has on file. I don't take crap from no one, so Nancy said we'd be the perfect fit." She flutters her lashes.

Although her sassy attitude dampens my worry that she can give as good as she gets, it won't stop me from saying, "Nancy is *way* off the mark."

I stop pulling my cell phone out of my pocket when Henley

announces, "And saved from your unjust tirade by a blissfully long weekend."

I cuss again when my eyes drink in the time on my phone screen. The agency closes at 5 p.m. It is five fifteen on the Friday of a holiday weekend.

"With that sorted, how about a re-introduction?" After waving her fingers at Lucy, who's watching our exchange curiously from the passenger seat of my truck, Henley holds out the same hand in offering. "Henley Seabourn, your *new* nanny."

This time, I accept her offer. "Brodie Davis, the *father* offering to comp you a hotel room for the weekend."

2

HENLEY

Good lord, it should be illegal for arrogant men to be so attractive. I'd never considered how Jax Teller would look in a pristine black suit until Brodie slipped out of the driver's seat of his big beastly truck. The sight hurts my eyes and makes me wonder if I have a daddy complex.

Brodie looks ten years my senior, if not a little older. The wrinkles in the corners of his eyes aren't from smiling too often, and the V etched between his dirty-blond brows appears older than me, but age brings its own qualities to a man's appeal.

Brodie's frown wouldn't look as attractive if worn by a younger face, nor would the slight sprinkling of gray hairs weaved throughout his manly bun. His age makes him as cultivated as the antique vase my grandmother never let me touch, and the "not allowed to touch" vibe beaming off him makes me want to bend the rules even more.

I've always dreamed of being a rule breaker.

My placement as Lucy's nanny gives me the opportunity to achieve that.

I grin when the creak of a door being opened ends our intense stare-down. I had no intention of losing, but the tension was reaching its boiling point.

"Can I come out now, Daddy?"

Not waiting for him to answer, Lucy jumps down from a truck that should emasculate its owner's mannish vibes but doesn't, before she sprints down the sidewalk I paced for almost an hour while waiting for my new family to arrive.

"Hello." She swivels on the spot as her teeth indent her plump bottom lip, and her big brown eyes scan my body as vigorously as her father's had. "You're pretty. I like your shirt. I have a shirt like that. We didn't get it from the shop." She cups her mouth with her hands like she's about to whisper, but her voice still comes out loud. "I cut it with scissors. Don't tell Ms. Mitchell. I'm not allowed to play with scissors."

As Lucy continues her story, Brodie announces, "She babbles when excited."

He sounds annoyed that his little bundle of joy is so welcoming. I love it. She demonstrates it'll take a lot of wit to get her father to fall in line, and I'm just the girl for the job.

After bobbing down to Lucy's level, I tuck a strand of her gorgeous yet wild hair behind her ear. "Scissors are okay on certain occasions, but what is one thing we should *never* do with them?"

Lucy's eyes bulge before her mighty voice rumbles through my chest. "Run with them."

"That's right. We should never run with scissors." I peer up at Brodie and grin. "But we're not carrying scissors now, are we? We can run all we like. So how about you yank up the cuffs of your jeans that survived their hacking better than mine and show me the fastest route to my room."

I don't think Lucy's eyes could pop any more. "You're my new nanny?"

"Uh-huh." My southern accent twangs my next five words. "Are you okay with that?"

Her squeal warms my heart. "Oh, yes, yes, yes!"

After looping our arms, she races us toward the front stairs of her home. Before I can trespass against the homeowner's wishes, she seals my fate as her nanny by charging back for her father.

My heart melts into a gooey puddle when she throws herself in Brodie's arms and smothers his hairy chin with kisses. "Thank you. Thank you. Thank you. I love her already!"

Brodie wants to deny her claim that I'm her latest toy. He tries to subdue her happiness in a manner any father would when their child becomes instantly besotted with a stranger, but the longer Lucy's praise fills his ears, the harder it is for him to steal her joy.

So instead of squashing her happiness, he peers at me over her golden locks and murmurs with a frown, "You're welcome."

"Oh my goodness, Lucy-Lou. This room is almost as precious as you."

Lucy grins at both my praise and the use of her nickname before trudging to her bed with her toy rabbit swishing the floorboards behind her. The past couple of hours have been as tiring on her as they have been on me. She gave me a tour of her home, which is modestly sized and well-decorated. We cooked chicken and rice for dinner, ate on the outdoor patio, bathed, then read one too many bedtime stories.

Every task was conducted under Brodie's watchful eye, so not only did I have to give the performance of my life as a doting nanny, but I also needed to ensure Lucy wasn't subjected to the tension teeming between her father and me.

Children, girls in particular, are less forgiving of their parents when there is an apparent rivalry with their friends. At such a young age, they don't understand that their parent is their biggest ally.

"Do you usually sleep with a night light?"

A smile graces my lips when Lucy shakes her head. "But can you leave the door open?"

"Of course." I help her to bed before tucking her in.

I step back from her half-wrapped cocoon when "That's my job" comes barreling from the hallway.

As Brodie enters Lucy's room, his manly swagger more noticeable in the tight confines, Lucy's eyes roll skyward. "When he's not working, but since he's returning soon, you should practice." Her lower lip drops into a pout. It is the first time it's hung so low in hours. "He won't be around much once he goes back to work."

Ouch. There's the guilt every working parent faces. I once gave my father hell about his hectic work schedule. I never got the chance to understand how unfair I was being.

Brodie takes Lucy's complaint on the chin with only the smallest rebuttal. "You know how important my job is, Lucy." His next set of words announces how closely he's been watching. "It's what allows you to sleep without a nightlight." He finishes getting her ready for bed before brushing back a lock that had fallen across her eye and kissing her forehead. "I love you."

"I love you too, Daddy," Lucy replies through a yawn, her earlier anguish forgotten.

I wait for her to wedge her hands under her cheek before I follow Brodie out. He leaves her door partially cracked open, saving me from announcing his child's wish, before he lifts his murky eyes to mine.

Lucy must have gotten her dark eyes from her mother, because Brodie's are light blue and utterly captivating. He is tall, muscular, and handsome, and something about his scent drives my insides wild.

My stomach hasn't stopped dancing all evening.

His hair is a little longer than you'd anticipate for an FBI agent, but its knotted appearance around his face gives him a youthful look he could pull off well into his forties. However, his frown is the sexiest thing about him.

I just wish it didn't directly follow every glance he tosses my way.

He doesn't want me here. I'm just skeptical if something I've already done awarded me his distrust or if it's something he's worried will occur in the future.

It could be a bit of both.

I've not exactly been honest with him.

Our stare-down is so intense I expect Brodie to say something far more profound than he does when he ends it by dropping his eyes to his feet. "Night."

I'm lost for a reply. Not only am I shocked by his nonchalant farewell, but it is also barely eight. If I go to bed now, I'll be wide awake by two in the morning.

When Brodie waits for me to reply before leaving, I stammer out, "Um... night?"

I cringe at the desperation in my voice before spinning on my heels and galloping down the stairs. Brodie has already cleaned the kitchen and filled the washing machine, so I gather my new cell phone from my suitcase and enter the living room with the hope of a good cable subscription service.

I'm not surprised when I discover a ton of messages from my best friend. She is the only person with this number, and the instant she was given it, she would have commenced blowing it up.

AMELIA:

What's he like?

Did he welcome you with open arms?

Is he open to visitors? I need to get out of town for a few days.

Beau was asking about you earlier. *gag* Do you want me to pass on a message?

I don't bother reading the messages following that. My reply to her question is too imperative for small talk.

> ME:
> Tell him we lost contact.

Considering the early hour, it's no surprise that an ellipsis trickles below my received message.

> AMELIA:
> I'd have a better chance of drilling off a massive chunk of the chip on his shoulder. Besties 4 life!

Her reply makes me laugh so hard that I snort.

Beau is my ex. He's arrogant and uptight and believes his shit doesn't stink. I've left him four times over the past two years. My returns weren't my choice, and this time, I've placed a ton of distance between us with the hope this break will be final.

I exhale a big breath when my phone vibrates with an incoming message.

> AMELIA:
> So... the new guy. Is he "daddy" material?

My fingers fly over my phone screen.

> ME:
> Don't make it weird. You know I'm here for his daughter, not him.

I flick on the television, pick at the varnish on my nails, and twirl my hair before I eventually give in and type the remainder of my reply within a shamefully short time.

ME:

But yes, he's seriously fucking hot.

I stab at the volume button with my thumb when the FaceTime ringtone bellows up the stairwell.

"Are you insane?" I say after connecting Amelia's call. "The volume was up full bore."

Springs of black curls bounce around the screen along with her smile. "You can't tell me he's 'seriously fucking hot' and not offer a sneak peek. You only swear when referencing guys who are gods. Beau only got a *damn*, and you had to bat women off him at every event you attended as his plus one."

A long breath eases out. "Thanks for the reminder."

She only takes in my eyeroll for half a second before asking, "What the hell are you wearing? Is that a Fluro pink bra under a see-through midriff top?"

"No." I tug down my shirt like it might suddenly gain three inches in length. "I didn't know how welcoming he'd be, so I tried what forever worked for Beau."

"You need to stop watching *Pretty Woman*." Amelia roars with laughter. "Not even deadbeat dads want their kids raised by a hooker."

"I didn't realize Lucy would get me over the line, so I tried to..." I stop talking, too embarrassed to continue.

Amelia will never let me off so easily. "So you..." When I remain quiet, she fills in the gaps. "Seduced him with your body?"

"It was pointless," I say with a huff, incapable of denying the truth. "He seemed more impressed when I called him out for age discrimination than my outfit."

"You didn't?" Amelia says, her mouth gaping.

I sit straighter, sighing. "I did. He was being an ass." Her laughter is infectious, but I try to play it cool. "Why are you laughing? We're always treated like idiots because we're not thirty." We gag at the same time. "But we probably have a higher IQ than the combined ages of the people judging us."

Finally she climbs over to my side of the fence. "This is true. Especially for you. Your brain is almost as big as that massive heart of yours." I could kiss her until she demands, "Now give me a look at the hunk you're hogging to yourself so I can hit the night scene early."

"You're going out tonight?" I ask, jealousy weighing heavily on my limbs.

Missing my forlorn look, she nods. "Mario and some guys want to check out a new band. They're playing at The Fort." After inspecting her lipstick and scrunching her curls, she shifts her eyes to me. "Give me a sneak peek, and I'll take you with me."

As much as I'm desperate to get to know Brodie better, I can't spy on him.

When I say that to Amelia, she replies, "Uh... yeah, you can. Just slowly meander past him while holding your phone out in front of you. Easy peasy."

"I'm not—" A grunt cuts me off. "Hold on. I think Lucy is awake."

I take the stairs two at a time, breaking up Amelia's reply so well I can't decipher it.

My lips twist when I spot Lucy in the middle of her bed, sound asleep.

Amelia's face fills the screen when a second grunt is loud enough for her to hear this time. "How short did you hack your jeans?" I'm lost on what she means until she asks, "Are they spank bank length?"

"Don't be absurd." Another grunt dampens the assurance in my tone. It is throaty and delicious and forces my knees to pull together.

"What direction are they coming from?" Amelia asks before demanding me to spin my camera around.

The frantic beat of my heart cuts through my reply. "From the bathroom. It's one of those two-way designs." I don't know why I'm whispering. "Should I make sure he's okay?"

"Uh... duh! Of course you should!"

"Shush," I plead, glaring at her gorgeous face even with the camera facing the portraits lining the hallway.

"I won't speak another peep." She locks her lips and throws away the imaginary key. "But I think you should hurry. He sounds like he needs help." My steps freeze when she gabbers, "You're still wearing jeans as underwear, right?"

"Amel—"

"I'm joking. Those aren't masturbating grunts." She couldn't lie straight in bed if her life depended on it, and when my silence calls her out on it, she demands, "Just go. If you're brave enough to walk in on Beau with his cousin's friends, you can do this."

Her reminder of my ex's cheating ways sees me marching into the bathroom without bothering to knock.

What I find isn't close to what I expected.

3

BRODIE

*T*he muscles in my shoulder lock even firmer when a singsong voice asks, "Do you need help?"

Since I never directed Ms. Mitchell to Walmart to pick up the undershirts I wear under my suits, I can't see a fucking thing. The rigid material stuck halfway up my back and over my head is the same color as Henley's shirt, but since it is ten times thicker, I have no clue if I am facing Henley with my junk hanging out, or the vanity sink.

I really hope it's the vanity sink.

While taking a mental note to remove my shirt before my pants from here on out, I reply, "No. I'm fine." Since I am frustrated, my next set of words is a mumble. "I just need to find the damn scissors."

When I recall Lucy's earlier confession, I cuss myself to hell. Earlier this week, she hacked the clothes I purchased for her with the scissors I keep in the bathroom drawer for incidences like this. Supposedly my selections made her look frumpy, so she fixed my mistake by halving the material of her outfits.

I lower the hand not stuck in my shirt to my crotch when Henley's accent echoes the deeper she comes into the bathroom. "It isn't a bother. It won't take a minute."

"I'm naked," I announce, like she hasn't reached that conclusion herself. The hem of my shirt is flapping at my nipples. There's no way she hasn't noticed I'm butt-fucking-naked. "And I need more than one hand for coverage, but my shoulder is locked. I can't move it."

She doesn't sound as sweet as her innocent face when she replies, "If it makes you feel any better, it isn't anything I haven't seen before."

It is inane that jealousy returns some color to my cheeks, so I keep my response to myself.

When Henley's breaths hit my back, I warn my cock to stay flaccid. I'd put away men for stunts like this before checking if their story was legitimate. And even then, I'd take my time running their credentials through the system.

I have a daughter, so it is my obligation to protect every female in my realm as if they are her, isn't it?

After a brief assessment, Henley asks, "Can you lower your arm at all?"

My chin-length hair slaps my cheeks when I shake my head. "The muscles spasm before locking up. It's called—"

"Upper limb spasticity." My shoulder flexes through a second set of spasms when Henley's fingertip glides over the bullet wound holes in the upper left quadrant of my back. "It is more common in stroke victims or people with diseases like multiple sclerosis and cerebral palsy, but these could also be the cause. When were you injured?"

"Eighteen months ago." Not wanting to have this conversation at all, much less while I'm naked, I once again attempt to remove my shirt. "I just need..." A painful spasm sending shockwaves down my spine stops me from shredding my shirt off my body. The pain is intense, and although I have a prescription that will take the edge off, I can't take it if I want to return to full duties. My veins must be free of narcotics, including painkillers.

"If you don't quit wiggling, you'll make it worse." I grunt in frustration at Henley's blasé response, but she acts ignorant. "I have to come around the front."

"No—"

Her reply snaps from her mouth as fast as my denial. "I'm not tall enough to pull your shirt over your head without increasing the pressure on your shoulder. You won't suffer additional pain if I use the vanity for leverage."

Everything she's saying makes sense, but I am as stubborn as a mule. "What if I bob down?" Certain things couldn't get more embarrassing, I grumble, "You'll be able to remove my shirt without having my junk thrust in your face."

"Okay." She hisses with me when the faintest dip rockets more pain through my body. "Slow down. We have all night. There's no need to rush."

Stay the fuck down, I mentally warn my cock before making sure it gets the message by squeezing my knees together, strangling it between my thighs.

Henley grunts and groans under the pressure of her pulls before asking, "Can I rip your shirt? The cuff is stuck on your bicep and isn't willing to leave for any amount of sweet talking." My embarrassment that I fell for the gimmick of the dad-bod craze isn't as noticeable when she whispers, "I understand its fascination."

"Yes. Do whatever you need. Just get it off me." My last five words correspond with the fracturing of stitches on my forty-dollar undershirt.

The price tag alone should have told me I was an idiot. I merely hated that none of my regular clothes fit me within a month of recovery. I know the reason. I ate out of boredom, then left my home gym the instant my shoulder started niggling, but it is easier to deny the truth than face it head on.

Tonight isn't giving me any other option, though.

I'm out of shape, which hopefully assures Henley that nothing happening right now is a ploy. I'm mortified that this is anyone's introduction to my body, much less someone with a body as tight and fit as hers.

Henley loosens the rigid material so well that she slips it up my neck before slowly easing it over my head. "We're almost there. Just your man bun to go."

I could laugh at her wittiness if I weren't so horrified.

"And... you're..."—another grunt—"free!"

I'm so relieved I jump up without considering how close Henley stands. I bump her chest with my still-locked shoulder, sending her flying backward.

Not thinking, I band my good arm around her back and tug her into me before she topples into the bathtub. "Whoa, careful."

The fringed edge of her jeans tickling the fine hairs splayed above my groin reminds me that I'm naked, not to mention Henley's quick inhalation of air when my dick brushes her thigh.

"Shit. Sorry."

"Don't let me go," she whispers on a plea when I try to back away. "I'm not exactly trusting of my legs right now."

As her cheeks redden to the color of beets, I re-firm my grip before drinking in the girly freckles on her face, hopeful they'll stop my body from reacting to her sweet honeysuckle scent. They're faint and dotted across the bridge of her nose and high on her cheekbones, adding to her roused coloring. Her almond-shaped eyes, her plump lips, and the perfect symmetry of her face reveal she will age well no matter her struggles. She is beautiful, but even if I were looking for something more, which I am not, she is far too young for me.

"I can't hold you much longer," I announce, hating the weakness the assault forced on me.

When Caroline and I first started dating, I could hold her against a wall and ravish her for hours.

Now I can barely hold my arm above my head for five minutes.

"Okay," Henley murmurs as her eyes bounce between mine. "Okay," she whispers again while slowly inching back.

Respectfully, she keeps her eyes on my face before she twists to face the door.

For the first time in ten minutes, I see the humor in the situation when she murmurs, "It's lucky I didn't take you up on your offer of a hotel room. You could have been stuck for hours."

Unease hiccups through my heartbeat when a girly squeal leaves the bathroom. Unlike earlier when my arm was stuck in the air and my pants were kicked too far across the room to contemplate yanking them on, this groan isn't filled with agony. Frustration, yes, but I doubt its owner is contemplating a lengthy stint in rehab to end a brutal cycle of pain.

If it weren't for the bottle of scotch Ms. Mitchell gifted me on her last day, the pain rocketing through my shoulder would have set my recovery back days.

Mercifully, alcohol is almost every agent's crutch, so I can use it as freely as I like—and the remembrance saw me guzzling half the bottle in under two hours.

I wasn't planning to get drunk, but when you're hiding in your room to save face, one nip soon turns into ten.

Fortunately, I don't lose my smarts when tipsy. Instead of racing into the bathroom to save Henley when she squeals for the second time, I press my ear to the door and ask, "Everything okay?"

Really, douche canoe? She's screamed twice. One more and your neighbors will call in backup.

It's happened before. More than once.

A reminder of the final time cuts through me like a knife.

After shaking my head to rid it of negative thoughts, I tilt nearer to the bathroom door and await Henley's reply. She delivers it two seconds later. "It's the water. It keeps going cold."

"The faucet is finicky. You need to turn it all the way to hot before slowly notching it back at a thirty-degree incline, but don't increase the pressure past half or it'll never warm up."

"What?" Henley asks, as confused as me. They don't stem from the same thing, but there is no doubt we're as confused as each other.

"The faucet. Only pull it out partway—"

"Can you show me? I'm decent... *for the most part.*"

My body's response to the last half of her sentence has me immediately shaking my head. I rarely have an issue keeping a rational mind, even when my veins are tainted with liquor, but something about this woman has me acting recklessly. The thoughts in my head this evening are insane. I've never experienced anything like this before, not even while courting Caroline, and the admittance of that makes matters worse.

I'm a thirty-seven-year-old widow. I should not be having the thoughts I am, especially when I am a father of a daughter. I can sure as hell tell you if a grown-ass man was sniffing around my barely legal daughter, I'd bury him where his remains would never be found.

When I realize Henley can't see my denial, I say, "Notch out the faucet to the halfway mark—"

My instructions are cut short when the bathroom door swings open and I stumble into the non-steamy space. It is as risqué as my deviant head imagined when the bathroom light flickered on. Henley is wearing a towel that leaves nothing to the imagination. Her hair is pulled up and off her neck, and the split in the material I starched to within an inch of its life while waiting for our latest recruit is dangerously close to gaping open when she juts out her hip and says, "By the time you talk me through the process, there'll be no hot water left." She steps to the side, tightens the scrap of material barely covering her plentiful chest, then waves her hand at the shower. "I learn better when shown instead of being told, so will you please teach me your ways, wise gentleman?"

Shut your mouth, fix the damn faucet, then leave.

"Pull it halfway out." I demonstrate what I mean on the tap. "Drag it all the way to hot." Henley watches me with her teeth digging into her plump bottom lip and her scent strong enough to announce her nipples are seconds from scratching my back. "Then slowly bring it back to cold on a thirty-degree incline until you find the right temperature."

A zap hits my balls when her murmured command flaps the locks around my ear. "Can you be a little gentler with your tugs, sir? I like my showers scorching *hot*." She's standing so close we're practically one, so there's no way for me to miss her big inhalation when she takes an unashamed whiff of my scent. As she exhales with a moan, she asks, "What brand is your aftershave? It smells good enough to eat."

There's something I want to feed you.

It isn't aftershave.

Needing distance before I say something stupid out loud, I ask, "Does this temperature work for you?"

Her breasts press against my good shoulder when she leans over me to check the water temperature. For someone preparing to shower, she smells fresh and innocent—unlike her throaty reply. "I think I can handle a little more."

She's twenty-two and your daughter's nanny. Get those thoughts out of your head.

After I adjust the faucet, she tests the water again, her erect nipples unmoving from my back. "More. I definitely need more."

For fuck's sake, Brodie. Leave now!

"More. Please. Just a little more."

You're a father! Fathers aren't meant to have thoughts like this.

"Perfect! There. That's great!"

I swear to God, if you don't leave this instant, anytime you attempt to strangle the sausage over the next month, I'll remind you how Mrs. Montebello's hairy top lip tickled your navel during your first assignment undercover.

No more words are needed.

I'm out.

"Thanks for your help, Brodie," Henley purrs with a giggle as I make a beeline for the door.

I throw my hand in the air to acknowledge I heard her, race into my room, and close the door behind me before working on forgetting that I have obligations in the morning that leave no room for a hangover.

I last two minutes in my room before it finally dawns that no amount of alcohol will have me forgetting that there is a beautiful naked woman only feet away from me.

It's been a long time since I've described someone as beautiful and naked back-to-back. It's been even longer than I've been dishonored with the widow title.

With my mood depleted, I snatch up the bottle, then gallop down the stairs to place much-needed distance between me and the house guest I'm adamant I still don't need.

Henley's hair is still wet when she finds me in the living room, aimlessly flicking through channels. Although her nightwear has around the same amount of material as the towel, it is far thinner and almost see-through. It clings to her body and exposes that she also isn't a fan of wearing undergarments under her nightwear.

There's nothing like the feeling of sleepwear brushing directly on your skin. It is erotic and sensual—on par with the visual of Henley's cotton nightie slinking past her nipples as she saunters into the living room to join me on the sofa.

"Hey." Her smile adds to her animated greeting. "I thought you had gone back to bed." After tucking her feet under her bottom, she angles her torso to face me. "I didn't wake you, did I?"

I wet my dry lips before replying. "No, I was awake."

"Doing?" When my brows furrow, her smile wanes. "Oh... So the tension during our first bathroom rodeo was one-sided? *Ouch.*" She sinks low into her seat before peering up at the television mounted on the wall. "Though I can't really complain. That was the biggest O I've experienced by myself. I usually need help."

What the fuck is she talking about?

Two seconds later, the truth smacks into me.

"You... Did..." *Either man the fuck up or leave.* "Do you often masturbate in strange environments?"

Not missing a beat, she replies, "You class your house a strange environment?"

"No, but you should. We're strangers."

She nonchalantly shrugs. "Strangers who have seen each other's junk—"

"I haven't seen your... *junk.*" Considering our conversation, my last word shouldn't have been delivered so weirdly.

I recoil as if she slapped me when Henley says, "Because you ran like a wimp." Her teeth make mine jealous when they munch on her lower lip. "I'm not a one-and-done girl. I still had plenty left in the gas tank." She rolls her eyes. "Though I could have sworn I charged my V the last time I used it."

"Your V?"

Her eyes shift from the television to me. "My vibrator." My cock instantly hardens when she asks, "Do you want to see it?" As her eyes rake my body, her tongue delves out to wet her lips. "I've heard this brand works just as well at relieving male tension as it does female." She stops her scan at my crotch. "You've just got to be open to some experimenting." She holds my gaze for almost thirty seconds before she bursts out laughing. "I'm joking, Brodie." She barges me with her shoulder. "I was hopeful a bit of banter would loosen you up a little. You seem a bit stiff."

I am. Just not where she thinks.

"And I thought it would make this a little less awkward."

When I follow the direction of her head nudge, I cuss. My channel surfing caught me in a massive barrel, leaving me no choice but to wipe out. I don't recognize either of the actors, but I hope they got a ton of money for this movie because their sex scene could only look more real if it were filmed on an adult entertainment industry set.

The two dark-haired actors are doing it on every surface of a yacht, and the close-ups have me reconsidering Caroline's assurance years ago that manscaping would soon go out of fashion.

Henley's laugh ripples through me when I switch off the television after a lengthy delay. "They won't win an Oscar anytime soon, but come on, you have to admit that scene was pretty hot." She twists to face me, her knee brushing my thigh. "I've never done it on a boat. I get crazy sea sickness, so more rocking and rolling would increase my chance of being sick, right?"

Assuming she is summarizing, I don't answer her.

I learn my mistake ten seconds later.

"You're not much of a talker, are you?"

The hair I've left down since I couldn't risk my arm getting stuck to pull it back swishes around my ears when I shake my head. "Why waste air for something of little sustenance?"

"Silent and brooding type. Got it."

I smirk but don't deny her claim. "And let me guess. You're the talkative, hyper type?" When she too cannot offer a rebuttal, I murmur, "Not exactly a compelling match."

"Says who?" I don't get the chance to fire off a syllable. "Robert Francis Winch, the professor recognized for the term 'opposites attract,' did multiple studies of spouses in the 1950s that showed it wasn't similarities that made a good match. It was complementarities. If you're unwilling to request the gravy you ordered with your dinner, you need someone who will ensure you won't just get the damn gravy you paid for, you'll get an extra serving of mashed potatoes as well."

"Been jibbed on gravy previously?"

She sighs and sinks low in her chair. "So many times." Her breasts hoist high when she folds her arms under them. "But I'm slowly learning to fight for what I want."

"And that is?"

She peers up at me, blinking and mute, until she finally whispers, "I thought it was to venture out of the South, but now I'm not so sure. The goalposts are adjusting faster than I can keep up."

When she scoots across the sofa, filling the minute gap between us, my brain screams at me to shut this down, but my feet refuse to move. My body doesn't want to get caught out by her any more than my brain, and at the moment, she has them both clutched by the throat.

"Can I?"

When I peer down to where she's looking, my heart rate kicks up a beat. With the night humid and my belief that I'd spend most of it in my room, I've forgone a shirt.

My dad bod is on display for the world to see.

Thank fuck Henley doesn't seem to mind. The need in her eyes grows the longer she stares at my tattooed pecs and full sleeve before she drops her gaze to the bullet wounds and shrapnel scars stretched from my shoulder to my stomach.

"I took a couple of remedial massage classes a few years back, and although your shoulder looks relatively unlocked compared to earlier, there is still a lot of tension in the surrounding muscles." Sparks zap through my body when she rubs her fingers over my serratus muscle, and my mind instantly goes to the gutter when she murmurs, "It is as hard as it looks."

Within a couple of rotations, my mind has no choice but to shift to controlling my groans of pain. Her massage hurts, but I can't remember a time when it hasn't. My muscles were patched back together. It's been one pain-filled day after the other ever since.

"What the fuck is that?" I ask when a crunching noise follows a handful of more rotations.

"That is just the beginning." Henley suggests for me to breathe out my nose before she moves my shoulder to a point that causes me to stiffen. "You need to trust me, or we will never get this knot out." The tension slackens when she murmurs, "And you're wearing pants this time, so what's the worst that could happen?"

I barely smirk when she uses my distraction to her advantage. A loud pop cracks from my shoulder before I let out a relieved sigh. "Now that's done, all the toxins clogged in there can make their way out." She grins at my shocked expression before inching back. "If you're unwilling to let it go in other means, sometimes you have to let others force you out of your comfort zones."

When her eyes drop to my crotch that displays how much I enjoyed having her hands on me, I yank over a pillow to cover the bulge. "That—"

"Is a perfectly natural response for a man as wound up as you." The hairs on my neck prickle to attention when she presses her lips to the shell of my ear. "So you should consider yourself lucky that I refuse to take advantage."

When my glassy eyes bounce between hers, confused, she nudges her head to the coffee table, which is housing an almost empty bottle of scotch.

Confident I understand her objective, she inches back, stands, then moseys toward the exit. I watch her stalk, my eyes only leaving her ass when she slings her head back and says, "If you have to go outside tonight, don't use the flashlight in the kitchen drawer. I wasn't lying when I said my V ran out of charge, and the flashlight batteries were the only ones I could find."

4

BRODIE

The following morning, as I enter the bathroom from my bedroom, hungover and with a dry mouth, I catch sight of my reflection in the vanity mirror. I grimace at the dark circles rimming my eyes before groaning about the flab circling my midsection.

Not that long ago, the only things I hated about my body were the nicks and scars I'd gathered during my years at the bureau. Dexter made my internal wounds visible for the world to see, and they're more hideous than any scar I own. He reminded me that I am a mere man and that my daughter would become an orphan if I didn't harness my wish for revenge.

Although the past eighteen months have taught me to slow down and smell the flowers, I still have a long way to go. There are perps to be caught and mass murderers to be taken down. I just need to balance parenthood with my wish to eradicate the world of scum.

After scrubbing the roadkill smell from my teeth and tongue and putting on the aftershave Lucy is adamant I wear even with a razor not touching my face in over six years, I tug open the top drawer of my bathroom cabinet. My heart beats out a funky tune when I take in the orange canister hidden at the back, but before I'm tempted to reach for it to silence my thudding skull, a sliver of silver steals my attention.

The scissors I sought last night have been returned to the drawer, and a shirt oddly similar to the one partly responsible for my hungover state is folded and resting on the vanity above it. It is one of those dad-bod-fit shirts, but it appears a little looser around the arms and midsection.

The one Henley helped me escape last night was meant to hug the favorable parts of my body while hiding less desirable assets.

I didn't get close to what I paid for.

Once I slam the drawer shut, I toss my leftover dad-bod shirts into the donation box filled with clothing I've yet to work up the courage to donate before pulling on the more generously fitted shirt from the bathroom. It is as soft as a cloud and the perfect fit.

"Lucy-Lou," I call out, walking down the hall with a newfound spring in my step.

Who knew a soft cotton shirt could make such a difference?

It's not the shirt that has you skipping like a schoolgirl, dipshit.

Ignoring my accurate inner monologue, I push open Lucy's door. She often sleeps in late, even during school holidays, so my unexpected sleep-in shouldn't have altered her schedule too much.

"Wakey wakey..." My words trail off when I find her bed empty and made and her pajamas folded on the top of her drawers.

"Lucy," I call out louder this time. I have no reason to freak out. I've not stumbled onto one case where the perp folded a victim's clothes before kidnapping them, but old habits die hard. The first and only time we played hide-and-seek was almost five and a half years ago. "Where are you?"

Henley's head pops out from the bottom of the stairs, her smile growing the longer she takes in my shirt. Once she's had her fill, she says, "She's down here with me." I slow my trudge down the stairs so she can appreciate the relaxed fit of my shirt while also giving me time to drink in the one she's wearing as if it is a dress, but she halts my inspection of her sweltering thighs by announcing, "But you're banned from the kitchen." Before I can utter a syllable, she clarifies. "We have a very delicate operation occurring, and a certain someone doesn't want the mess decreasing the deliciousness of her creation."

I groan when the truth smacks into me. Henley's shirt slash dress was a decoy. Even with Ms. Mitchell cooking at least twice a day in the years she lived with us, she only let Lucy cook with her once. That's how much of a messy "creator" she is.

After smirking at how well flour blends with Henley's light-colored hair, I ask, "Is the dining room safe?"

"The dining room is perfectly A-okay." My earlier grimace jumps onto her face. "But I'm not sure how long that will last. Lucy's creations are... all-encompassing."

Laughing, I head to the dining room before remembering I owe her my gratitude for her assistance and massage last night. This morning was the first time I hadn't woken up in sweats from lying on a bum shoulder throughout the night.

When I spin around, Henley snaps her eyes away from my denim-covered ass. Even though I shouldn't, I sigh in relief that the interest isn't blatantly one-sided. There's less chance of me getting sued if she instigates our exchanges instead of dodging them.

Upon spotting my smile, Henley drags her teeth over the lips I dreamed about last night. "Unlike last night's numerous attempts to make you squirm, that wasn't what it looked like." She is the worst liar I've ever met. "I was looking at your ass, but purely from a designer's perspective."

She's lost me, but I remember my objectives before her gorgeous face and barely covered body can turn my brain to mush. "Talking about last night, I forgot to thank you for your help."

She brushes off my praise with a wave of her flour-covered hand.

"No thanks needed. It was my pleasure." She swallows when she realizes what she said before locking her rapidly dilating eyes with mine. "Not like that. I... ah..." She pauses for several painfully long seconds before she twists her lips. "I can't dig myself out of that hole, so I'm just going to say if you don't want to go broke, you should consider purchasing rechargeable batteries." She hits me with a frisky wink before breezing through the swinging kitchen door like there isn't enough room for both her and the hundreds of images bombarding my head. "Oh, and I'm glad you like the shirt I made you enough to wear it."

Shock echoes when I ask, "You made my shirt?"

Her head returns to the hallway, but her body remains in the kitchen. "Uh-huh. After that short skit in the living room"—*why does my mind go to her massage instead of the twenty-minute yacht-fucking scene we watched?*—"I had a heap of adrenaline to disperse but only a handful of materials and a steady hand to get the job done."

Trying in vain to keep my mind out of the gutter, I ask, "You hand-stitched me a shirt?"

Henley takes a moment to register if my high tone is shock or disappointment before bobbing her head. "Looks like the measurements I took were spot on." A faint grin furls her lips at one side. "I usually break out the trusty tape measure to ensure the perfect fit." Again, she drags her eyes down my frame before biting her lower lip. "I need to give my new method more thought. It could gain me a heap of new customers."

Before I can fake that I'm not jealous, a smoke cloud billows out of the kitchen. "Should I—?"

"No!" Lucy and Henley shout at the same time.

A grin tugs at my lips when Lucy's head pops out of the kitchen several inches lower than Henley's. "We got this, Daddy, so please take a seat, and someone will serve you shortly."

When Henley giggles at the cute impersonation of her southern twang, Lucy snaps her eyes, which are crinkled in the corners, to her. "Sorry," Henley caves, her apology not authentic. "It won't happen again, boss."

Quicker than her scowl can turn into a smile, Henley scoops Lucy into her arms, tickles her belly, and disappears into the smoke-filled kitchen.

I'd follow them with a fire extinguisher if the texture and taste of the cloud didn't register as familiar. A dangerous inferno isn't destroying my kitchen. It is the wholesale bags of flour Ms. Mitchell left in the butler's pantry in case our new nanny had a hankering for baking.

Henley is the first to accept her challenge, but I wouldn't say she's winning.

5

BRODIE

The whoosh of an email landing in my inbox piques my interest, but only as long as it takes to spot the out-of-office automated reply Nancy's server issues when she's out of town. It announces what Henley broadcasted yesterday. The agency I've used since Lucy was six months is closed until Tuesday morning, and Nancy, the lead nanny recruitment officer, is uncontactable even longer than that.

She is on a two-week hiatus to visit her family in Sweden, and although her team could assist in fixing her error when they reopen on Tuesday, I'm not sure I will survive the wait.

It is only three days away, but those three days may very well kill me.

I'm thirty-fucking-seven, but the maturity that should come with digits that high didn't free me from spending most of the night having inappropriate thoughts about my twenty-two-year-old employee.

Even once the jumping sheep succeeded in their plan to have me nodding off, Henley invaded my dreams. Her fresh smell before showering. Her wonky smile when she's riling me. *Those fucking shorts.*

They played through my head on repeat all night, making me the most restless and horniest I've ever been.

Fuck! I am officially one of the creeps I regularly lock away.

This is why I veer for older, more mature nannies. *If she hasn't celebrated her sixtieth birthday, I don't want her* is the motto I've lived by the past five plus years.

A motto I remind Nancy of when I email her while waiting for Lucy and Henley to find the detonation button in the kitchen. I keep my correspondence professional. Fuck only enters the equation once, and it is more in response to how my responsibility as a father only extends to not fucking up my daughter's life. My moral compass doesn't swing to a stranger's offspring.

She's young.

I sign off with.

Too damn young.

As I click the send button, Lucy and Henley enter the dining room from the other end. Their cheeks are dusted with flour, jam is smeared across Lucy's lips, and her teeth are stained with chocolate syrup, but they're in one piece.

I can't say the same for the pancakes balanced in their hands. It looks like mixing the ingredients was an afterthought. They are gooey and floury—an odd combination for a cooked product.

"That isn't sherbet," Henley warns while placing a large stack of pancakes in front of me. "I would suggest eating from the outside in."

"Do you like your surprise breakfast, Daddy?" Lucy asks, stealing my focus from the humored twinkle in Henley's eyes. "I know you like *big* pancakes, so I added extra ingredients for you." She stumbles over "ingredients." She finds large words like that hard.

While ruffling her hair, I ask, "In the middle of the batter after Henley scooped it on the skillet?"

Henley's eyes sparkle with laughter at my questioning tone, but all Lucy hears is pride.

She nods before leaning across the table to hand me the syrup. "You go first. It's your special treat."

"Thank you. That's very polite of you."

I was wrong when I said Henley's stay might kill me.

Death by pancakes will be the only slogan written on my headstone.

―――――――――

"Thanks for the tip of eating the pancakes from the outside in."

Henley grunts out a laugh at my grumbled praise before scraping the clumps of unmixed batter into the bin and placing my plate in the dishwasher. "She can't cook to save her life, but she's so precious. How could anyone ever get mad at that face?"

"You say that now, but ask me after you've finished bringing up breakfast for three hours straight."

She chuckles again but doesn't refute my claim we could get food poisoning from Lucy's breakfast surprise. Eating uncooked eggs is rarely recommended.

While Lucy draws in the dining room, Henley and I move around the kitchen with ease, cleaning up the mess stretched from one counter to the next. I've done the same multiple times with Ms. Mitchell's replacements, particularly on Sundays when they were meant to have the day off, but it feels different today. Henley's presence still demands the space, but it isn't suffocating this time around. We work together as a team instead of opponents at opposite ends of the court.

Henley peers up at me with her big blue eyes blinking when I ask,

"Is this something you've always wanted to do?"

"Ah... not exactly." Her honesty is refreshing. "It was more expected because of who my father was."

Noting she said "was," I try to be empathetic with my next question. "Your father was also a nanny?"

She screws up her face before barking out with a laugh, "What?" As quickly as her humor arrived, it vanishes. "No. He was... ah..." She switches the direction of our conversation. "Wiping smelly bottoms isn't what I envisioned while studying fashion." An expression I can't quite work out crosses her face. "I was patenting my own unique flare and getting rave reviews across the industry, but then life happened, and I had to give it up." She locks eyes with me. There's only the slightest bit of shimmer to them when she confesses, "You settle for pretty much anything when bills start piling up."

Mindful not everyone is raised with a silver spoon in their mouth like Caroline was, I ask, "Have you ever considered finishing your studies?"

Locks of snow-white hair swish past her cheeks when she shakes her head. "It's not an option for me right now, but I never say never."

I cough out a laugh. It is as foreign to me as having a conversation with anyone and it not being about work or Lucy. "I once lived by that motto."

After playfully bumping me with her hip, Henley asks, "Not anymore?"

"Huh?" I ask, praying she isn't offering me more pancakes.

With the island clean, she shifts her focus to the counters surrounding it. "Never say never. Why was that 'once' your motto?"

I take a moment to ponder before hitting her with the honesty she deserves. After last night's antics, she could have made brunch awkward, but I felt more at home in my home than I have in years. "Lucy. She put a new perspective on everything."

When Henley peers at me with more affection than I'm used to, I slant my head and glare at a greasy blob running down one of the overhead cabinets. "Is that what I think it is?"

She grimaces before switching her rumpled expression to a smile. "I was teaching Lucy how to juggle." I grin when she looks at me apologetically. "I learned quick smart that one egg is her limit." After soaking a washcloth, she slowly saunters to the other side of the kitchen, her hips swinging. "With how expensive eggs are, should I be hopeful or worried you bring your handcuffs home?"

She hits me with a flirty wink before balancing on her tippy-toes to mop up the mess.

Even extended to her full height, which I'd guess to be around five eight, she still can't reach the blob of egg yolk splattered on the glossy wood, so it is only fitting that I step forward to help her.

"Here, let me."

I blame the lack of sleep and my hangover for my stupidity. I don't wait for Henley to move out of the way. I lean over her, and since the island hogs most of the space Caroline's mother had refitted not long after I moved in, barely an inch of air floats between us when I crowd her into the overhead cabinets with my body.

"Definitely hopeful," she murmurs when the front of my shorts brushes the skin high on her bare thighs.

I inwardly cuss when she flattens her feet to the floor. She barely drops an inch, but the slightest movement sees her ass grinding against my crotch—my rapidly extending crotch.

She smells good. Too fucking good, and it takes everything I have not to lean in for a big whiff like she did in the bathroom last night.

Fortunately for me, I don't need to move to learn her shampoo is scented. Within a second of her ass pressing against my crotch, Henley braces her head on my chest and cranes her neck to look at me.

When I see the need in her eyes, I tell myself to walk away, to place distance between us now, but instead of doing what is morally right, I cage her to the counter by placing my hands on the cabinets beside her head and leaning in deeper.

I wondered for hours last night how easily her tight, compact body would fit mine. Now I know without a doubt that it's a perfect fit.

You'd swear she was made for me.

Step back, asshole. Shut down this insanity.

My dick is as hard as a rock, and the endorphins thickening my veins are potent enough to disintegrate my smarts. Nothing but learning the taste of Henley's lip gloss is on my mind, so my feet won't budge no matter how loudly my morals yell.

I can't kiss her. She's too young for me and way too fucking sweet. I just don't have the willpower to pull away from her, so I try to force her to do it.

"Tell me to walk."

Recently shampooed hair wafts into my nostrils when Henley shakes her head, denying my suggestion without words.

When I remain quiet, still battling with myself, she spins to face me. Her twirl has my cock fighting to burst through my zipper, and I feel my cheeks heating. It's been a long time since I was this close to a woman, and the last time she was this beautiful, I was standing across from my wife.

The reminder sees me taking a step back. I only manage one because before I can force additional space between us, Henley hooks her finger into a belt loop of my shorts, leaps onto the counter, then tugs me forward until her thighs have no choice but to part so I can fit between them.

"You're not drunk now, so neither of us has to walk."

Once she's confident the heat between her legs has me determined to stay, she slides her hand up and over my chest before curling it around my prickly jaw.

Just one taste, I convince myself. *Then it'll be out of your system.*

Though I'm certain you'll make a fool of yourself.

How long has it been again?

"I can't."

I step back again, confident this can't happen. I haven't touched a woman since my wife died, but that isn't the sole cause of my apprehension. There are many more excuses, and almost every one involves Lucy.

"We—"

Lips as soft and sugary as marshmallows halt my reply a second before they part to invite my tongue between them.

My mind is overloaded by her smell, her taste, and the little moans that erupt from her throat when I drag my tongue along the roof of her mouth. It is a needy, desperate kiss. A kiss I've never experienced before. It is urgent and hurried and arrives with a ton of grinding that has me on the verge of making a mess in my pants.

This is the first non-solo expedition I've participated in over the past five years. A mishap is bound to occur. Fortunately, Henley tastes sweeter than the syrup on our pancakes, but my roguish palate has me craving so much more.

Rushing to the finish line is the last thing on my mind.

Banding one arm around her back, I tug her ass off the counter before the other drops to the base of her neck. I hold her mouth hostage to mine while she explores my body. Her hand slips under my shirt to tickle the hairs once spread across rock-hard abs as her tongue dances with mine.

Like last night, she doesn't seem bothered by my dad bod. Her musky scent strengthens the longer her briefest touches scorch my skin, and I'm eager to learn how heady it can be.

Henley thrusts her head back with a grunt when I lower my lips to her neck. I nibble on the skin dotted with flour and sweat while palming her breast through her shirt.

The heat of her pussy as she rubs herself against my cock has me the firmest I've ever been. Pre-cum leaks from the head like water from a tap, and the thin material of my shorts is doing a terrible job hiding the stain.

I'm spiraling out of control but defenseless to stop it.

This train is only ending one way.

With me balls-deep inside her.

Henley's hand freezes partway into my shorts when the creak of the kitchen door swinging open reminds me that we're not alone. This isn't the bachelor pad I purchased my first year out of college. It is my family home. *My daughter's home.*

"Daddy, I don't feel good."

We rip apart so fast Henley's head smacks into the kitchen cabinet while my ass almost takes out the island. Although we're panting and out of breath, Lucy doesn't pay our odd response any attention. She slowly enters the kitchen, the woes of her stomach more vital than her wish to learn her father isn't a respectable man.

"I don't think my tummy is happy about the pancakes. It's rumbling like a tiger with a splinter in his foot."

"That's not good, honey," Henley replies, jumping into action so I'm not forced to interact with my daughter with pre-cum-stained shorts.

After pushing off the kitchen cabinets, she scoops Lucy into her arms and makes a beeline for the door still swinging in the aftermath of Lucy's push.

"Do you think a soak in the tub will make it better?"

Lucy barely nods before they break through the kitchen door, leaving me to clean up more of a mess than there was to begin with.

6

HENLEY

"*H*ave you had her tested for gluten intolerance?"

Brodie pulls Lucy's door almost all the way closed before shaking his head. "It isn't something I thought I'd need to look in to. She eats a wide variety of food."

"It's probably more a gluttonous stomach than a food intolerance, but it wouldn't hurt to get her checked. I can make an appointment with a pediatrician if you'd like?"

Lucy recovered quickly after her upset stomach this morning, but she went downhill for the second time today after we had pasta for dinner. It could be because her stomach can't stop flipping with excitement like mine has been since the thrilling kiss I shared with her father, but I'd rather be safe than sorry. Food intolerances shouldn't be messed with.

"There's no need. I have contacts." We haven't been alone since our kiss, so I'm delighted when Brodie nudges his head to the stairwell and asks, "Do you have a minute to talk?"

"Yes!"

Calm down, Henley. You're meant to be playing hard to get since you practically threw yourself at him like a desperate harlot in the kitchen.

Brodie smirks at my girlie squawk before gesturing for me to lead the way. Our brief trek to the living room veers us past the kitchen. I can't help but smile while recalling the way Brodie pinned me to the cabinets without a snippet of pain crossing his face. His bad arm wasn't above his head—it was too busy groping my ass to creep higher than my neck—but I don't think even a three-hour-long marathon would have seen him bowing out because of an injury.

Only one thing derailed my campaign to seduce him, and she's currently snuggled into her pillow, fast asleep.

I'm wet just at the thought of how many "alone" hours Brodie and I now have.

He let slip yesterday that Lucy loves to sleep in, so I scheduled our craft and dressmaking classes for after brunch so she has no excuse to wake early.

My nipples pucker when Brodie scratches his beard. Recalling his taste and how his prickles tickled my collarbone when he ravished my neck has me fighting not to fidget. I've never experienced a kiss as mind-hazing as the one we shared in the kitchen. It sparked more tingles than all of Beau's kisses combined.

Brodie ravished me.

Consumed me.

Made me an instant addict.

I am desperate for a second helping.

Regretfully, Brodie has other ideas. After gesturing for me to sit on the armchair across from the two-seater sofa I'd hoped we would play tonsil hockey on, he blurts out the last words I want to hear. "What occurred this morning can't happen again."

His obvious internal conflict makes the sting of his rejection not as hurtful, but it won't stop me from asking, "Can I ask why?"

"Because you're too young—"

"I'm twenty-two."

He continues talking as if I never interrupted him. "And my daughter's nanny."

I have a rebuttal for that, but not one I can give him, so I go on the defensive instead. "Are you saying our kiss was a mistake?"

The veins in my neck stop threatening to burst when he shakes his head. "No. But it can't happen again. I'm thirty-fucking-seven."

"So?"

He stares at me as if I am insane.

"I'm an adult, Brodie. So if I want to fuck a thirty-seven-year-old man, I can fuck a thirty-seven-year-old man."

His groan rumbles through my chest. "We're not fucking. How did this go from kissing to fucking? That wasn't even on the table. It will *never* be on the table."

Ouch!

"Okay," I murmur, too hurt to continue our conversation. "Thank you for letting me know that will *never* be on the table."

His hand shoots out to grip my elbow when I attempt to skirt past him. He doesn't look at me, but I can hear the strain in his voice when he says, "I'm trying to protect you."

"From what?"

My eyes bounce between his as I wait for an answer.

If I were holding my breath, I would have collapsed by now.

"Henley..." Brodie groans again when I yank out of his hold and storm for the stairs.

"It's fine. I'm fine. It was just a stupid kiss."

I replay that kiss on repeat as I lie in my room for hours on end. I haven't been to bed this early since I was a kid, and since I'd risk my ego being beaten to within an inch of recognition for the second time tonight if I were to collect my phone from the kitchen counter, time is passing at a snail's pace.

Ugh! I can't believe I was so stupid to think it was something more.

I thought my numerous decisions yesterday made me bold and risky.

It all feels like a lie now.

With my mind a little clearer than it was hours ago, I crack open my bedroom door and enter the hallway. The house is quiet, eerily so.

After checking on Lucy, I head for the bathroom. A glass of wine, my Kindle, and millions of bubbles are calling me. I'll give myself thirty minutes to recoup, and then it is back to business.

I came here with a purpose, and I can't let anything get in the way of that.

Once I have a glass of red in my hand, my hair pulled up off my neck, and my Kindle resting on a stool next to the bath, I tiptoe to the door that enters the master suite.

The curtains are closed and the lamps are off, so I can't tell if the lump in the middle of the bed is Brodie or the laundry basket he removed from my grasp before I could fold the clothes while waiting for the pasta to cook. He explicitly stated that I am his child's nanny, not a housemaid, so laundering his clothes isn't my responsibility.

At the time, I thought he was chivalrous, but now I wonder if he was putting barriers up because he realized we would be alone for hours once Lucy went to bed.

"Stubborn man," I murmur before closing his door and fixing the lock in place.

Once I've closed the main door enough to offer privacy but with a gap that allows me to hear Lucy no matter how thick the walls are between us, I fill the tub, undress, then slip into the heavenly warm water.

In an instant, the tension in my shoulders relaxes, and my thumping head gets a moment of reprieve.

I'd pay a million dollars for a device that keeps the tub water piping hot. I'd never leave if I weren't forced out when the water turns cold.

I've just finalized my third refill when the main entrance door bursts open and Brodie enters. When he fails to notice me straight-away, I sink below the bubbleless water before following his trek across the room.

His white sleeveless undershirt is drenched with sweat that adds a pungent, manly aroma to the air, and his sweaty hair can't hide the cause of his ignorance. He's wearing EarPods, so he fails to hear my quick inhalation when he pulls open the shower door and cranks on the water full blast with only the slightest bit of fiddling.

It took almost ten minutes to get the water right last night, but I'll only ever need cold showers from here on out when Brodie peels off his shirt with only the slightest grimace of pain before he tackles his running shorts.

I shouldn't look when he bends down to gather his clothes and dump them into the laundry basket, but tell me one girl who wouldn't? He not only has a body that makes my pussy have its own pulse, but he also knows how to put his dirty clothes in the basket.

I couldn't be hornier if I tried.

"For the love of god," I murmur to myself when he steps into the shower.

He has so much length, even when I view his package through the gap of his stride, its impressive size can't be missed. But I barely get the chance to peruse everything he has on offer. A second after he enters the shower stall, he steps back out while grumbling a curse word under his breath.

His cock swings like a pendulum on an antique clock when he tugs his EarPods out and dumps them onto the vanity. As he spins back to face the shower, his eyes lift to admire the visual thickening my tongue.

He startles when he realizes he isn't alone, but anger isn't the first expression to cross his face.

Need is.

The bubbles dissolved over thirty minutes ago, so bar the flutters of the water as it ripples over my rapidly rising and falling chest, I don't have a single ounce of coverage.

Good.

My nakedness exposes Brodie lied when he said the prospect of us fucking was never a possibility.

His cock can't share the same lies as his mouth, and I am slowly learning that I'm not a girl who needs to shy away from controversy.

7

BRODIE

My muscles are aching after a five-mile run. I'm exhausted and on the brink of collapse, but not a single ache I've endured the past eighteen months comes close to the throb that thuds through my cock when my eyes land on Henley naked in the tub.

I knew from our kiss that her body was tight and compact. I tasted the deliciousness of her skin, but the visual is beyond what I could have comprehended, and it greatens when she braces her foot on the edge of the tub and slowly cranes open her thighs.

My first instinct should be to bark out an apology before leaving the bathroom as quickly as I entered it, but the instant her eyes drop to my cock and she licks her lips like she's imagining tasting the droplet of pre-cum beaded at the top, I know I'm not going anywhere.

She's using my body for inspiration as I did hers while pounding the pavement with my feet. I hadn't been on a run in years, but it was the only defense I had at my disposal to stop me from sprinting to her room and telling her I lied when I said the possibility of us hooking up was never on the table.

If Lucy hadn't interrupted us this morning, I doubt anything could have stopped us.

"Jesus fucking Christ," I murmur under my breath when Henley slides her hand from her midsection to the delicate lines between her legs.

As she strokes her pussy, water splashes her collarbone and her breasts that sit perkily on her chest despite her odd angle, before it careens down the smooth planes of her stomach to join her hand at the apex of her thighs.

When her index finger rolls over her clit and the faint ripple of her moan fills my ears, my body clenches like it is seconds from orgasm. I'm hard and fighting like hell not to wrap my hand around my cock while imagining it is my finger slowly sinking inside her.

Her breathing comes out harder and faster as she finger fucks herself with controlled movements. She doesn't race for the finish line. Her pace is as steady and audacious as the lusty stare she hits me with before toying with her clit with her thumb.

Everything tightens when she murmurs, "This could have been your tongue."

I can't fight the urge a second longer when I imagine her widening the span of her legs and inviting me to devour her sweet pussy. I fist the head of my cock before dragging my hand to the base. I strangle it as well as Henley's presence strangles my self-control.

My hand refuses to unclench its brutal clutch when Henley hardens me further by pinching her nipples with her free hand. She rolls the peaked buds between her index and thumb until they're as stiff as my cock and begging for attention.

A droplet of pre-cum rolls over my knuckles when she whispers, "And this could have been your teeth."

My skin hums and my body tightens when she swivels her clit so firmly she has to fight her eyes to remain open. "God... just the thought of your big fat cock inside me has me on the brink of release."

"Show me."

Those words weren't meant to leave my mouth. They should be buried deep down in the crevice where my morals seem to have slipped. But I'm glad I couldn't hold them back when Henley accepts my challenge.

She struggles to breathe as she rotates her clit with her thumb. My breath catches as she thrusts her head back with a throaty moan. Her arched back forces her breasts above the water. They bounce in the shakes of her pleasure, tortuously teasing me as I imagine my lips circling the taut, puckered buds.

I almost lose all sense of control when she looks up at me before giving in to an orgasm so intense, she can't breathe, speak, or think.

Her climax blindsides her. It floods her cheeks with heat while forcing the air from her lungs with frantic, needy moans. But it doesn't keep her down for long.

With the gracefulness of a ballerina, she rises from the bath. Not even my firm grip on my cock can weaken its throbs when my eyes follow the bath water's weave down her unblemished skin. The dreaded lighting in the bathroom fails to point out a single flaw. She is perfect and aware of that as she slowly prances my way.

Since her face is flushed with ecstasy, the sprinkling of freckles across her nose is even more noticeable when she stops in front of me. The tension teeming between us is so white-hot the water that drips off her breasts onto my cock sizzles.

It also proves my response to her kiss had nothing to do with dirty old man vibes. We have a connection. I'm just too shit-fucking-scared to admit that.

Fortunately for me, Henley gives me no choice.

After plucking a towel from behind me, her breasts close enough to scrape my arm, she wraps it around her body, murmurs a brief "Night," then exits the bathroom without so much as a backward glance.

8

BRODIE

"*E*verything okay?" Henley asks from her station at the corner of the kitchen, her brows crinkled like she hasn't witnessed my rumpled expression numerous times over the past three days. "You appear deep in thought."

Her calm, collected approach since our third bathroom rodeo would have you convinced it didn't happen. I swear I didn't imagine it. When I commenced rehab, my painkillers were strong enough to cause hallucinations, but I've not touched them in weeks, so they can't excuse the inanity of that night.

Henley's orgasm was as real as the one I tried to strangle into submission. I smelled it, witnessed it. Not even the most vivid imagination could conjure up something so inspiring it enters your thoughts every time you close your eyes.

It happened, but neither of us is willing to bring it up first.

"I'm good."

I close my laptop before forwarding the email I sent Nancy to the nanny agency's generic email. The agency reopens first thing tomorrow morning, but I'm struggling to decide whether I should assign another recruitment officer to find Henley's replacement or ruminate on Nancy's recommendation a little longer.

Get your mind out of the gutter. My change of heart has nothing to do with our kiss or numerous bathroom exchanges. Henley has only been Lucy's nanny for three days, but I've already noticed profound changes in my little girl, who's faced more sadness than happiness in her life. She wakes up every morning smiling and goes to bed grinning ear to ear.

She even smiles in her sleep.

I haven't seen her this happy in months, and as much as I want to credit the change up to the delay in me returning to work, I can't. Between Lucy and Henley's crafting and dressmaking classes, and how often they copy crazy hairstyles from YouTube tutorials, I've barely seen Lucy over the past three days. She is in the Henley-obsessed bubble I'm attempting to dodge as if it is the plague.

I've never spent so much time in my room.

My hand also hasn't seen so much action.

When Henley remains staring, wordlessly demanding more of an answer with eyes that can see through to my soul, I reply, "I was factoring in a change to my routine." *A change I didn't know I needed until now.*

As much as the tension bristling between us has me considering a plea of insanity, I've never felt more alive. I'm running twice a day and working out, and I even tackled a mountain of paperwork I've been avoiding since Caroline's death.

It is funny how different things look when you stop peering at them through grief-tinted glasses. It still fucking hurts, and I'll never stop grieving, but the steps Caroline put into place in the event of our daughter losing one of her parents show she knew the risks of our relationship.

She didn't walk in blind—unlike Henley.

She thinks her placement is the innocent meddling of a sixty-year -old matchmaker.

Only I know it could be direr than that.

That's why I need to keep my distance no matter how tempting things become.

Henley struggles to hide her pout when I place the kitchen island between us before she switches to interrogative. "What kind of change?" She finishes wiping up flour from the counter, which is surprisingly clean considering the near disaster it faced multiple times this weekend, and rinses out the cloth in the sink. "Should I grab my planner? I'm sure I'll have an hour or two free between beading and pancake demolitions sometime this week."

Her wittiness reminds me this wouldn't be so hard if I stopped valuing our exchanges ahead of how much Lucy loves having her around. Henley is a good nanny, and that should rate higher than how unbelievably gorgeous she is.

"Bar having me home more than she'd like, this change won't affect Lucy too much." Henley peers at me as if I have rocks in my head, but before she can assure me that I haven't already fucked up my daughter's life, I add, "It's work. I was meant to return last week, but an issue with paperwork means I can't go back for a couple more weeks."

"Oh..." She tries to act nonchalant, but her tone gives away her surprise. "Is that why you were so apprehensive to have me? You wanted to keep Lucy-Lou to your greedy self for a little while longer." She walks around the island wedged between us, her swinging hips as teasing as her grin. "Don't fret. There are enough beads for all of us."

"Great..." My breathy chuckle is as fake as the numerous times I've tried to act disinterested in Henley, but before she can call me out on it, I'm saved by Lucy for the umpteenth time today.

"Grandma Stell wants to speak to you." After climbing onto a stool wedged under the counter, she hands me my cell phone.

As Henley asks Lucy if she'd like a glass of milk, I squash my phone to my ear. "Hi, Stella."

"Hello, darling. How are you?" I once thought Lucy earned the ability to talk underwater from her mother, but when I met Stella, I soon realized it is a multigenerational thing. You can barely get a word in. "I was calling to make sure you're still coming to the barbecue today. Everyone is dying to see you."

The Ashburns have held an annual Fourth of July barbecue since before Caroline was born. I've only ever missed the one. It was the year Caroline was killed. I was grieving and reacted fiercely when I believed the only person giving me a reason to breathe was taken from me.

I wouldn't have survived those first few months if Lucy weren't relying on me. I couldn't drown my sorrows with liquor or spend several weeks in bed because she needed me, so you can imagine how angrily I reacted when Chelsea, Caroline's twin sister, tried to fill her sister's motherly shoes.

Although we've patched things up now, mostly due to court-ordered documents, it is still a little strained. It is hard to look into eyes identical to your wife's and not recall the last time you saw them.

The memory isn't pleasant, and it takes Stella saying my name three times to remember she asked a question.

"Yeah, we'll be there. Lucy has been looking forward to it all month."

When I ruffle Lucy's hair, she nudges her head to Henley and asks, "Can Henley come too? Please, Daddy. I asked Grandma Stell. She said it would be okay."

"She did, and I'm fine with you bringing a plus one. The more the merrier."

"Um—"

My reply is cut off by a man who hasn't been to an Ashburn barbecue in years. "Who the fuck is your plus one? If you say Mrs.

Palmer and her five daughters, I'm out. Our friendship is over. You'll never come back from that."

"Uncle Thane!" Lucy squeals when she stops gulping her milk down so fast she hears him over her gluttonous swallows. After snatching my phone out of my hand, she activates the speaker function. I'm not sure why. She never gives Thane the chance to speak. "I have a new nanny! She is the most prettiest, nicest nanny I've ever had. We do crafts, she's helping me make a dress, and she doesn't get mad when I blow my nose on a towel instead of a tissue."

Thane's deep, rumbling laugh cuts her off. "Wow... She sounds like a hoot! But I think you made a mistake, Lulu. No one is prettier than you."

"Henley is," she instantly denies. "She is the prettiest person I've ever seen."

"Henley?" Thane checks, his tone raised with suspicion.

Lucy's chubby cheeks bounce when she nods. "Uh-huh."

Mistrust echoes down the line with Thane's grumbling voice when he confirms, "The nanny who arrived Friday afternoon after you went with your dad to his work?"

"Uh-huh," Lucy repeats, louder this time.

"The smoking-hot blonde with a fantastic pair of—"

"Swans!" I interrupt before throwing an apologetic stare at Henley.

There's no way I can cover this up with the innocence of an almost six-year-old, so I leave it to Lucy.

She digs my hole deeper.

"Daddy was talking about Henley? I thought the swans were in the sky." Her mouth gapes open as her eyes bug. Hope is all over her face. "Where do you think they are now?"

When she hops off the stool to search for the pets she's convinced Henley is hiding, I hear Thane ask, "Maybe they're in the nanny's bedroom and that's why Henley has to sleep in your daddy's bed?"

It dawns that we're doing well at hiding the tension when Lucy replies with a giggle, "Henley hasn't been sleeping in Daddy's room, silly. She has her own room!" Her chuckled words are gobbled up by the swinging kitchen door and her dash up the stairs.

I take a moment to contemplate how to pull myself from the trench in one piece before spinning to face Henley. Her eyes are sparked with amusement, but it won't stop me from attempting an apology. "I was out of line, and when my commentary got out of hand, Thane tried to save me."

Her brows furrow. "Out of line for looking?"

"*Yes.*" That didn't come out as strong as hoped. Not even after we married did Caroline see looking as disrespectful. She was a firm believer in admiring what deserved to be admired. I loathed when she reminded me of her logic while we vacationed in Sweden, but the playfulness that came with my jealousy made our sex life out-of-this-world good.

I'm torn between my past and the present when Henley says, "If looking is out of line, how bad were the charges after I..."—her teeth get friendly with her lower lip—"you know... flicked the bean in front of you. I wasn't just looking. I took a ton of mental snapshots for future use. They came in handy both last night and this morning."

Needing to shut down our conversation before I pin her to the kitchen cabinets and clean out her filthy mouth with my tongue, I nudge my head to the stairs. "You should probably head up and get ready. Stella is a stickler for her guests being on time."

Henley's face is so ageless, even when she's confused it is without a single wrinkle. "Are we going somewhere?"

I nod. "Fourth of July barbecue." I gather my laptop, then angle my head so it hides the frustrated groove down the middle of my forehead. "If you have plans, I can tell Lucy you need to sit this one out. Her previous nannies joined us for most functions, but I'm sure she will understand."

"No, I'm happy to come. It's just..." She licks her lips before ripping off the Band-Aid as effectively as her presence shreds my smarts. "I accepted this placement because they said you rarely leave your home. Considering we've been inside the past three days, I assumed the rumors were true."

Her reply shocks me, but I keep my expression neutral. "That isn't exactly a lie, but functions like today are important for Lucy. She needs Caroline's family in her life." That was harder to admit than I care to share. I hate that I hurt Caroline's family, but they weren't the only ones who suffered from her loss.

"Who's Caroline?" Henley queries, forever curious. She asks as many personal questions as Lucy.

The smile she hasn't stopped wearing since she awarded me the show of my life slips when I answer with an honesty I don't give many people. "My wife."

"You mean your ex-wife?" She frowns, certain I dropped the beginning of Caroline's title.

"No," I disagree. "She is *still* my wife. Her death didn't change that." Eager for the mood not to sour with more words, I tell her we will meet out front in half an hour before exiting the kitchen. "Pack a swimsuit. Lucy is a water baby."

9

HENLEY

"I'm sure you're overreacting." Amelia rolls onto her back before adjusting the angle of her phone so I'm watching her from above. "Sometimes that's the consequence of having a big-ass brain."

I roll my eyes before shifting the focus off my stupidity. "How was last night's band? Any better than the Friday night disaster?"

"I'm up, talking to you before midday. How do you think it went?"

I screw up my face. "That bad? What is that, the fifth flop this month?"

Amelia's chest rises and falls with her big sigh. "Perhaps Raven-shoe has lost its knack for finding mega stars?"

Her gripe reminds me of an important fact I forgot to tell her last night when we FaceTimed from the second-story balcony so I didn't wake up Brodie, who has gone to bed as early as Lucy the last three nights.

His early bedtime routine would have you convinced he didn't enjoy the preview of how sparking we could be if he stopped pulling the age card.

It is a pity for him his body can't tell the same lies as his mouth. The remembrance is the only thing stopping my ego from dropping off a steep cliff.

"Guess who Brodie once worked for?"

Amelia taps her lips for barely a second. "The Dalai Lama?" When I scoff, she grins. "What? I could have said Trump."

"He's a federal agent, not a bodyguard."

"And the exact reason I stand by my guesses."

My eyes face their second strain this morning before I shut up her giggles by flipping my phone's camera to face a group of picture frames on the hallway table.

Her squeal is so loud the speakers in my cell almost blow up. "What the fuck? No way! How the hell does he know Rise Up!"

"Lucy didn't say"—*and I'm too chicken to ask Brodie*—"but this isn't the only image I've seen of them. The ones in Lucy's room are personalized to her, and she has a Jenni Holt dress in her wardrobe."

"Shut the front door!" She looks mind-blown. "She's your favorite designer, and Rise Up is your all-time favorite band. Slater and Noah got you off more than Beau ever could freshman year!" Her eyes bulge before she suddenly jackknifes into a half-seated position. "Do you think you'll have a chance to meet them?" Her eyes bug even more. "What if they're at the barbecue you're about to attend?"

When her quick moves blur the screen, I ask, "What are you doing?"

"Looking for my suitcase. I'm sure your southern charm will keep them put until I arrive. It's only a twenty-two-hour cross-country journey. No time at all."

"We're not going to a friend's barbecue." Amelia stops packing long enough to take in my disgruntled expression. "It is his wife's family's annual get-together."

"Oh... so that's how you fucked up by mentioning his dead wife?"

"I didn't know she was dead," I contest. "And when you go to a man's house and there are no pictures of a woman to be seen, he's either divorced or—"

"A cheating scumbag," she interrupts.

"Exactly." I stuff my swimsuit—that goes nicely with Brodie's old-aged personality since it is frumpy and floral—into my day bag before adding, "Since my brain impressed him more than my outfit, I assumed he was divorced."

"You fucked up." Yes, that was voiced like the TikTok sound clip.

"I did, and now I have to spend the next several hours with people who probably think I want to replace his wife. I'd never do that. Lucy will only ever have one mother."

"You don't need to explain yourself to me, Hen, but I'd appreciate it if you'd stop lying to me." When I arch a brow and gape my mouth, she *pffts* at me. "He gave you an out, but you're still packing."

"He gave me an out before I knew about his *dead* wife."

She continues talking as if I didn't interrupt her. "Because you're curious enough to continually step out of your comfort zone for this man." Again, she taps her lips. "You've never masturbated in your life, but the one time you decide to give it a whirl, you do it in front of your boss!"

"Amelia Josephine Lockhart! If you were here—"

"You'd be batting me off Brodie with a stick. My god. That man and his massive trunk need their own zip code. It's been days and I still haven't stopped thinking about it."

"He was facing the vanity, and you weren't meant to look!" I swear, I only rounded the corner of the attached bathroom for a nanosecond before closing down the FaceTime app.

The instant I realized Brodie was naked, Amelia's access to him was denied.

"Ah... he has a thigh gap and enough length for his johnson to dangle between them." She clicks her fingers together, praises the lord, then closes her eyes to relive the memory. "Shadows also can't be misinterpreted. If you don't believe me, ask the guy who sent me that beach dick pic." Her next words are barely audible through her snorting laughs. "It must have been really cold that day!"

"Amelia!"

"Okay. I'll stop. I'm sorry."

She's a damn liar.

"Not about anything I said about Brodie," she murmurs when she spots my expression. "I'll *never* be sorry about that. I'm preempting the apology I'll need to give you when he finally pulls his head out of his ass and ruins your insides with his foot-long sub."

It is not the time for me to laugh, but I can't help it. She is hilarious when jealous.

"I appreciate your belief that he wants to jackhammer my uterus, but—"

My head slings to the side when a tiny voice says, "What's a jackhammer?" Lucy enters my room, climbs onto my bed, then peers up at me with her adorable face no longer covered with flour. "Is that the name of Uncle Thane's new cat?" I warn Amelia to keep her mouth shut with a glare when Lucy screws up her nose and says, "I thought it was called clit slap."

With Amelia on the verge of cracking, I mouth that I'll call her later before shutting down my phone and directing Lucy's focus to something more suitable for a child her age. "Tate the Tortoise or Barry the Bandicoot?"

She points to the beach towel with bandicoots printed on it before asking, "What's a bandicoot?"

"A bandicoot is a marsupial that lives in Australia and the New Guinea region." Lines indent her nose when I say, "They kind of look like big rats, but they're *much* cuter and a lot more sanitary."

I take a mental note to choose better words when she asks, "What does sanitary mean?"

"It means they're clean." I tug on her ponytail we fixed into place this morning before she asked me to help her make her father break-fast for the third time this weekend. My heart broke the first morning when she said, "Mommy made him breakfast all the time." She sounded very confident, so I wasn't expecting a whispered "I think" to arrive shortly after. "Kind of like your hair. Where did the flour go? I thought we were meant to be twins today?"

"We were." Her bottom lip droops. "But Daddy said Grandma Stell would be upset if she couldn't see my golden locks." She blinks back tears before confessing, "My mommy had golden hair."

I wait, confident her sentence is not finished.

I don't often hate being right, but today is that day.

"I think."

"That's okay. I love your golden hair too." She peers up at me when I say, "And thanks to Ms. Mitchell, we have heaps of flour, so there's always next time. Okay?"

She nods. "Okay."

I smile, loving how easy she is to pacify. She has been a dream the past three days. It is like I have a new best friend. She is just several years younger than me—although our age gap isn't that much different from mine and Brodie's.

Even though that should put Brodie's apprehension into perspec-tive, it does little to douse the flames that ignited in my stomach when my eyes landed on him for the first time. He's a wonderful father, and when he's not dodging me like the plague, he's funny and incredibly endearing.

Those should have been the first clues that he isn't divorced. Who in their right mind would give up the ultimate representation of manliness? He's protective, sweet, and insanely attractive. A true triple threat.

When Lucy giggles at my loved-up expression, I ruffle her hair before asking, "Did you remember to pack your swimsuit? I hear there's water where we're going."

"There is. Grandma Stell has a huge pool and a lake!"

As I follow her to her room to fetch her things, I say, "But we're only swimming in the pool, right?"

She shrugs.

That's it. A teeny, tiny shoulder lift.

"Luc..."

A wolf whistle leaves my mouth as Brodie guides his truck down the driveway of a stately manor. His in-laws' residence is huge, and the driveway is littered with expensive cars.

"It's just a barbecue," Brodie assures me when I lower my eyes to the overlarge shirt I'm wearing as a dress. I jazzed it up with a belt, but it is still as casual and low end as it gets.

His arm brushes my thigh when he leans over to lower the radio. We were running late, and we didn't have time to move Lucy's booster seat to the middle of the single cab, so I'm riding bitch.

I don't know what's been more torturous. The faintest connection of Brodie's hand with my thigh each time he changed gears, or when he busted me taking a whiff of his aftershave. His scent is almost as appealing as his handsome face. It is unique and sexy but oddly comforting.

"Does Caroline's family work in the same industry as you?"

Another torture device joins Brodie's collection. His laugh.

It is delicious and pussy-tingling.

"No."

Before he can elaborate on his reply, Lucy screams, "Grandma Stell!"

"Wait until I pull up, Lucy," Brodie demands.

We've barely stopped when she throws open her door, tosses off her belt, then leaps down from the truck at a million miles an hour.

I laugh when Brodie mutters, "You'd swear they didn't see each other only last week."

"I think it's sweet." An appreciative grin lifts his lips when I add, "And as you said, this is important for Lucy. Having a stable family basis is necessary for every child."

Before I can shove my foot in my mouth, I slip out the door Lucy left open, then head for the bed of the truck to grab the cooler and bags.

"Please, allow me." I startle when a man with a fancy hat leans over me to remove the cooler from my grip and pull it from the tray.

"That's Riggs, the Ashburns' butler." When Riggs walks away with my bag, Brodie chuckles. "It takes a little getting used to. He still hasn't forgiven me for accusing him of stealing my stuff the first time I came here."

"You didn't."

His grin lights up my insides more than any fireworks tonight will. "I did. I was from—"

I want to scream when we're interrupted. "Brodie, darling..." The beautiful middle-aged lady with gorgeous red hair trails off when she spots me standing awkwardly at the side. "Oh..." She blinks three times before composing herself. "Please excuse my rudeness. I wasn't anticipating someone so..."

"Young?" I fill in when words elude her.

"I was going to say beautiful, but young suits just as well." Her laugh makes her comment endearing instead of bitchy. "Oh my goodness, I'm making a fool of myself." She slings her arm around my waist before guiding me inside. "It's been so long since we've had someone new to the festivities I went and lost my manners." I jump when her shout pierces my ears. "Herbert!"

A man with salt-and-pepper hair twists to face us. He's more casually dressed than Mrs. Ashburn, with an open Hawaiian-printed shirt and matching boardshorts, but even out of the suits I'm sure he wears on the daily, he is undoubtedly handsome.

"Come meet..." Her greeting stops again before she cranes her neck to look at me. "I'm sorry, we've not been formally introduced. I'm Stella. Most people call me Stell, and you are—?"

The room falls silent when Lucy wraps her arms around my thigh and says, "My new mommy."

"Oh... No... I... Ah." Not wanting to hurt Lucy's feelings, I cup her ear and tug her in closer to my thigh before saying, "I've never implied that. I swear." My eyes are for Stella, but my words are for Brodie. Even if he eventually gives in to the tension burning between us, replacing Lucy's mother would never be a part of the terms.

Brodie remains frozen at the side of the foyer, but Stella takes Lucy's comment in stride. "Well, aren't you lucky?" She bobs down to Lucy's height before lowering my hand from her ear. "But I think people will look at me a little funny if I call her Mommy." Lucy and a handful of the people surrounding us laugh when she murmurs, "She's almost old enough to be my sister." She tickles her tummy, assuring her she hasn't done anything wrong. "So what should I call her instead?"

"Henley," Lucy answers. "You can call her Henley."

"Henley? What a beautiful name." After returning to her full height, Stella squeezes my hand in silent support before mouthing for me to take all the time I need before I join everyone out back for lunch.

"Thank you," I murmur, grateful she isn't mad.

I can't say the same for Brodie. He looks seconds from blowing his top.

"I didn't—" He follows Lucy and Stella to the patio before I can assure him I've never given Lucy any assumptions that I am here to replace her mother.

"Let him cool off. He's always been a hothead."

I sling my eyes to the voice, gasping when I see a beautiful blonde with many identical features to Lucy. If I didn't know any better, I'd swear she was her mother.

"And please don't look at me like that. I get enough glares from Brodie to last me a lifetime." She saunters across the room before holding out her hand in offering. "I'm Chelsea, Caroline's sister."

"Identical twins?" I ask while shaking her hand.

"Uh-huh. But only in looks." She laughs a dainty giggle. "Caroline was always the more reserved of our duo." She signals for me to join her by the bar near the exit doors of the patio before asking, "I hope you don't see this as rude, but how did you get in?"

Her question stumps me for a couple of seconds. "Ah... Brodie invited me."

Chelsea laughs again, louder this time. "Not here. In Brodie's house. How did you manage the impossible?"

This question is simple for me to answer. "I'm Lucy's new nanny."

I feel as stupid as I sound when she rolls her eyes. "Yes, but how? He only ever hires old grannies with smelly armpits and no sense of fashion." She nudges her head to my shirt slash dress. "I love your outfit, by the way. Very retro."

"Thank you." I could leave our conversation here, but if I don't keep talking, she won't either. "I may have told a couple of fibs on my application."

Chelsea almost chokes on her drink. "You only needed to fudge one." She locks eyes with me. "Your age. Brodie has a thing about not associating with anyone close to his age. He keeps us all at arm's length like harm may come to us if he lets us get too close." Her expression sours. "If it weren't for the courts, I doubt we'd see Lucy." My heart pains for Lucy. Her excitement was palpable on the short drive to her grandparents' house. "And I can't remember the last time he looked me in the eye."

"It probably hurts."

I realize I said my comment out loud when she murmurs, "Perhaps." She squeezes my arm in the same manner as her mother before nudging her head to the double French doors. "You're being summoned."

Lucy has her face squashed against the glass, waving me over. "Grandma Stell has a trampoline in the lake! Can we have a turn, please?"

Nodding, I shift my focus to Chelsea as my cheeks whiten. "Did she say the trampoline is in the lake?"

10

BRODIE

*B*eer squirts from my nose, and my balls shrivel up, when Thane whacks me in the nuts.

"What the fuck, Thane!" I cough through wheezy pants. "You got me in the dick."

With his eyes locked on the patio doors and his mouth ajar, he replies, "Don't act like it hurts. You're either wearing a steel plate, or you're so fucking old your dick doesn't work anymore, because there's no way *any* man, not even one still wading in grief he doesn't deserve, could sit next to that for ten minutes straight and not exit his truck with a raging boner. She was practically sitting on your lap!"

"What the hell are you talking about?"

He nudges his head in the direction he can't tear his eyes away from. When I follow the path of his gaze, my cock assures me his hit didn't cause any permanent damage.

"Jesus fucking Christ."

Henley's bikini leaves *nothing* to the imagination. It is tiny and triangular, and although I can't see the back of her bikini bottoms, I'm reasonably sure it is the equivalent of dental floss. The amount of skin reflecting in the patio doors announces this, not to mention the number of dirty gawks she gets from men old enough to be her father.

You're old enough to be her father, I remind myself.

I lost my virginity at fifteen. Right around the time Henley was conceived.

The thought makes me shudder.

My eyes sling back to Thane when he asks, "Are you gay?"

"No. I married your sister, for crying out loud."

"And?" he replies with a cocked brow. "Alana was married to a dude for three years before she switched teams. Her wife was a huge loss for all of humanity."

I backhand his chest. "Stop fucking horn-dogging over your cousin's wife and get your damn eyes off my nanny's ass." As suspected, Henley's bikini bottoms don't have a back. Her ass is hanging out for the world to see, and even after telling myself multiple times that I shouldn't be looking, I can't tear my eyes away from the spectacular visual.

"Man, if she's going to show it, I'm gonna look."

I hit Thane for the second time, winding him up before putting steps in place to ensure he can't look.

"Henley..."

She tells Lucy to grab a lifejacket from the dock near the lake before spinning around to face me. When she spots my red cheeks and dilated eyes, she smiles the same grin she issued when I checked the flashlight in the top kitchen drawer for batteries three mornings ago.

"Hey." Her smile is even wider now. "We're about to go on a trampoline on the lake. If you want to join us, you're more than welcome. The more the merrier."

"Um..." Her offer stumps me for two seconds, not to mention her using a saying Stella tosses into almost every sentence. "Sounds good. But before then, don't you think you should cover up?"

I sound like her father, which doubles the heat of the blood roaring through my veins.

Henley accepts a lifejacket from Lucy before bobbing down to put it on her. Her kneeling position makes the situation worse. It has the hungry vultures hovering in close, desperate for an unhindered view.

The Ashburn men have seen it all before, but the investment bankers they pluck from universities straight after they receive their degrees are on the verge of coronary failure.

They've never seen so much skin, and Herbert, Caroline's father, rarely wears a shirt, even with his chest having more gray hairs than dark ones.

Henley takes so long doing up Lucy's zipper, I re-ask my question, assuming she didn't hear me.

"I heard you the first time," she murmurs before clicking the safety buckle into place to stop the lifejacket from slipping over Lucy's head. "I'm just a little unsure why you want me to cover up."

"Ah... your swimsuit. It's missing a big chunk of material."

When she stares at me as if confused, I nudge my head to her naked backside.

She laughs. "That's the design. You're meant to wear them like this."

The envious gawks bombarding her have words cracking out of my mouth like a whip. "I don't give a shit if that's how they were designed. Your ass is hanging out for the world to see."

"Daddy!"

I apologize to Lucy for my potty mouth before suggesting she ask Grandma to put sunscreen on her.

Lucy folds her arms over her chest. "Nuh-uh. You owe me two dollars."

I yank my wallet out of my shorts and thrust it into her chest before twisting her to face her grandmother, who is waiting near the water's edge.

Once she's out of earshot, as excited to test out the new toy Stella purchased as she is to empty my wallet of bills, I shift my focus back to Henley. I want to march her inside and cover her head to toe with cotton, but I try to remember I'm the elder of our duo, so I can't act like a Neanderthal, no matter how strong the urge is. "The people here are... conservative. They're not used to *those* types of swimsuits."

"My swimsuit is worn around the world, and this is just a barbecue," Henley quotes, her tone low and brimming with annoyance. "I'm also wearing far more clothing than you wore my first two nights as your nanny."

I realize our exchange is being witnessed by more than Thane when the crowd snickers in response to her reply. It won't have me backing down, though. "I would like you to put on a shirt."

I balk when she snaps out, "No."

"Henley."

Not even my stern grumble of her name sees her backing down. "You told me to pack a swimsuit. I packed a swimsuit. Next time you might need to be more specific."

She stops galloping down the stairs Lucy just raced down when I say, "I didn't realize I had to request no dental floss bikinis at an event with children."

"The only child here is you, Brodie," she gabbers before continuing down the stairs, her steps unfazed.

———

"Sit the fuck down, Thane," I murmur, pulling him back into his seat.

He's been running around after Henley all day, fetching her towels and drinks and pulling out the chair next to him when we sat down to eat. He's fawning over her, and it is pissing me off more than Lucy hoisting her swimsuit up her backside so her bottoms matched Henley's when they got off the trampoline.

I was two seconds from marching Lucy out of the festivities and leaving Henley at the mercy of my in-laws. I didn't because Stella pulled me aside and told me a story about Caroline doing a similar stunt when she was eleven.

"We'd vacationed in Miami for a week and were clueless of the influence strangers could have on a child's confidence." She threw her head back and laughed. "She sauntered around the living room and pool house for days with literal dental floss wedged between her butt cheeks. I was horrified." Her face softened. "Until I realized that for the first time in a long time, she wasn't hating on herself. Her confidence to wear something like that said far more than a person's response to her wearing it." She turned me to face Lucy and Henley playing at the water's edge. "Tell me one time you've seen that child's face lit up like that?"

I couldn't answer her. I'd never seen Lucy's face gleam as it did while making sandcastles with Henley. It was always sadder and more downcast than her peers' faces. It didn't even gleam that bright when Marcus invited us to a private rehearsal with his band.

She loves life and is forever appreciative, but something has been missing from her eyes for a long time.

I thought it was because of the constant reminder that her mother had passed, so I stored away Caroline's things and made out we'd always been a single-unit family.

Was that wrong of me to do? Probably, but grief doesn't come with a handbook. There's no step-by-step process on how to go about it. I did what I thought was right at the time, and I will save my judgment until Lucy is at an age where she can tell me how badly I fucked up.

"I was just gonna fetch her bag for her," Thane says, reminding me that I still have my hand splayed across his bare chest.

Henley's lack of clothing the past few hours reminded everyone that this was meant to be a pool party. They stripped down shortly after her first backflip on the inflatable trampoline. I haven't seen this much skin since I first entered Chains, the exclusive BDSM club.

No, I am not a part of the BDSM community. Marcus, my former detail, owns Chains. He kept his private life secret for years until he exposed it to bring his girlfriend's stalker out of hiding. We had no clue we were looking in the wrong direction until Dexter popped three bullets into me before pinning me to my unmarked car with a steel garden rake.

"You have a butler, remember?" My words come out pissy since my past popped in for a visit.

"And a maid, two pool men, and a piano teacher who gives fantastic head, but I'd still give it all away for ten seconds beneath the sheets with Hen—"

I wallop him so hard that nothing but battered breaths leave his mouth before I snatch Henley's bag out of Riggs's grip and guide her and Lucy to my truck.

Thane's voice is still wheezy when he checks, "Thursday, right?"

It's the fight of my life not to slam the passenger side door shut before Lucy can climb in when Henley stops clambering over her booster seat to answer Thane's question with a head bob. "But it will have to be after two. Lucy has her first dance class Thursday morning."

"Since when?"

Henley slots her backside into her seat before lifting her eyes to mine. "Since Chelsea offered during lunch. Don't worry, it won't cost you anything. She's doing it pro bono."

"And then Uncle Thane is going to teach us self-defense," Lucy announces as I place her into her seat. "Then we won't have to worry about snakes like Nathan Banks." Her face brightens. "That rhymes."

Henley saves me from asking what the fuck I missed by whispering in my ear. "He told her she must have bought her swimsuit from the grandma section because it was ugly and made her look fat."

Lucy proves what I have always suspected. She has supersonic hearing. "Henley punched him in the nose for saying I'm fat."

"I did not," Henley defends, her squeal ear-piercing. "I told him if his momma doesn't teach him better manners, I'd punch *her* in the nose."

"He ran away crying," Lucy announces, pleased with herself. "Then Aunt Molly got cranky."

"I didn't know she was your sister-in-law until after I threatened to punch her," Henley explains, spinning my head further. You can barely get a word in with Lucy as it is, but it's been impossible since Henley arrived. They can both talk underwater. "You didn't introduce me."

"Because she isn't my sister-in-law," I reply with a grimace. "The Ashburns have been trying to get rid of her since Thorin's Vegas elevator quickie."

"Uncle Thorin is away on business," Lucy explains, as capable of reading Henley's shocked expression as I am. She shifts her focus back to me. "What's an elevator quickie?"

Certain this isn't a conversation I can participate in today, I buckle Lucy in, jog around my truck, then slot behind the steering wheel.

Henley hisses when I crank the ignition and put the gearstick into first. A noise always popped from her lips when my hand made contact with her thigh on the drive here, but this one sounds more from pain than excitement.

"You okay?"

With her eyes facing the front, she nods.

I'm confident she is lying, but instead of calling her out in front of my in-laws, who are stretched across the stairs of their family home, farewelling us, I grind my back molars together before commencing our short drive home.

For every bump I hit, a groan escapes Henley's lips. I try to tell myself they're groans of pain, but my fucked-up head isn't hearing them that way. It sounds like she's moaning, and every whimper has me giving Thane's rambling more credit than it deserves.

A steel plate may be the only way I can leave my truck without making a spectacle of myself.

Henley saves me the embarrassment by ramming her elbow into my ribs as we enter the driveway of our home.

My home, I mentally chastise.

A grin tugs on my lips when I realize what she is pointing out. Lucy is out cold in her car seat, sleeping with her mouth open.

"I can't recall a Fourth of July event when she hasn't crashed on the way home. She loves swimming, but it zaps all her energy. After filling her belly and washing off the dirty water, she'll be out until tomorrow."

I park, shut down my truck, then jog to the passenger side door to lift a sleeping Lucy into my arms.

Henley's smile competes with the moon when Lucy mumbles, "I love you, Daddy," into my chest as I pull her in close, but it has nothing on how bright her face becomes when she adds, "I love you too, Henley." Since she's tired, her "love" sounds more like "wuv." "I knew you'd come." She cracks open her groggy eyes before whispering, "I just had to be patient."

With my life only weeks away from being hectic again, I should feel grateful when she holds out her arms for Henley to take her, but all I want to do is whine like a bitch.

Lucy loved Ms. Mitchell, but she never once picked her over me.

"It's okay. I've got her," Henley assures me as my hands shoot to catch Lucy when Henley groans like she's heavy. "Are you okay with the bags?"

When I jerk up my chin, Henley carries Lucy into the house with only the faintest whimper escaping her mouth.

By the time I finish unpacking the truck and have put away the cooler and inflatables for the next Ashburn family get-together, Henley has Lucy fed, bathed, and tucked into bed.

I'm not as butthurt as I was when I walk into Lucy's room and spot her blissfully happy face. She had the time of her life today, and although at one stage I thought going it alone would be best for everyone involved, the grin she can't hide even while sleeping proves I went about things the wrong way.

Stella and Herbert's wealth wasn't responsible for the target on Caroline's back or Chelsea's antics after her death that saw them almost lose their granddaughter as well.

The blame belongs on solely my shoulders, and the only way it won't be forced onto someone else's is by maintaining the solidarity I've enforced in my personal life over the past five years.

So, with my mind made up, I tuck in my daughter like she isn't already wrapped in blankets, then head for my bedroom like I'm clueless only a wall separates me from my twenty-two-year-old nanny showering naked in the room next door.

11

HENLEY

*W*ith Lucy bathed, fed, and tucked in bed, I finally had five minutes to work on an issue I wouldn't have if I hadn't taken relationship advice from a woman with gorgeous tanned skin. Chelsea was adamant my placement in Brodie's home would be short-lived if I didn't find a way for him to admit he isn't as ancient as the people who usually care for Lucy, but I didn't place my pasty-white skin into the equation.

I'm from the South, but my skin is alabaster white. It doesn't take kindly to the sun in general, but when you limit your clothing to force a response, you pay for the consequences of your decision fast.

Even after a shower cold enough to make my teeth chatter, my ass still feels like it is on fire.

"Sweet baby Jesus, this isn't good," I murmur to my reflection when I peel off my towel to inspect the damage.

I could feel the sting of my burn in the shower, but it's worse than predicted. My bikini straps are the only part of my back not as red as a Coke can, and most of my skin looks well past cooked.

"Is that a blister?"

My eyes widen as I struggle to take in the glossy bubble-like curve in the middle of my spine. It is just above the two dimples in my lower back—right at a region Brodie burned a hole in all day.

No wonder it is festering.

I freeze like a statue when "Is everything okay?" barrels through the unlocked bathroom door.

Although I wore a bikini to gain this man's attention, I don't want him to see me like this. I look as foolish as I feel.

"Yeah. I just..." I get desperate when a big stretch still doesn't offer me any relief. "I'm burned... *badly*. My back is blistering."

"Blistering?" Brodie double-checks, assuming he heard me wrong.

He didn't. "Yeah. I'm fairly sure it's a blister, although it's hard to tell since I can't twist my neck enough to see it."

After what feels like two lifetimes, he finally asks, "Are you covered?"

I curl the damp towel back around me, hissing when it hugs my skin, before replying, "Yep... for the most part."

Brodie doesn't enter the bathroom at the speed of a rocket like he did two nights ago. His pace is as slow as the drop of his eyes when they leave my blemished face. Thankfully, embarrassment is the cause of my colored cheeks. I was smart enough to put sunscreen on my face. My wish to make Brodie squirm as I had the previous seventy-six hours made me forget the rest of my body.

The sting of rejection burns worse than the sun when it dawns on me that Brodie isn't checking me out. He's hunting for the offending blister. "Where do you think the blister is?"

"On my back." Spinning away from him, I attempt to lower my towel without fully dropping it. This is no easy task. It isn't anything he hasn't seen before. I just hate that it is under these circumstances. You can't exactly woo someone when you look like a lobster.

I'm reminded of when my grandmother had a massive boil on her inner thigh when Brodie hisses while inspecting my back.

"Is it bad? Will it scar?"

Desperate to check for myself, I pivot toward the mirror. It fans out my towel, leaving my rear end fully exposed, and sees me coming face-to-face with Brodie. He stands a couple of inches taller than me, but several important regions of our bodies line up with perfection. I'm an inch from a pussy grind that would send me toppling into ecstasy.

"It isn't that bad." He forces me back around before crowding me against the vanity. His body temperature must be astronomical because the hand he brushes down my back is warmer than my scalded skin. "It also isn't a blister."

"Then what is it?"

I hold my breath when his touch sends a thrilling zap down my spine. It also forces goosebumps to rise to the surface of my skin, but I try to act ignorant. He is inspecting my stupidity, not undressing me with his teeth as I've dreamed about multiple times the past few nights. However, you wouldn't believe that with how erratic my pulse is.

I sigh in relief when he holds up his goop-covered finger in front of me. The "blister" is the body gel I was too scared to lather on my skin with a loofa. I used my hand because I was worried the scratchiness of the loofa would cause more damage.

I had no reason to fret. Brodie's calloused fingers feel divine, and I'd give anything to switch the mess on them to something more sinister.

After washing away the goop in the sink, his body close and hot in the tight confines of the bathroom, Brodie contemplates using my towel to dry his hands before thinking better of it.

He shake-dries them before making a beeline for the door while grumbling, "Night."

"Before you go," I push out, stopping him.

He shoves his hands into the pockets of his shorts before slowly spinning to face me. The apprehension on his face makes my chest so tight I can hardly breathe, but it won't stop me from asking, "Would you mind?" I jingle a bottle of aloe vera in the air. "I can't reach the middle of my back, and it's even more burned than my ass."

A victorious grin threatens to stretch across my face when his eyes snap to the vanity mirror for the quickest second before he cusses, adjusts his crotch without removing his hands from his pockets, then returns his eyes to my face. "I..." He stops and then tries again. "I can't."

Feeding off the tension that teemed between us during the short ride home, I say, "It's just a bit of aloe vera. What's the worst that could happen?"

His blurted confession gives my battered ego a moment of reprieve. "If I touch you again, I won't be able to stop."

"And that's a problem because...?"

"Because you drive me fucking insane." He thrusts his hand at the bathroom door like the Ashburn mansion is on the other side. "I was at my wife's childhood home with her damn family, yet all I kept thinking about was how I'd give anything to tan your ass redder than the sun ever could for denying my request for you to cover up."

Okay, now we're getting somewhere.

"And you're young. So fucking young."

I roll my eyes. "Then I guess it's lucky I have connections with people my own age."

"Thane—"

We're interrupted by a likely source, but not in a way anyone would anticipate.

A painful groan closely follows Lucy's entrance into the bathroom. "I-I don't feel good."

As Brodie scoops her up into his arms, I slip on the silk kimono I plucked from my suitcase with the hope its softness will caress my skin more than inflame it, before moving to Lucy to check if she has a temperature.

"I noticed her cheeks were a little red when bathing her, but I was hopeful it was from excitement." I grimace when her forehead feels as hot as a furnace. "Do you have children's pain relief?"

Brodie nods. "In the vanity cupboard, third shelf on the right."

After gathering the Tylenol and wetting a washcloth, I follow Brodie into his bedroom. Like the past several days when we've worked side by side, caring for Lucy together, we move in sync naturally—almost as one.

"She often gets heatstroke," Brodie announces after placing her on one side of his bed and fetching a bucket from the linen closet in the hallway.

Fortunately, he moves fast. A second after placing the bucket under her chin, Lucy brings up everything she ate and drank tonight.

"Oh, honey, it's okay," I promise when a scared whimper leaves her mouth between hurls.

After climbing onto Brodie's bed, I slip behind Lucy to ensure none of her freshly shampooed hair gets caught in the aftermath of her day in the sun. "It is better to get it out than hold it in. I know it feels yucky, but I promise you'll feel better once you get it all out."

Once she's tremored through the awful eviction of her supper, Brodie wipes up the mess on her chin with the washcloth before wetting a second one for her forehead.

"A little more, Lucy-Lou," Brodie instructs before pushing the last of the Tylenol through the needleless syringe and into her mouth.

"Good girl," I praise her when she takes her medicine without additional tears. "You're so brave."

When Brodie bobs down to issue his approval eye-to-eye and with a ruffle of her hair, I attempt to scoot back in case he wants to comfort his daughter with more than silent praise.

I barely get an inch away when Lucy begs, "S-stay with me." My heart whacks my ribs when she rolls and buries her tear-stained face into my chest.

"It's okay," Brodie murmurs when I peer up at him to request permission. I don't want to leave her, especially since much of her sickness is my fault. I spent most of the day outside so I'd have no reason to cover up the cause of Brodie's ticking jaw. I liked his jealousy because it made my inane feelings for him since day one more understandable. "I can sleep on the couch."

"Are you sure?"

He nods before pulling up the blanket at the foot of the mattress to cover us.

I smile against the tickling springs of Lucy's hair when he tucks us in tight. "Thank you."

With a second nod, he sits at the foot of Lucy's curled frame until sleep is close to overwhelming us both before he leaves his room with the faintest sigh.

12

BRODIE

$\mathcal{F}$orever alert for home invasions, I jackknife into a half-seated position when a light in the kitchen turns on. From a young age, I taught Lucy to maneuver throughout our home without lighting. By intimately learning the floor plan of our house, we have an advantage over anyone foreign to it.

I stop moving for the gun taped under the top shelf of a bookcase when I recognize the silhouette of the person in the kitchen. It is slim with a handful of enticing curves that will keep you awake all hours of the night.

After checking the time and noticing it is a little after four, I kick off the blanket I collected from the linen cupboard after checking on Lucy and Henley for the umpteenth time tonight, scrub the gunk out of my eyes, then make my way to the kitchen.

A grin curls on my lips when Henley busts my approach. A spoonful of ice cream is stuffed into her mouth, and the back half of her body is swamping the upright freezer. She is clearly cold—her nipples are puckered and erect—but her face isn't showing a smidge of discomfort.

"Sorry," she apologizes, talking around the spoon. "My skin still feels like it is on fire, so the thought of icy conditions became too tempting to ignore." She angles the ice cream container my way. "Want to join me for a late-night snack?"

I shake my head before switching on the coffee pot. "I'm more of a dark brew before breakfast kind of man."

"Breakfast?" She scoffs as if I am an idiot. "It's barely midnight..." Her words trail off when she takes in the time displayed by the electronic planner on the kitchen counter. "I told you I'd be up before the sparrows if I went to bed at eight."

Some of the heat coloring her chest creeps up her neck when I murmur, "You must have needed it. I closed your mouth three times in the past hour alone."

She makes a face like I'm an adorable puppy before her expression goes deadpan. "You were checking on Lucy, not me."

I nod. I've always found it easier to lie without words.

"Her fever broke pretty quickly." She stops shoveling a generous spoonful of ice cream into her mouth to look up at me, blinking and confused when I say, "Yours hung around for a while longer."

The look of adoration is back on her face. "You checked me for a temperature?"

Nodding, I pace closer to her to fetch the milk from the refrigerator.

My strides falter when she asks, "You don't have a rectal thermometer, right?"

I'm tired, functioning off approximately thirty minutes of broken sleep and paying too much attention to how her fleshy lips curl around the girthy end of the spoon with ease, but I don't hold back my laugh.

Her wittiness deserves a reply.

My laugh adds to Henley's roused coloring, and it doubles the electricity firing between us. It cracks and hisses in the air, and I swear to God, the faintest brush of our arm hairs sends a current roaring through my body. It clusters low in my groin and makes me hard as stone in an instant.

I snatch up the milk jug before my hands are tempted to explore something far more enticing than caffeine, then head back to the coffee pot. "No. But..."

Henley doesn't breathe while waiting for me to finish my sentence.

I relish the quiet. I've barely had an ounce of it since she joined the chaos I call my life. However, I'm not eager to go back to silence either. I was lost during those first couple of hours of peace tonight. Chaos is hectic, but it is also therapeutic when you associate death with silence.

Once my mug is full of murky goodness, I spin to face Henley. She's still watching me with awe, her early morning treat no longer her focus. "I might have to consider getting one if you remain standing in the freezer." When she slants her head and arches a brow, confused, I expand on my reply. "The thermometer."

"Oh." After popping the lid onto the tub, she stores the ice cream away, then joins me at the island. "I was too busy contemplating if you have somnophilia to remember my comment about a rectal thermometer."

"What?"

She props her hip on the counter. "Somnophilia is—"

"Someone who gets sexually aroused by having sex with someone who is asleep. I know what it is." It isn't the father side of my brain speaking when I add, "I'm more trying to work out why the heat on your chest extended to your cheeks during your contemplation."

Henley replies without a single balk or any signs of repulsion. "You have to admit it is pretty hot."

"To not give consent?"

"To be wanted so unapologetically," she corrects. "And consent can still be given." She stares me deadpan in the face. "If you're too impatient to wait, I give you permission to wake me in any way you see fit."

"For fuck's sake."

That isn't for Henley. It is for my cock, which is acting as if none of my objections are serious. Its response to Henley sleeping in my bed is why I had to sleep downstairs, and it wasn't even behaving as devious as it is now. It was imagining itself snuggled in her curvy backside, nestled between the cheeks I struggled not to spank when she ignored my numerous requests for her to cover up.

"I need to check on Lucy," I announce, using her as an excuse to dodge human interaction as I have the past five and a half years.

Henley must be a pro at hiding her emotions. She barely sighs before she jerks up her chin. "I've done a solid eight hours, so I might just hang out and watch TV." Her fondness for Lucy can't be misunderstood when she shifts to face the stairs before saying, "If she asks for me, will you come get me?"

"Of course." I rub her arm like a principal would a student, then grumble about stupidity while taking the stairs two at a time.

I'm expecting Lucy to be sound asleep, so you can imagine my shock when I find her in the bathroom, climbing up onto the vanity. She still sleeps like she did as a newborn, her necessity of twelve hours on par with her uncle's. Thane whines like a baby when he's woken before midday.

"Lucy, what are you doing?" I ask when she almost slips. After scooping her off the drawer handle she's using as a ladder, I plonk her backside onto the vanity. "Are you thirsty?"

Blonde curls tickle her cheeks when she shakes her head before she scrubs at her tired eyes. "I need to help Henley." I don't get a chance to announce my confusion. "She's sick too, Daddy. We need to help her." She reaches for the aloe vera gel bottle. "She made me all better, so now I have to help her." I feel like a fucking ass when she confesses, "Her skin is hot. Dis will make it better." She never pronounces her words properly when tired. She slurs like a drunken sailor. "Aunt Chelsea said. She gave it to Henley when she said she didn't want to wear her swimsuit."

"What?"

Lucy is more forgiving of my daftness than Henley. "Aunt Chelsea wanted Henley to look pretty for you, so she gave her the butt-hungry swimsuit to wear." Her giggles bounce around the bathroom. "That's what Henley called her new swimsuit when she saw the bottom half. She said it would make it look like her bottom got hungry and ate her swimsuit." She yawns before leaning in close. "I wanted you to think she is pretty too, so I told her you like butt-hungry swimsuits." My heart enlarges when she peers up at me. Her eyes are identical to her mother's in every way. "You did like them, didn't you, Daddy? That's why you got mad."

"I didn't get mad."

"Yes, you did!" With a huff, she leaps off the counter and then hits me with some of the sass I'm sure I'll get smacked with a hundred times a day once she is a teen. "You were mean to Henley, and now she might leave."

"She won't leave."

I realize she has a way to my soul when she huffs so loud that steam billows out of her ears. "You need to make it better. You have to fix it like you did my rollerblades."

"Fix what? Nothing is broken."

"Her butt! You need to fix Henley's butt."

My denial is fast and direct. "I can't do that, Lucy-Lou."

"Why not?"

She cocks her hip and taps her foot, impatiently waiting for the answer she will dismiss within an instant of it being given. She has no intention of backing down.

It is times like this I hate that she got my stubbornness.

"Because—"

She thrusts the aloe vera gel into my chest before I get out half a reply. "That's not an acceptable answer." For once, she mimics my voice instead of Henley's. "That was the worst excuse I've ever heard." I realize she listens in on my conversations with Thane more than believed when she hits me with another one of the lines I regularly use on him. "You're a man, so you need to act like one."

The floorboards creak under my weight when she pushes me out of the bathroom. I wouldn't budge if I didn't want to, but I won't ever make her feel like she can't defend herself, especially in her home.

"I'll help Henley," I announce, slowing her barges, "on one condition."

She waits for me to spin and face her before replying. "Name your terms."

I said one condition, but I refuse to give up an opportunity of parenting her on the unfairness of life. "One, you have to go back to bed. The last time you woke up at 4 a.m. resulted in you *and* Thane having a tantrum in the middle of the grocery store."

She giggles but doesn't refute my claims Thane's tantrum was on par with hers.

I wait for her to enter her room and climb onto her bed before I continue our negotiation. "Two, you need to hang up your baker's hat." The tears springing in her eyes have me backtracking in an instant on what I was certain was a good idea. "For a week. Henley loves baking with you, but she has so many more things she wants to teach you." I pull down her blanket and gesture for her to slip beneath. "She can't do that if she's spending half the day cleaning the mess in the kitchen."

"That's true," she murmurs through a yawn, her eyes fluttering as her head lands on her pillow. "So I guess I could save my creations for next week." My stomach flips for the wrong reason when she smiles and says, "That will give me heaps of time to come up with some new recipes."

"Yay..." I hide my grimace with a smile.

Lucy giggles as if aware of the reason for the grumble of my stomach before rolling onto her side and tucking her hands under her cheek. "What's the final term, Daddy? You say they always come in threes."

With my stomach being saved for a week and the possibility of an imminent tantrum almost eradicated, I shift my focus to an earlier anguish. "Can we schedule your butt-hungry swimwear's return for after graduation?"

"High school or college?" she asks, her words groggy.

"Coll—" Her glare cuts me off. "High school?"

She thrusts out her hand in offering. "Deal!" Once we shake hands, she confesses, "I'm happy to skip the butt chafe for a few more years." Through another big yawn, she murmurs, "Wet material and walking aren't a good com-bin-ation." She stumbles over her last word. "I got a sore tooshie."

Trying not to laugh, I ask, "Are you okay?"

"Yeah." She nods. "'Cause Henley took care of me. She put talcy powder on my butt." Her smile grows, which reduces the width of her eyes more than her tiredness. "It makes my tooties smell fresh." A small toot leaves her backside. "See? No stinkies."

"Lucy?"

"Yes, Daddy?" she answers, blinking as she struggles to keep her eyes open.

"I'm going to write down everything you just said and share it during your twenty-first birthday celebration."

She appears disgusted for barely half a second. "That's okay. You can." The reason for her carefree attitude is exposed when she murmurs, "You said I can't have a boyfriend until I'm thirty, so I'll have another"—she quickly calculates—"nine years from then before he finds out that bubbles turn into puff clouds when you're not in the bath."

13

HENLEY

$\mathcal{M}$y hunt for the aloe vera gel I could have sworn I left on the shelf above the vanity stops when "Are you looking for this?" rumbles through the bathroom.

I twist to face the voice, my legs shaky due to the huskiness of Brodie's question. He sounds like he spent the last thirty minutes sleeping, so I tiptoed up the stairs instead of galloping. I didn't want to wake him if he finally gave in to the exhaustion on his face.

When I spot the aloe vera in his hands, I sigh in relief. "Yes. I thought I had misplaced it." As quickly as relief bombards me, fret takes its place. "Is Lucy okay? She didn't get burned, did she? She said her tooshie hurt, but I thought she had chafing, so I put talcum powder on her bottom to soothe any further irritation."

"Lucy is fine." His smile makes him look less tired. "Excluding some badly placed chafing. I doubt she'll wear a butt-hungry swimsuit again anytime soon." With his confession rendering me silent, he enters the bathroom without protest before asking, "Do you still need help?"

"With?"

Another outfit that will have you tripping over your tongue?

The key to unlocking your secrets?

A new pair of panties since the scent of your aftershave disintegrated the ones I'm not wearing?

I'm left a little gob-smacked when he replies, "With the gel." I take a mental note to let Lucy destroy the kitchen for the next month when Brodie nudges his head to her closed bedroom door and confesses, "She promised not to wear a G-string until after graduation if I agreed to fix your butt."

"I can reach my butt."

I'm not turning him down. I simply don't want his daughter pushing him out of his comfort zone.

That's my job.

When disappointment crosses his face long before relief, I say, "But I wouldn't say no to some assistance with my back. I can't reach the middle."

He takes a moment to deliberate before lifting his chin.

Our eyes remain locked even with me spinning to face away from him. The mirror stretched from one side of the double vanity to the next is perfect for keeping the tension high. It crackles and hisses in the air along with Brodie's groan when his attempt to rub lotion into my back is foiled by the satin dressing gown I'm wearing sans panties.

"I need to take it off."

I wait for him to fire off an objection.

When he doesn't, I unknot the silky material and let it drop where it falls.

The hiss that escapes Brodie's mouth when he realizes I am without panties matches the one that leaves my mouth when his gel-loaded fingers land on my heated skin. I'm not hissing in pain. I am moaning about the spasm his briefest touch causes my skin.

I'm on fire again but for an entirely different reason this time around.

"You should never take Chelsea's advice." His fingertips tickle my spine as his hand floats down my back. "Rarely is it right. She forever steered Caroline in the *wrong* direction."

His voice is not as angry as anticipated, so I say, "I wouldn't say her plan was brilliant, but it achieved the effect we were aiming for."

He peers at me over my shoulder, his hand still soothing to my back. "How?"

"I wanted to make you jealous," I answer, the truth not missed in my tone.

His hand slips a little lower and to the left, his fingertips teasing my rib. "Why?"

"Because until your confession last night, I was beginning to wonder if the fireworks were one-sided."

His fingers tickle my side boob when I spin to face him, but he drops his hand before its gooey surface can add to the bumps in my areolas.

I don't mind. The tension is so white hot I don't need to hear words to feel wanted. I can feel it radiating out of him, smell it on his skin. He wants this as badly as I do. He's just too scared to make the first move.

For once in my life, I'm not.

I step closer until my erect nipples scratch his chest, then confess, "You were meant to follow me to my room." Confusion barely graces his face before I strive to eradicate it. "The night you watched me." I stray my eyes to the bathtub before returning them to his face, smiling when no amount of distance could have me mistaking his body's reaction to my reminder that I masturbated in front of him. He's hard. I'd put money on it. "You were meant to follow me to my room and finish what you started. But instead, you—"

"Finished in the shower... with my hand..." His breaths are hot and heavy on my lips. "Thinking about you." As his eyes drop to my lips, his tongue darts out to wet his mouth. "Your taste. Lips." A ghost-like grin stretches across my face when he groans. "Those fucking shorts." You'd swear I didn't put sunscreen on my face when he drags the back of his index finger across my cheeks. "Even these came up." He pays so much dedicated attention to my freckles that I wonder if they're an erogenous zone on my body I didn't know about before he once again lowers his hand. "But no matter how shiny the fruit, sometimes you can't bite into the apple." Finally, his eyes give in and drop to my breasts for the quickest second before they return to my face. "You need me to walk away." He ignores my headshake. "And I need to respect that more than my wish to fuck you senseless."

My hand instinctively shoots out to grab his shirt when he attempts to walk away. My clutch is pathetic, he could easily escape it, but my lusty head tells me he doesn't want to.

"Tell me you don't want me." He remains facing the front, unblinking and unmoving, but it won't stop my campaign. "If you can do that, I'll drop this immediately and never bring it up again."

Brodie watches me through a sheet of hair that has fallen in front of his eye for what feels like a lifetime before he says, "You're—"

"An adult who can make her own decisions," I interrupt when the same excuses flood his eyes. "And I know what I want." His eyes bounce between mine as I say, "I want you." When panic flares through his eyes, I quickly clarify, "To fuck me. I want you to fuck me."

"Jesus Christ, Henley. You can't say that to me."

"Why?" I ask, giving his brief interrogation trick a run for its money.

His reply isn't close to what I expected, but it is better than a straight-up no. "Because if that's all you want, a night of fun with no attachments, I might not have the strength to fight anymore."

There's the confession I've been dying to hear.

"So you feel it too?"

"Yes!" He throws his hand into the air before dragging it over his head. "But we can't—"

I shut him up before he says another stupid word by kissing him.

I'm not talking about your ninety-year-old grandma kissing her husband farewell. I'm talking fireworks in the sky, a greasy breakfast after a night of drinking, and tingles that have you wondering if you've ever truly orgasmed. It is an intense, blistering embrace that knocks Brodie's hesitations out of the park.

My head bumps into the door when he braces me against it after guiding my legs around his waist.

"Shit," he whispers over my kiss-swollen lips a short time later.

"Is it your shoulder?" I ask, panicked our stumble to the door overexerted him.

"No," he answers between placing hungry kisses on my neck. "My shoulder is fine. I'm worried about your burn."

"The burn that feels nonexistent when compared to the heat of your kisses?" When he peers up at me, his smirk almost nonexistent, I cock a brow. "Please don't tell me you're one of those people who have sex with the blanket on?" The vibration of his chuckle is as delicious as the tingles racing through the conjoined areas of our bodies. "I don't care if it is minus thirty, bedding is the first thing to go." I give him a look. "If it isn't, you're fooling around with the wrong person."

He nods like he agrees with me but still inches me away from the door.

As I stroke Brodie through his shorts, he shuffles us to the other side of the bathroom. The marble top of the vanity feels cool on my backside when he sets me down on it, but a second after his lips lower to my breasts, my core body temperature climbs to a dangerous level.

"Sweet lord," I murmur when he sucks my nipple into his mouth and swirls his tongue around the aching bud.

After playing with my breast long enough to bring me to the brink of ecstasy, he kisses a path down my stomach. When he reaches the apex of my thighs, my eyes shoot to the open bathroom door. I'm already panting in excess. I can't guarantee my moans won't wake Lucy.

"Should we close the door?" I ask between big breaths, my body reeling. "I don't want to wake—" I'm cut short by my own moan when he pushes apart my thighs and buries his head between my legs.

One sweep of his tongue across my clit has me vaulting off the vanity.

A second has me moaning like I'm possessed.

"You need to be quiet," Brodie murmurs, his mouth barely an inch from my pussy. "Lucy can sleep through a hurricane, but when it comes to you and the possibility of you being in pain, she'll hear everything."

It is not the time to smile, but I can't help it.

I'm smitten with that little girl and am so glad she feels the same way.

"Henley," Brodie growls in warning when his hot breath blowing over my throbbing clit almost sets me off.

"I can't help it," I gripe while endeavoring to return his mouth to my pussy. "It feels too good. I need a gag. Do you have one of them?"

I was hoping he'd silence me with his cock. Instead, he uses his hand. He clamps it over my mouth before spearing his tongue inside me. He licks, bites, and eats until his palm muffles my screams, then doubles the flare of my nostrils by slowly sliding a finger inside me.

"Christ, Henley. You're so tight."

"It's been a while," I murmur into his hand, my words hardly coherent as my hips swivel to lessen the burn.

I don't know if my mumbled reply is responsible for the lowering of his hand, or if it's his wish to make me so wet he won't face any resistance when he switches from one finger to two. Whatever it is, I'm grateful when the hand he had clamped around my mouth drops to my stomach. He pushes down just above the region pubic hair is meant to be before he drags the tips of the fingers inside me along the roof of my pussy.

"Damn..." My thighs shake along with my words. "I don't think I can't scream."

"Keep them inside, and I'll teach you how you should have gotten yourself off when you teased me in the tub." The sting that came with his underhanded dig at my inexperience doesn't hurt as much when he murmurs, "I need to taste you again." He blows a hot breath over my clit before locking eyes with me. "But you need to be quiet, okay? We don't want any interruptions."

"Okay," I murmur, willing to say anything to get his mouth back on me.

When the bumps on his tongue make contact with my clit, I slap my hand over my mouth a second before my throaty groan can erupt. Brodie's lips lift against my scalding skin for barely a second before he circles his tongue around the aching bud and sucks it into his mouth.

"That's my good girl," he murmurs against my pussy when my moan comes out as a long, nasally exhale instead of the scream a rush of euphoria like this usually demands.

I'm biting on my palm, hopeful a sting of pain will stop me from screaming, but it adds to the tension bubbling in the lower half of my stomach. I'm seconds from detonation, as turned on now as I was when I pretended it was Brodie's hand wandering over my body in the tub nights ago.

"Oh..." That sounds more like a moan than a breathy chant, but it can't be helped. The sensation is amazing. He's eating me and finger fucking me at the same time. My senses are overloaded. I've never experienced such a need before. "Please..."

"Fuck," Brodie murmurs when he hears the plea in my voice as easily as I do. I'm desperate to scream, and he's just as eager to hear me.

When his eyes flash to the door that separates his room from the bathroom, and hesitation crosses his face, I say, "My room. It's the furthest from Lucy's. She won't hear us there."

He appears pleased by my suggestion for half a second. "You only have a single bed."

"Which has more than enough room for you to pin me to the mattress and fuck me senseless."

The hesitation on his face seconds ago jumps onto mine when he says, "How did you ever get through nanny school with such a filthy mouth?"

"They have schools for nannies?"

I'm saved from wrenching my foot out of my mouth when Brodie shrugs. "Fucked if I know, but if they do, there's no way you'd pass with flying colors."

"It isn't easy to be quiet when someone has their head between your legs."

When Brodie pulls a face as if to say *I wouldn't face an issue*, I accept his nonverbal challenge by falling to my knees, taking his shorts with me, and curling my hand around his cock.

"Jesus. Fucking. Christ."

Brodie's hand shoots out to scratch at the wall when I wrap my lips around the head of his thick cock.

"Shhh," I demand before drawing him to the back of my throat.

His nostrils flare as ruefully as mine did when he had his head between my legs as I withdraw to the tip before using the droplet at the end to gloss up my lips. The slippery wetness of his pre-cum makes my descent the second time around a lot smoother and has Brodie's breath trapping in his throat.

His cock is so rigidly thick it is almost beastly. It is also long and beautiful, a perfect representation of the male anatomy. It's too big for my mouth, so I can only imagine how snug it will be once our exchange switches from foreplay to the finale.

My pussy wets at the thought of being stretched so wide.

I want it all.

Every bit of him.

Even if it is painful.

"More," Brodie demands as his hand finds its way to my hair. "Take me deeper."

He groans with me when a gag vibrates on his knob. It is the most erotic noise I've heard, but it doesn't stop me from shushing him before attempting to generate more noises of pleasure for me to silence.

I fuck him with my mouth until the tension reaches boiling point, and Brodie pulls me off his cock with a rough tug on my hair. "I haven't come with company in years, so the first time won't be down your throat."

Hold on, what? Is that why it is so thick and veiny? Is he holding back far more than just days of sexual tension?

Before my thoughts can get away from me, Brodie plucks me up off the floor, then walks me into his bedroom, kicking the door closed on the way. The main door is already shut.

Despite the humid July night, the bedding feels cool against my burning skin when he places me down in the middle of the bed before leaning over to dig a condom out of his bedside table.

The way he rips it with his teeth before guiding it down his shaft is almost as erotic as him positioning himself between my legs. He's impatient. Almost desperate. And before I can secure a full breath, he slowly notches inside me.

The burn as he pushes in inch after steely inch is excruciating, but I suck in a few big breaths while remembering that the pain will be a small price to pay to relieve so much sexual buildup.

"Christ, Henley."

Just the way Brodie growls my name takes the edge off. It has me acclimating to the pain of being stretched so far and encouraging the faintest roll of his hips.

"I don't need to move yet. Take all the time you need."

"I don't need time," I assure him. "I need you."

Again, a flare of panic darts through his eyes.

"To stop pussyfooting around and get the job done."

He smirks before slowly rocking his hips backward. I expect him to slam back in, but his pace during reentrance is more timed than his exit. His slow speed should be infuriating, but the flick he adds at the end of his roll snaps the last bit of restraint I have left. I beg him to take me hard and fast, to fuck me senseless as promised.

I need him to let go of the restraints holding him back for a few more blinding minutes.

"Be patient."

"No. I want you to fuck me."

"I'll tear you."

"I. Don't. Care." I slam down on him as each word rings in my ears, forcing him deeper with every thrust. "I want to feel where you've been. How deep you went. I want to remember how you couldn't hold back no matter how hard you fought."

The pads of my feet dig into the mattress when he slams in so fast my eyes roll into the back of my head.

I've never been more full.

"Yes," I hiss through gritted teeth when the rock of his hips turns undulating. He pounds into me without constraint, drawing moans out of me with barely any effort. It feels good. Wildly intense. I've never experienced such an indulgent sensation.

Brodie knows how to fuck. He has the cock of a god and the moves to match its size.

Our connection is better than I could have ever imagined.

Over and over again, he drives into me. He takes me to the brink before forcing me over the axis. I come again and again and again. Yet, he still doesn't stop. He fucks me until my entire body collapses with pleasure, and I am so spent that the only thing I can do is roll over and hug my pillow while fighting to breathe.

14

HENLEY

*M*y muscles are deliciously sore as I descend the stairs siding the kitchen. My exhaustion saw me oversleeping, so I wasn't shocked to wake up alone. It is a little after ten following the Fourth of July weekend. It could have ended worse.

"Good morning, Lucy-Lou," I greet when I spot her at the island in the kitchen, playing on her father's laptop. "Are you meant to be on that? Daddy could have important stuff on there he doesn't want you to see."

"I'm allowed when my iPad is dead." She screws up her nose. "I think."

"Maybe hop off until you can check with your dad." I ruffle her hair when she immediately jumps to my command. "Then there's less chance of us getting in trouble when we make a mess." After filling a mug with coffee from a pot that looks like it's been sitting for days, even with Brodie making a fresh batch every morning, I pull on an apron and tie it at the waist. "What's on the baking menu today?"

"Um..."

I move closer to Lucy when she drops her eyes to her feet. "Is everything okay? I've never heard you so quiet."

She smiles and nods before turning her bottom lip into her infamous pout. "I promised Daddy I wouldn't bake for a week." She must see something I wasn't meant to show. "He said you had lots of other stuff to teach me, but you wouldn't get the chance if you're always cleaning up my mess."

"That's true. We still have that dress to finish." Her pout decreases when I ask, "A bowl of Cheerios and then a dressmaking class?"

Her happiness has me convinced she will jump at the chance to sew, so you can picture my shock when she replies, "Can't. We're going to the movies."

"Oh, fun! What are we going to see?"

I sling my head to the swinging kitchen door when Brodie answers on Lucy's behalf. "*We* are seeing a remake of a movie her mother loved as a child."

When he ruffles Lucy's hair before suggesting that she fetch her shoes, I can't take his "we" as anything but a rejection.

I'm not invited.

His lack of eye contact assures this, not to mention his cool demeanor.

I wait for Lucy to be out of earshot before asking, "Did you decide to go to the movies before or after what happened last night?"

A big knife stabs into my chest when Brodie places his empty mug into the sink before replying, "Last night?" He doesn't bother facing me. He peers at the window like the scenery he witnesses every day is far more interesting than me. "Did something happen last night?"

Is he seriously going down this route?

Is he honestly going to pretend nothing happened?

He can't if I don't let him off the hook.

"Last night when we fuc—"

"Can I wear flip-flops?" Lucy giggles before locking her big eyes with me. Their lack of worry exposes she didn't hear the anger of my last word. "They're like butt-hungry swimsuits for your feet."

Her innocence is so beautiful I can hold back my anger when she is around. "They are, so you better get sunscreen on your tiny white toes. You don't want them looking like a lobster tail, or I might be tempted to eat them."

As I chase Lucy around the kitchen while clapping my hands like a crocodile, I recall how much difference a couple of hours makes to a child's recovery from heatstroke.

Is that why Brodie is acting daft? Did I hallucinate the entire thing?

I couldn't have.

A connection like ours can't be fake.

We created more fireworks than the nation dispersed last night.

I also woke in his bed, although the condom wrapper he left on the floor last night was nowhere to be found, and the new box he opened was no longer in his bedside table.

I shake off my confusion when Lucy says with a boisterous giggle, "You can't get burned inside, silly." Her eyes bulge as her mouth gapes. "You should wear flip-flops too. Then we'll match."

"Henley can't come with us," Brodie announces, saving me from lying to a little girl who doesn't deserve to be deceived. "She... ah... has to study."

"But you said she was coming," Lucy argues, unafraid of the brooding tension bouncing off Brodie in invisible waves. She requests to be put down before shifting on her feet to face her father. "I want her to come."

"No," Brodie corrects, uncaring of her foot stomp. "I said it would make it seem as if your mother is with us." For the first time this morning, his eyes lock with mine. "Henley is not your mother."

"Because you won't let her be!" Lucy storms off. "If Henley isn't coming, I'm not going either!"

"Lucy!"

"It's okay." I step into Brodie's path before he can chase Lucy down. "I've got this."

Not giving Brodie a chance to deny my offer or to apologize for being an ass, I barge past him before finding Lucy in her room. She is on her stomach on her bed, crying into her pillow.

"Hey, what's with the tears? I thought we promised yesterday never to shed tears over stupid, immature boys."

"Daddy isn't a boy," she whimpers. "He's a man."

Now is the wrong time for images of his manliness to flash into my head, so I won't mention it.

"I don't want to go to the stupid movie anymore."

The mattress dips when I sit on the edge and rub her back to soothe her hiccups. "How do you know it's stupid? Have you watched it before?" She shakes her head. "Then you can't give it a fair judgment, can you?" When she remains quiet, I pull back the locks she's using to hide her face, before angling my head so she can see my eyes. "Your dad also said your mom loved this movie." Not wanting to upset her more, I brush away her tears while whispering, "I thought you wanted to learn about your mom?"

"I do." Her sobs break my heart. "But not without you."

"I'll be here when you get back. You couldn't get rid of me even if you wanted to." That gets a smile out of her. Not a big one, but it is better than nothing. "And your dad has to return to work soon, so maybe he just wants some time with you by himself."

"M-maybe."

I clean away her tears with my shirt sleeve when she sits up. "Do you think you'd feel like going more if we make your toes match your flip-flops?" When confusion crosses her face, I say, "Please don't tell me you've never been introduced to a pedi?"

"What's a pedi?"

"It's the best thing since sliced bread." My saying is as lost on her as it was on me when I was first told it years ago. "How about I show you really quick? What time does the movie start?"

"Ten thirty."

Yikes.

"Is the movie theater close by?"

I breathe a little easier when Lucy nods.

"Great! We have time. I'll be right back. I need nail polish."

Lucy's excitement is so high she bounces on the bed, missing me colliding with her father in the hallway.

He's snooping—again.

"She'll be ready in ten minutes," I say matter-of-factly, too angry to play games. "You can wait downstairs."

"I—"

I squash my finger to his lips and tsk him for thinking he has a say before I head for my room, swinging my hips like they're not marked from the deep dig of his fingers when he fucked me ten ways from Sunday.

"Amelia—"

"I'm sorry. I just need a minute to decompress everything. It's a lot to take in. His cock is as large as imagined, possibly larger, he fucks like a god, but he's an ass the following morning." She twists her lips before saying, "Things could be worse."

"He's denying we were even together. It can't get more fucked up than that."

She murmurs her disapproval before adding words into the mix. "He could have slipped out while you were sleeping, and you'd never see him again."

"It's his damn house."

Her brows drop low. "True. But..."

She has nothing. Not a single thing.

Except, "He did kind of warn you that it was a one-night-only hookup."

"When?" I deny, my voice so loud it echoes through the empty living room. Brodie and Lucy left thirty minutes ago for the theater.

My phone screen goes blank when she scans back through the messages I bombarded her phone with. I told her everything, in detail, via messenger.

She must be proud.

Amelia's face fills the screen again. "Found it." With her accent mimicking a man, she says, "Because if that's all you want, a night of fun with no attachments, I might not have the strength to fight anymore." She glares at me. "That screams one-night stand."

"But that was before we fucked."

If she wore glasses, I'd see her pulling them off sideways to emphasize her glare. "A one-night stand usually entails fucking."

"But the connection—"

"Doesn't matter with a one-night stand."

"We created magic."

"For *one* night only."

"And it was beautiful."

"I'm glad, because from what I read, you might need the memories for future taco-tickling Tuesdays."

I groan and flop onto the couch. She's right, but I can't admit that.

Aware she's won, Amelia's smile shines brighter than the early morning sun.

"I really loathe you sometimes."

She takes my insult as a compliment. "Aww... you're so sweet when you've had all the kinks banged out of you." She stops humping the corner of her couch when a strange ring trickles through the living room. "What is that?"

I shrug. "Brodie took his cell with him."

"And he's about ancient enough to have a ringtone that old."

I laugh like his maturity isn't one of the things I like the most about him.

"Does Lucy have a cell phone?" Amelia asks when the noise continues.

I shake my head just as "You've reached the Davis residence. We're not home right now, so if you leave a message, we'll get back to you" comes from the entryway table.

"No fucking way," Amelia murmurs when we find the cause of the noise. It is a voicemail but in a box. "Are you sure he's thirty-seven? You might have gotten the numbers mixed up."

"You've seen him—"

"And Botox does wonders. Look at Cher."

I startle when she is interrupted. "Brodie, it's Laura from the nanny agency. I just read your email about Henley—"

"Answer it now!" Amelia demands, scaring me for the second time in the past minute.

"Answer what?"

"The phone. The voicemail gadget should have a phone attached to it. It will be big and clunky. Pick it up!"

When I find a white oblong-shaped object beside the still-talking machine, I pick it up, push the answer button, then squash it to my ear. "Hello..."

"Oh, hello. Ah. Is this Henley?"

I lower my voice and make it sound old. "Who, dear?"

"Henley..." Papers ruffle. "Seabourn. She is the nanny placement Brodie cited for Lucy Davis."

"Ohh. Hillary Seabourn? Yes, I'm Hillary. It is these damn dentures. I can't speak without a whistle. He must have misheard me. Is everything okay?"

"Um. Yes." She is a bad liar. "Brodie, ah... Mr. Davis forwarded some concerns to us this morning." She realizes she said too much too late. "I'll return his email. If you could ask him to check it, that would be wonderful. Have a pleasant day."

She disconnects our call before I can reply.

"Shit. *Shit.* SHIT!"

As Amelia remains quiet, the room spins around me. I can't believe my ruse has been busted so soon. I thought I'd at least have a week or two.

"What are you going to do?" Amelia asks, drawing my focus away from hyperventilating. "You could pack and leave before they get home."

"I can't do that to Lucy. I promised I'd be here when she got back."

"You don't ow—"

"Don't finish your sentence, Amelia. Not if you want us to stay friends."

She appears frustrated but doesn't sound it when she says, "I'm just trying to look out for you, Henley. It's what friends do." Her brows furrow before her face smooths. "Do you have access to Brodie's email server?"

"If it's on his laptop, yep."

"Get it. Go. Now. Move. I tried to watch that remake three times already. It is so bad I left the theater at the exact same scene. They could be home in ten minutes." My stomach gurgles as I race into the kitchen for the laptop Lucy was tinkering with earlier. "How many stars are in the password box?"

"Doesn't say," I reply, defeated.

"Try Lucy."

My heart pumps out a crazy tune when it is denied.

"What about her birthday?"

Once again, we come up empty-handed.

"His name?" When I glare at her, she shrugs. "What? If I had a dick as big as his, I'd be in love with myself too."

She has a point, so I punch in Brodie's name.

"It isn't his name, and we only have one more attempt before we're locked out for thirty minutes."

"Shit." Amelia peers around the kitchen like the answer might present itself, before the color drains from her cheeks, and she murmurs, "What about his wife's name?"

I hate myself for the bitchiness of my reply. "From what I can tell, she died years ago. Do you truly think she'd still be his password?"

"If he hasn't gotten over her, yeah, it's a strong possibility. But I'll leave the decision up to you because it isn't my life on the line."

"Life?"

"He used your first name in an email, Henley. There could be a handful of Henleys in the world, but how many aren't of British descent and don't have using assholes on the lookout for her?"

"Fuck."

With shaky hands, I type "Caroline" into the login box.

It gains me instant access to Brodie's inbox that displays he sent his message to the nanny agency minutes before confronting me in the kitchen.

"Delete it and her reply, then block her email."

I do as asked while mumbling, "It won't stop her from calling him."

"It will when we disconnect the landline phone. If she had Brodie's cell, she would have called it immediately after hanging up. She wouldn't have emailed him."

Her assumption makes sense, but I can't harness my curiosity. "What the hell is a landline?"

"Get rid of that first, and then I'll walk you through the ancient world of old people."

15

BRODIE

*a*fter how I've acted the past few days, I have no right to get jealous when Thane cozies up to Henley's back while attempting to teach her how to defend herself if an attacker approaches her from behind.

It could be construed as an innocent gesture if he didn't waggle his brows every time our eyes collide. He's riling me, and it's fucking working. I'm pissed, jealous, and fighting like hell not to storm into the basement and take over the self-defense class he's been running the past hour.

Thane knows what he's doing. I'm just annoyed as fuck that he can do whatever he wants without consequences.

I'm not so lucky.

My every move is watched—even the ones that occur in the privacy of my home.

I fucking hope Caroline wasn't looking down on me three nights ago when I screwed our daughter's nanny on the bed she purchased when we moved in together. Lucy was conceived on that bed, but with my head in a lust cloud and my smarts shut down, I couldn't stop what was happening.

It seems as if I have no willpower when it comes to Henley. She drops my defenses like a bomb and has me acting as if I am a decade younger than I am.

God, that night.

Fuck. I'm hard now just thinking about it.

I treated Henley like a whore, and she loved every damn minute of it.

Caroline was beautiful but more reserved in the bedroom —almost shy.

We didn't fuck. We made love.

That phrase can't be used to describe my exchange with Henley. We fucked like wild animals, and at the time, I couldn't get enough.

Then the guilt set in.

Our house isn't the one Caroline and I purchased following our wedding, and neither is half of the furniture. But that mattress, the one I sullied and stained, was ours. I couldn't stop replaying the last time she told me she loved me on that same bed, her lazy smile when I kissed her goodbye for the final time. She was no longer on maternity leave, but Lucy slept peacefully in a crib beside our bed.

Don't get me wrong. I'm expected to move on. Caroline wouldn't want me to be miserable, but I could have picked a better spot to do that.

I should have respected my wife.

Instead, I took my anger out on Henley because she was the easiest target.

I am a fucking coward.

And the situation grew worse when we returned from the movies. Henley appeared set to rip me a new asshole the instant we were alone before we left that morning, but she's had a handful of opportunities over the past three days that she let slip by with the quickest farewell.

It has me panicked she didn't enjoy herself as much as I did. Perhaps she didn't want to be fucked like a whore and forced to orgasm an incalculable number of times.

She couldn't have been faking. Her shakes, those moans, the wetness, that couldn't have been made up. She was as into it as I was.

Wasn't she?

It's probably the dad bod that turned her off. I'm putting steps into place to fix it. I haven't worked out this much since my early twenties, which is facetious considering I'm adamant we can't do that again.

At least not on your wife's damn bed.

I shut down my frustration when Lucy plops her backside onto the warped wooden step. I've been watching their self-defense class for the past thirty minutes. I missed the first half because Chelsea decided to hang around after Lucy's dance lesson and have lunch with the girls.

If you haven't worked this out yet, I am a stubborn man. I've forgiven Chelsea for stuff that happened in the months following Caroline's death, but I won't ever forget.

I grin when Lucy chugs half the bottle of water I hand her before resting her sweat-dotted head on my shoulder. She's been a part of the action as much as Henley has, and it has me kicking myself that I didn't think about teaching her some moves earlier. It is never too early to know how to protect yourself.

"You better be quick, Daddy, or you might lose, and we know how much you hate losing."

"I don't hate losing."

Even sitting, Lucy cocks out her hip and fans her tiny hand across it. "You do so. You told the man at the fair that his duck game was fra-due-lant." She struggles with her last word.

"It was rigged!" I defend, giving her an easy word to use next time. "I hit every damn duck, but only three went down." She giggles when I won't let it go. "I had every right to inspect his gear. Ricocheting pellets are extremely dangerous." When she rolls her eyes, I band my arm around her shoulders and pull her to my chest. "And what have I got to lose? My most valuable possession is at my side, where she belongs."

I stop noogying her head when she murmurs, "Henley." When I free her, she gives me a miffed look while fixing her hair into place. Once all the static I created has settled, she locks her eyes with mine before proving she is far wiser than her almost six years. "Uncle Thane likes her a lot." She shouts her last two words. "So if you don't stop lying, Henley might start looking at him like she looks at you when you think she's not looking." Confusion mars her face until she runs her sentence through her head a hundred times to ensure it is right. She returns her focus to me once she is confident her tongue twister makes sense. "You look at her too. You just keep your tongue in your mouth..." Her head flings back to the main area of the finished basement. "Unlike Uncle Thane."

The annoyance in her voice jumps onto my face when I follow the direction of her gaze. Not an ounce of air is between Thane and Henley's bodies. They're joined at the hip, and with Henley needing leverage as she endeavors to throw him over her shoulder, her ass is grinding against his crotch.

Thane looks one grind away from climax.

"You need to distribute your weight more evenly." Lucy's face gleams with excitement when I enter the basement instead of hiding my watch on the stairs. "Especially when your attacker weighs more than you." I peel Thane off Henley's back before showing her the correct stance. "Widen your feet to the width of your shoulders, then use the strength in your legs to lift him from the ground. Your ass should bring him up and over you, not give him an erection."

Thane holds his hands in the air non-defensively when I shoot him a riled look.

Lucy asks, "What's an erection?"

I pretend not to hear her while instructing Henley on the correct procedure for fending off an attacker. She implements my instructions but won't look at me while I give them.

Her lack of eye contact pisses me off more than Thane's murmur after Henley tosses him to the ground like a ragdoll. "After all this action, I need a cold shower and a stiff drink." He locks his eyes on me. "You cool to wrap up this session while I take care of business?"

Lucy is clueless about what he's referencing, but Henley has no issues deciphering it. She tells him to wait, that after back-to-back dance and self-defense classes, she is also in desperate need of a shower.

"Maybe I should join you?"

This isn't the first time she's flirted with Thane today. However, it is the first time I have responded. Before she can get an inch away from me, I snatch up her wrist and tug her back.

I haven't had my hands on her in days, so the zap isn't just intense. It is palpable enough for Thane and Lucy to feel.

"Or maybe I just need ice cream?"

Lucy's eyes bulge before they rocket to her uncle.

Thane bounces on his heels, loving her attention. "What do you say, Lulu? Should we head to the ice cream parlor for a pre-dinner treat?"

"Yes!" Lucy leaps into the air before twisting to face me. "Can we, Daddy? Please."

"They can't come with us. Your dad isn't a fan of pre-dinner treats, and you heard Henley." Thane plugs his nose. "She's stinky." He ignores Henley's huff. "She needs to shower, and I don't know how your showers here work, but if they're anything like mine, she might need help."

"Daddy knows how they work," Lucy says, her face glowing. "Maybe he can help her?"

Her offer is as innocent as her face, but it doubles the heat burning between Henley and me.

Almost every incident we've had has been in the bathroom.

"That sounds like a good plan." I appreciate Thane handing over the baton for a game he should have never been participating in, but he ensures I know it won't be a long changeover. "We can only hope it won't take them all night to clear up the murkiness." Before climbing the basement stairs, he scoops Lucy up like she doesn't have legs. "We'll be back in an hour max. If you need longer than that, you have my number."

The thumps of his stomps have barely stopped booming in my ear when Henley yanks out of my hold before moving to the side of the makeshift gym to fetch a bottle of water and a towel.

She drags it over her sweat-drenched head, her eyes never veering near mine. Things have changed between us so dramatically. I fucking hate it. It wasn't like this before we fucked. And yeah, I can admit that I stuffed up with how I handled it the following morning, but what's Henley's excuse? She's acting as if it meant nothing to her.

Too annoyed to hold my tongue a second longer, I say, "This is the exact reason I tried to stay away. I gave into temptation once, and now everything is ruined."

Don't take that the wrong way. Henley is a brilliant nanny to Lucy. Her love and attention to detail for every aspect of her inclusion in Lucy's life can't be improved. I'm talking about how royally I screwed this up by giving in to the tension burning between us.

"Did I take it too far?" My next question comes out like my words were dragged over gravel first. "Did I hurt you? Is that why you're not talking to me?"

"Are you kidding me?" Those four words are the most she's spoken to me in three days. "You stopped talking to me."

"Because I couldn't get any words out through the guilt clogged in my throat." That was more honest than I'm used to, but it finally sees Henley's eyes locking with mine, so I continue. "I shouldn't have let things go that far, especially not there."

Her anger has her missing my last three words. "Don't worry, your actions over the past three days have ensured it won't happen again. Thane—"

"Will lose teeth before I ever let him touch you."

Henley is as surprised by my jealous outburst as I am, but she takes it in stride. "He thinks you'll never stop using Caroline's death as an excuse not to move on."

"Don't bring her into this." She hit a nerve. My tone announces this, let alone the groove between my brows. "You can't talk about shit you have no clue about."

I realize she's gunning for blood when she drags another innocent bystander into the mess we've created. "I know what it's like for Lucy." She dumps the towel in the laundry basket, her back facing me as she adds, "I know what she's going through and that you have no right to keep her mother's family from her."

After gritting my teeth and throwing her a disdained glare that should burn more than her sunburn ever did, I exit the basement before I say something I'll later regret.

Henley follows me, her impairment too clouded by anger to let this go. "That little girl is in the midst of an identity crisis because she has no clue about her heritage."

"Are you fucking kidding me?" I roar, my anger palpable when she thrusts her hand at a portrait of Lucy in the hallway. "We just spent hours with her uncle and aunt today after a nine-hour stint with her grandparents over the weekend."

"Because a court ordered you to associate with them."

My laugh is brittle and low. "Oh. Let me guess... you've been speaking with Chelsea?" I don't wait for her to confirm. "Did she mention how she took Lucy from her crib when she was six months old? How she left me a fucking note saying she'd take care of my daughter while I grieved the death of her sister?"

Henley doesn't speak. Her mouth only opens and closes.

"Or how about when a delivery driver mistook her for Lucy's mother, and she didn't correct him? Did she take any of the blame for the rift she caused between me and Lucy's family?" When she shakes her head, I scoff. "Of course she didn't. Because it is so much easier to blame everyone but the person responsible." I step closer to her, my anger too perverse to shut down. "You come into my home, into my life, but you don't know the first thing about me or my daughter. Yeah, I could have handled matters differently both now and back then, but I was holding on by a fucking thread."

Tears burn my eyes, but Henley's spill over when I confess, "My wife was dead, and the daughter she didn't get the chance to raise was living three states over without my fucking permission. Was I an ass? Yeah, I was. Did I bring up every one of their family's secrets during the drawn-out court proceedings to grant me custody of my own damn child? Fucking oath I did. Do I regret it? Not for a single second. Why? Because Lucy is mine, and I will never let *anyone* take her away from me. Not Caroline's parents, her twin sister, or Thane..." I could stop there, but when have I been sensible around this woman? "Not even you."

"I—"

Before she can speak another word, I climb the main stairs of the house I purchased with a massive mortgage since no one wanted to live in the "murder house."

This time, Henley doesn't follow me.

16

BRODIE

*W*hen I hear the patter of tiny feet, I scrub at my mouth to remove the whiskey from my lips, then hide the bottle Thane and I are sharing in the bottom drawer of my desk.

"Hey, baby. What are you doing down here? I thought you were heading up to bed."

Lucy walks into my office with her stuffed rabbit dragging behind her. When she reaches my desk, I push back my chair and pick her up. She can smell the alcohol on my breath—her screwed-up nose announces this—but she's not up for more antics today.

With my conversation with Henley not needing longer than an hour, Thane took that as meaning I was refusing the baton, so he stayed for both dinner and dessert.

It is a pity for him Henley hasn't left her room in hours.

She didn't even come down for dinner.

I can't say I blame her. Thane is a worse cook than Lucy.

"If you're worried Daddy and Thane will be upset about Henley tucking you in, you have no reason to fret. We were planning to come up and make sure you were settled after your bedtime stories."

"We didn't read any stories. Not even one."

"You didn't?" I ask, surprise in my tone. She suckers Henley into reading her two to three bedtime stories a night. I usually only do one.

When Lucy shakes her head, blonde locks catch in my cropped beard. "Henley isn't in her room. She isn't in the bathroom either. I can't find her anywhere."

When I peer at Thane, he scrubs at the stubble on his chin before placing his glass of whiskey down and heading for the stairs before us. He tried to coerce Henley out of her room earlier, but that was hours ago.

Upon noticing how worried Lucy is, I try to calm her. "Maybe she's tired and went to bed early."

"She's not in her bed. I checked. She's gone." I pull her in close to my chest when her lower lip quivers, before climbing the stairs several paces behind Thane.

As I reach the door of Lucy's room, Thane exits Henley's at the end of the hall.

My heart sinks to my feet when he inconspicuously shakes his head, wordlessly announcing that Henley's room is empty, but I play it cool. Lucy wasn't old enough to remember the horrible way her mother was killed, and I want to keep it that way.

"I guess it's my lucky night." After placing Lucy on her feet, I nudge my head to her bookshelf. "Pick a book." When she peers up at me, blinking and pleading, I hold my finger in the air. "One book. It's already past your bedtime, so I'm not risking a tantrum, especially not with him sleeping over." I nudge my head to Thane, whose shoulder is propped against Lucy's bedroom door as he soundlessly seeks instructions.

"Uncle Thane is sleeping over?" Lucy's words roar from her mouth.

When Thane answers on my behalf with a head bob, Lucy plucks the first book she sees on the shelf, charges for her bed, and dives in. I realize her acting skills are on par with mine when she says, "Henley will read me three stories tomorrow. She won't let me down." She hides the wetness welling in her eyes with a slanted head. "Right, Daddy?"

Not wanting to break her heart, I nod.

It appeases her worry, but only a smidge.

It takes reading her a story and running my fingers through her hair for almost ten minutes before she finally lets go of the tension keeping her shoulders taut.

Thane's eyes lift to mine when I enter the office we were commiserating in earlier. I'm not exactly sure what he had to commiserate, but it was clear his mood after dinner wasn't as embellished as it was when he was grinding against Henley's ass.

As much as I wanted to pretend Henley's presence wasn't missed this evening, it couldn't be denied. My mood has been in the toilet right along with Thane's, and it worsens when I notice a cell phone on my desk. It is new but not the latest model.

"I found that on her bed," Thane announces when I pick up Henley's cell phone to scroll through an endless list of messages from the only friend she talks about, Amelia.

"Her things?"

I breathe a little easier when Thane replies, "Still in her closet." He plops down a bottle oddly similar to the one I lost myself in this afternoon, but the scant bit of liquid at the bottom is clear. "That was full when I gave it to her. Her friend swears it had to have been half empty."

Sliding over the fact he gave my nanny alcohol during a shift, I ask, "You've spoken to her friend?"

As he scrubs at his jaw, he lifts his chin. "She said what I had suspected, that drinking isn't Henley's go-to coping mechanism, and she's usually smarter than that." His eyes drop to the almost empty bottle. "She must have been real upset to down a bottle of vodka in under two hours." When I remain quiet, silenced by guilt, Thane angles his head so I can't lie straight to his face before asking, "You fucked your nanny, didn't you?"

"No." My lie barely lasts a second. "I didn't mean to take it that far. I thought one taste would be enough."

"Come on, man. When is one taste *ever* enough?" He props his ass on my desk and folds his arms over his chest. "When did it happen?"

"Does that matter?"

"Yeah, it does," he immediately fires back. "Because from what her friend told me, it was days ago, so why would she respond to your piss-poor attempt of acting like you don't need anyone in your life now? Why wasn't it an immediate response?"

"Did it ever occur to you that it was because I was doing a good job keeping things professional between us?"

He throws his head back and laughs. It isn't his real laugh. It is the one he does when he knows I'm full of shit. "I love how you only ever jump when you think there's competition. Caroline—"

"Keep my fucking wife out of this."

My angry roar gives me away in an instant. "So it wasn't anything Henley said that pissed you off." He stands to his full height, bringing him an inch taller than me. "I'm a big boy, Brodie. If I said something that made you angry, you should have taken it out on me."

"I didn't take anything out on her." My voice lowers as the truth slips from my lips. "I just told her that she doesn't know shit about Lucy and me and that she will never really have the chance to learn."

"You're a fucking ass—"

"Those aren't the exact words I said."

"So?" Thane bites back. "You hurled abuse at a girl who should be scared of her own shadow but for some fucking reason isn't." When my expression deadpans, he *tsks* me. "You're so caught up in your own woes, you think no other fucker has any." He nudges his head to the door like Henley is standing on the other side. "I offered self-defense classes because she flinches around any man who isn't you." I don't get the chance to register my shock or my anger. "And Chelsea encouraged her to wear a bikini because when she pulled out the frumpy one piece she had packed, she let slip that she's never purchased her own swimsuit." His fond smile pisses me off. "And do you notice how often she tugs on the hem of her shirt?"

"She fiddles when nervous."

He *tsks* me again. "She has body issues."

"No, she fucking doesn't," I instantly deny. The woman who has stood in front of me naked time and time again can't have body dysmorphia. "How could she when she's perfect?"

I realize I said my last statement out loud when Thane throws his hands in the air. "Finally we're getting somewhere." He drops his arms and glares at me. "But maybe you should mention that to her occasionally instead of emailing the nanny agency, begging for her replacement." He backhands me like it is the only thing stopping him from turning our exchange physical. "Caroline said you were daft at reading people, but I had no clue it was this bad."

I let his comment slide since it is accurate. I've always been bad at reading people. It is one of the reasons I'll never be anything more than hired muscle to the bureau. I can't profile to save my life.

My brows furrow when part of his reply smacks into me. "What do you mean I emailed the agency for a replacement? I forwarded my concerns to Nancy, but she isn't back for another week."

Before he can answer me, Henley's cell phone rings.

"Put it on speaker," I demand when Thane picks it up to answer it.

"I found her," a girlie voice shrieks down the line before Thane can get in a word. "She's at a bar a couple of clicks from your location."

"Name?" Thane asks, his head not as clouded with information as mine.

A keyboard being clicked sounds down the line before she answers, "Aeros Club. It is a—"

"Known mafia location," I interrupt, cussing. "How'd you find her so fast?"

When she remains quiet, Thane offers an introduction. "Amelia, meet Brodie. Brodie, Amelia, Henley's BFF."

"Nice to..." Her words trail off for barely a second before they come back fast and heavy. "Henley is gaining a lot of interest."

Not needing any clarification to decipher what she means, I snatch Henley's phone out of Thane's hand and then demand, "Watch Lucy until I get back."

"I can get Henley."

Ignoring him, I grab my gun from the safe in my office, stuff it down the back of my trousers, then commence calling in a suspected possession charge for the Aeros Club. "Units should be advised suspects may be armed. Approach with caution."

I head for the garage as a nine-one-one operator dispatches my call over numerous channels.

"You're taking your bike?" Thane asks when I rip off its dust cover and unplug the battery saver. "You haven't ridden that since Caroline died."

"It'll be faster than my truck since I can take a walker's route."

"And you need to be quick," Amelia interrupts, backing me up. "She's a mouse in a snake pit, seconds from being bitten."

When an image pops up on the phone screen showing Henley butting shoulders with two known gangsters, I throw my leg over my bike, kick-start it, toss on my helmet, then crank my neck back to Thane.

He reads the fret on my face like no one else. "I won't let anything happen to her. I swear to fucking God."

He's only just finished crossing his heart when I fly out of the garage at the speed of a bullet leaving a gun. This is the one thing I loved about my numerous placements with the bureau over the past sixteen years. How easily you can pretend to be someone you're not.

An outlaw.

A biker.

The cousin of a mafia kingpin.

I can be anyone I want to be, bar the title I never wanted.

A widower.

That never opens doors. It only ever closes them.

I shake my head to rid it of horrid thoughts before taking the corner at a speed faster than safe. Once I narrowly miss an oncoming vehicle, I seek an update from Henley's friend. "Is she still at the bar?"

"No." Her voice is projected through my helmet now. "They're walking her toward the back exit."

"They?"

I hear her swallow before she answers, "There are three of them. One on each arm and a third trailing behind. He's wearing a suit and a sleezy grin."

I push the bike to its absolute limits. I thrash the living shit out of it before practically diving off it when I reach the back entrance of Aeros.

As the paintwork that cost more than I could afford at the time scrapes along the concrete, my fist finds its way into the first man's face, and my spare hand bands around Henley's waist to pull her behind me.

He lands on his ass with a thud as the ringleader pulls his phone from his ear. He is clearly in charge when he signals for the second goon to approach me.

Since his face looks like it's taken a hundred hits in the past week alone, I aim my fist lower. I hit him in the Adam's apple. It is a kill shot for someone who doesn't know what they're doing, but for me, it will keep him down long enough to get Henley to safety. Currently, she's leaning against a dumpster, too intoxicated to stand without assistance.

"I'd think long and hard before you reach for the piece stuffed under your jacket," I murmur when the man in the sleek black suit slides his hand across his waist. "If Henry finds out you're operating on his turf without a permit, you won't make it back to the dump you call headquarters."

Henry is a common name, but when it comes to gangsters, it is the only name that matters. He is the boss of all bosses and a recent associate of mine.

With his hand back at his side, the unnamed man mutters, "I'm not operating." He peers past my shoulder to Henley. "I asked if she wanted to get out of here. She said yes."

"She can't stand, but I'm meant to believe she agreed to go with you willingly?" When he jerks up his chin, I scoff out a brittle laugh. "Get the fuck out of here before I send a snapshot of that ugly ass neck tat to Storm." Storm is Henry's hacker. She can get shit not even the bureau can find. "I bet she'll find it in a heap of places like this." I wave my hand at the club. "And every single image will show you walking a drugged woman out, won't it?"

My jaw tics when he doesn't deny my claim. Sex trafficking is rampant now, and they've moved on from kidnapping women no one will search for. They take anyone they want.

The remembrance sees me putting my boot into the man withering at my feet before I pull out my cell phone to assist in his identification.

The fact I'm beating into him so freely convinces the goon that I'm not better than him. "All right, all right," he interrupts. His hands are in the air, but his smirk is more in amusement than fear. "We're leaving." He drags up the first man I took down before I snap his profile. "Get in the fucking car."

His eyes remain on me as he loads his men into his vehicle minus the asset they came for. My gaze only drifts to the rearview mirror for the quickest second when flashing lights project from a few streets over.

My eagerness to get Henley out of the alleyway before she is forced to sober up in lockup leaves the goon none the wiser that I'm a federal agent. He tosses me a gang symbol before he exits the alleyway in a smoke cloud.

The scent of burning rubber adds to the redness of Henley's cheeks. "Brodie?"

"Yeah," I reply far too smugly. I should hate how she can recognize me so easily, but I don't.

"I don't feel good."

"I'm sorry to hear that, but you'll need to hold it in until we get home."

I'm not sorry. Not a single fucking bit. I'm angry and my veins are clogged with adrenaline, but since I can't guarantee the goon didn't slip something into her drink, I can't announce how frustrated I am right now.

I need to get her home first.

And safe.

Making sure she is safe is my main priority.

I pick up my bike, then roll it close to the dumpster like the scrapes down one side aren't breaking my heart. Once my helmet protects Henley's head, I straddle my bike the best I can without letting go of her hand before gesturing for her to slip in behind me.

She backs away, shaking her head. "I-I can't. I don't feel good."

"Those lights aren't disco lights, Henley. They're the cops, so if you don't get on my bike, they will question why you were drinking in an establishment owned by the mob."

My reply sobers her up quickly. "What?"

"Get on, and I will explain when we get home."

"I-I—"

"Now, Henley!" I hate myself and everything I am about when she startles from my shout before scampering for the bike as fast as her wobbly legs can take her.

She shakes the entire way and long after I pull into the garage of my home. She even shakes when Thane curls a blanket around her back before digging her cell phone out of my pocket.

I was so focused on Henley that I forgot Amelia was on hold.

"Yeah, he's got her," Thane updates Amelia. "I'll make sure she calls you as soon as she wakes up. All right, bye."

"Leave her," I demand when a second after he dumps her phone on the shelf in my garage, he attempts to assist Henley off my bike. "I've got her."

"You sure?" he checks upon noticing Henley isn't the only one shaking.

My adrenaline is high, dangerously so.

"Yeah." I pretend to shake off my fear as if it is an overload of testosterone before dismounting my bike and pulling a silent Henley into my arms. "Take Henley's room. I'll put her in my room to ensure she's close to the bathroom."

"That's a good idea. She smells like a brewery."

My lips tug at one side when Henley murmurs, "I'm drunk, not deaf."

"And in a fuckton of trouble with Amelia," Thane torments before twanging her bottom lip and then leading our helm inside.

Henley's glassy eyes bulge before she buries her head between my pecs. "You should have let them take me. Doubt their torture would have been worse than Amelia's."

It is wrong of me to pry while she is intoxicated, but could I call myself an agent if I didn't? "Amelia really knows her stuff with security and surveillance, doesn't she? She found you fast."

Her praise comes in just as quick. "She is a genius hacker. She can find anyone this quick." She pulls her hand out of the blanket to click her fingers. "But everyone treats her like an idiot because she's young." I can't tell if she is looking at me or through me when she murmurs, "She tried to join the bureau. They told her to come back when she's thirty." She rolls her eyes before shooting her hand up to cover them. "That hurts."

Even with the lights off, Lucy knows when people are sneaking around. I've taught her every creak of our old home. "Daddy?"

"Yeah, baby, it's me. Go back to sleep."

With her eyes more adjusted to the dark than mine, she asks, "Is Henley okay?"

"Yeah, she's fine. She's just feeling a little unwell. Daddy will take care of her."

"I am not sick," Henley denies loudly. "I'm drunk." She hiccups, widens her eyes, then slaps a hand over her mouth when Lucy giggles at her reply. Her eyes are more sad than amused when she murmurs, "You can fire me now. I understand. I'm not good enough to be your daughter's nanny, so you had every right to seek a replacement."

"She must be sick if she believes that," Lucy pipes up. "I'll get a washcloth."

As she makes a beeline for the bathroom, I enter my room and place Henley on my bed. Her hand is still clamped over her mouth, and her eyes are full of apologies.

With the likelihood of her remembering our conversation in the morning weak, I admit, "I sent an 'are you sure she's a good fit' email to Nancy the morning following your first sleepover, but I never contacted the agency directly to seek your replacement." I move to her feet to remove her shoes. "I don't know where you got that information, but it is wrong."

"That's not true." Henley waits for me to remove her shoes before confessing, "I saw the email on your laptop. It was in the sent folder."

"That isn't poss—"

"It was me," Lucy admits, her words barely a squeak. "I was trying to find some new recipes, and there was an unsent message on the screen, so I sent it so it would disappear." Her watering eyes shift to

Henley. "I'm sorry. I didn't know what it said. I wouldn't have sent it if I knew about the mean things Daddy was telling them."

I don't get the chance to defend my actions. "Oh, honey, it's okay," Henley assures her. "You didn't do anything wrong."

"I did. I sent it, but I didn't know what it said. I swear. I don't want you to go." When Lucy's bottom lip quivers, Henley holds out her arms for her. She dumps the washcloth on the floor, sidesteps me like Elvis Carlton does the defensive line every game, and throws herself into Henley's arms before hiding her wet face in her chest. "I'm s-so sorry."

I try to comfort her too, but I'm shunted away.

It doubles the guilt in Henley's eyes, but I only see it for a second before she focuses all her attention on Lucy.

I don't know what she whispers in her ear, but in a matter of minutes, Lucy pulls away from her chest, wipes away her tears, then rolls back her shoulders.

I am anticipating the dressing down of my life, so you can picture my shock when she squeezes the life out of my thigh before she exits my room without so much as a backward glance.

17

BRODIE

"What the hell did you do with my daughter? And where can I find her?" Lucy scares the shit out of me more than any other girl I know, but that's one of the things I love about her the most. She doesn't put up with my crap.

Henley stares at the door Lucy passed through a few seconds ago before shifting her dilated eyes back to me. "I told her she shouldn't be so hard on you. That a daddy's job is to protect their children, and although she may not want to believe it"—she swallows three times before finishing her sentence—"she probably needs protecting from me more than anyone." She fans her face, but it does little to bring back its color. "I also reminded her that Uncle Thane is sleeping over..." She stops, then starts again. "He—" A dangerous heave interrupts her this time. "I'm going to be sick."

I dive for her at the same time she lurches forward, so my shirt catches most of her first lot of vomit.

The toilet bowl handles the rest.

"I—" Another stream of liquidity vomit cuts her off.

"We'll talk once you've sobered up." I pull her hair back from her face before opening the drawer under the vanity and finding an elastic hair tie. My stomach is rock hard—on the inside. Nothing makes me queasy, but I'd rather sleep on vomit-free sheets.

"Why aren't you mad?" Henley asks after expelling half of the alcohol she'd consumed before going out to search for more. "Beau would have been horrified."

The churns of her stomach when I aid her to her feet are so loud they hurt me.

Needing to keep the focus off the massacre occurring inside her, I ask, "Who's Beau?"

"He's my ex." Her feet more drag than stomp along the tiles when we move for the door, so I return her to my arms to make the journey easier. "He was an asshole." I deserve her jab when she murmurs, "I seem to have a thing for assholes." My knuckles are already bruised, but they're primed for a second round when she quietly adds, "He's the reason I'm a lightweight. The last time I drank of my own will, he chipped my tooth."

"I'm not exactly sure you can call a whole bottle of vodka a lightweight drinker's companion." I place her onto the bed before pretending our conversation is casual and not an interrogation for information. "Is Beau from the South like you?" Her lips purse in confusion, so I add, "Does he have an accent like yours?"

Her *pfft* sends spit flying in the air. "I don't have an accent." Her throat works through a hard swallow when her eyes drop to her gym pants. "But I do have vomit on my pants."

I face my eyes to the wall when she commences pulling them off, but within seconds, I'm left with no choice but to gawk. Her gym pants are stuck halfway down her thighs, and no amount of grunting and groaning will remove them.

"If you're wearing butt-hungry panties, I can't be held accountable for my actions."

Henley's smile does stupid things to my insides. It makes my heart flutter faster and my stomach not feel so twisted up in knots. "I'm not. I don't own any G-strings."

As I move closer to the bed to offer her assistance, I say, "Did Chelsea not offer you extra sets?"

She stills before locking her eyes with mine. I'm already struggling to keep a rational head, so you can imagine how hard it becomes when her teeth graze her bottom lip before she confesses, "I accepted her offer because I wanted to make you jealous."

"You succeeded."

My honesty awards me the same from her. "And angry."

As I yank on her skintight pants, I ask, "You wanted to make me angry?"

Henley shakes her head, then pulls a face like she regrets her decision. "I made you angry." Giving up on her campaign to free herself from her vomit-stained pants, she flops onto the bed with a sigh. "I guess I shouldn't be surprised. I had my butt hanging out for the world to see even with this ugly thing on it."

She flips over like she's dying to be taken from behind, before highlighting a scar I hadn't noticed before. It is faint but long and jagged.

"Did Beau do that?"

After taking a moment to assess if the edginess in my tone is jealousy or fury, she shakes her head. "But I don't want to talk about him and his weird eyes." A second after she's freed from her pants, she crawls up my bed with her floral printed-backside swinging high in the air, slips under the comforter, then buries her head into my pillow. "I'm tired."

With her eyes already closed, I place the dedicated vomit bucket at her side of the bed, then tiptoe to the door.

I almost make it outside before the faintest plea stops me. "Stay with me."

"I—"

"Please." Just the plead in her voice won't see me issuing another denial, much less what she says next. "I'm scared."

"I'll stay with you until you fall asleep, but then I have to check on Lucy."

Henley nods before scooting over to the half of the bed Caroline always slept on. As I toe off my boots, I scrub at my beard. This is a bad idea. I know it is. I just can't help myself. The last time I raced to find someone, it didn't end with her sleeping in my bed.

She died.

Left.

I never had the chance to make things right.

"Is it my breath?" Henley asks, mistaking my forlorn look. "It's bad, isn't it?" She cups her mouth and breathes into her hand. A second after her nose screws up, she slips out of bed and makes a stumbling dash to the bathroom. "I'll brush them. There are a lot of nasties in vomit that could hurt my teeth if I don't wash them off. Considering I hate the dentist, I should lessen the chance of a visit."

Her race for her toothbrush slows when I ask, "Do you think you can handle a full brush? Maybe rinse out your mouth first and see how your stomach handles it."

After a short deliberation, she says, "I can brush. My stomach will be fine."

She knocks over the toothbrush holder and the brushes inside when she launches for them. Her perceptiveness is off since her veins are still primed with alcohol.

I can't help but grin when she murmurs, "Maybe I should gargle."

"Good idea." I clutch the mouthwash so firmly the bottle indents when Henley traces the grooves of my smile with her index finger. I don't have dimples—more creases from smiling too often. I also wasn't aware of how close I was standing to her until she didn't have to overextend her arm to touch me.

With her fingertip still exploring, she asks, "You were happy once, weren't you?"

I wait for her eyes to lift to mine before nodding.

"Then she died, and you became sad."

"Not exactly," I reply, shocking us both with my honesty.

Things weren't great between Caroline and me before she passed. My hours were draining, Caroline was itching to get back to work, and we hadn't been intimate since Lucy was born.

I often wondered if that is why Chelsea responded how she did. Perhaps she knew we were fighting and that much of the tension centered around Caroline's family wanting her to return to work sooner than I'd hoped.

For a drunk woman, Henley has way too much wisdom. "No matter what was happening between you two when she died, you shouldn't keep who she was a secret from Lucy. She deserves to know what her mother was like."

"I tried," I reply before I can stop myself. "It just..."

When words elude me, Henley fills in the blanks. "Hurts?"

Again, I nod. "I kissed her goodbye, but I was still angry that she was returning to work sooner than we had agreed, so I didn't wish her well. I didn't hope she'd have a great day. I resented her putting her position above our daughter's needs." My laugh is brittle and echoes in the bathroom. "I was a fucking hypocrite. She always put Lucy first. Even right at the end."

I cough, hopeful it will hide the croakiness of my voice, before filling the cap of the mouthwash with minty blue liquid and handing it to Henley.

She appears as if she still wants to talk, but she instead downs the burning liquid, swishes it around her mouth, then spits out the now-frothy concoction into the sink.

When she heads back to my room, I assume our conversation is over, but the faintest mumble announces even if we talked for hours, I still have so much to learn about this woman. "I was older than Lucy when I lost my mother, so my memories are stronger, but as the years move on, they fade more and more." She looks me dead in the eyes. "I don't know if I could have forgiven my father if I found out he was purposely hiding memories of her from me. He was hurting too, but he never pretended she didn't exist." She stops, slowly breathes out her nose, then whispers, "I was the only one he forgot about."

The tip of her nose reddens when she rubs her hand over it. "He wouldn't look at me after she died, and it was only after you ignored me the same way that I realized how much it hurt me." She scrubs at a tear rolling down her cheek. "I get that it hurt him to look at me, and that he was reminded of what he lost, but I was grieving too. I was just as upset. I didn't deserve to be ignored."

"You didn't," I agree, mindful not all my agreeance stems from how her father handled the loss of his wife. "Not back then or now. I just..." I stop talking when I fail to find the right words.

Several long sniffles pass before I give the truth a whirl. "I fucked up. Grief makes you stupid. It affects you in ways you can't comprehend even while wading knee-deep in it. I—"

There is so much more I want to say, but Henley's interruption assures my focus remains on Lucy. "Promise you won't do to Lucy what my father did to me. That you won't put your grief above hers." I feel like a complete fucking ass for how I responded at the Fourth of July barbecue when she says, "You lost your wife, but Lucy lost her mother, and as much as she is desperate to find her replacement, deep down inside she knows Caroline is irreplaceable. She lives inside her. She has her blood pumping through her veins, so she will *always* be her mother."

When her words overturn every worry I had about her trying to replace Caroline, I murmur, "I promise."

My pledge should mean nothing to her, but with a sheepish grin that announces she's apologetic for the sorrow on my face, she accepts it, bobs down to collect the spew bucket from the floor, and slips out of my room via the bathroom a second before Lucy enters my room via the main door.

Impulses have me wanting to chase Henley down, but with a lot of what she said making sense, I scoop my daughter in my arms and tickle her stomach. "What are you still doing up, missy moo? You were meant to be in bed hours ago."

"I forgot Uncle Thane snores!" she replies while scrubbing at her eye with her balled hand.

"Uncle Thane is already asleep?"

Lucy shakes her head. "No, he's out there." She thrust her hand at my partially open bedroom door. "Spying on you."

"I'm not spying," Thane refutes, proving Lucy's assumption is on the money. After pushing open the door his shoulder was propped against, he says, "I was going to fetch a glass of water for Lucy when I realized the bathroom was occupied."

"You could have gone to the kitchen."

"Yeah, Uncle Thane, you could have gone to the kitchen," Lucy repeats, backing me up. "You scared Henley away."

"That isn't what happened." I don't know why I'm tossing Thane a life vest. I should let him tread water alongside me since it was the jealousy he instigated that fueled my fight with Henley. "Henley was feeling better, so she went downstairs to heat up some leftovers."

"That doesn't sound like someone who feels better," Lucy contradicts when the sound of someone being sick slips through the floorboards. After wiggling to be placed down, she says, "I'll get a washcloth."

"No!" I shout, stopping her. "It is time for you to go to bed. For real this time."

Thane looks misty-eyed when I hand him Lucy. It is understandable when you learn I haven't left her in the care of anyone but Ms. Mitchell since I was regranted custody of her six weeks shy of her first birthday, and that was only because Ms. Mitchell survived three months of intense one-on-one training. I shadowed her for weeks on end. If she hadn't passed with flying colors, I wouldn't have returned to work.

Considering that would have left a heap of bad guys on the streets, I'm glad she was as tenacious as I am stubborn. She raised Lucy how I would have if I weren't tracking down my wife's killer, and never once forced me to face the guilt I dumped on Caroline when I didn't understand she was more than a wife and a mother.

I made mistakes back then, big ones.

I won't do it again.

18

HENLEY

*W*hoever said death isn't painful lied. It hurts. A lot. My head is thumping, my body is aching, and my neck is kinked like I spent the night sleeping upright.

It dawns on me that is in fact the case when I slowly crack open my eyes. I'm on the three-seater couch in the living room, leaning on something that feels stiff and poky.

My heart rate jumps astronomically when I discover what is propping me up. It isn't a pillow. It isn't even a what. It is a who. A very handsome who even though he appears as if his sleep was as lackluster as mine over the past few nights.

Brodie is slotted on the couch next to me. His mouth is slightly ajar as his chest rises and falls in rhythm to his faint snores. He's wearing a white sleeveless undershirt similar to the one he wears while jogging, and it announces that his hard work the past week is paying dividends. Almost every bump my eyes drink in is muscle, even the ones in his midsection that I liked a little squishier.

His dad bod suits him as much as his chin-length hair and frown lines.

The giddy feeling overtaking my hangover gets sideswiped when portions of my night filter back into my head. My argument with Brodie. The chugs of vodka. The fool who wouldn't take no for an answer.

My eyes bulge when I remember Brodie's fist flying through the air a second before he pulled me behind him. I warned the men that there'd be consequences for taking me. I had no idea they would come in the form of Brodie.

The memories stop at Brodie's impressive fighting skills. I recall a talking helmet and a dread unlike anything I've ever felt, but the rest is a fog.

"Oh god," I groan when I stretch high enough to spot a bucket at my feet. It is empty, but droplets of water have dried along the rim, announcing it was recently cleaned.

I should have known I'd be a messy drunk. It gives Beau's numerous requests for me not to drink more credit. I thought he was worried about his club being busted for underage drinking. How stupid was I?

I swear when I met him I had no idea what he was involved in. It was one horrifying unveil after another until I could no longer deny the truth.

He was a horrible person, and I had to do anything I could to get away from him.

When the remembrance of how desperate things got floods my mind, I swish my tongue around my suddenly dry mouth. It worsens the churns of my stomach. My mouth tastes like roadkill, and my teeth are furry.

Never one to leave a bad impression, I carefully pry myself out from beneath the blanket spread across my thigh, cover Brodie, then creep toward the stairs. The creak of the floorboard gives away my flee, but instead of revealing he is awake like his no longer gaped mouth does, Brodie pretends he is still asleep.

It would hurt like hell if I hadn't caught my reflection in the hallway mirror. I look as bad as I feel. My hair is knotted, my skin is pale and blotchy, and I'm not wearing pants.

Great!

I didn't think matters could get worse, but I'm proven wrong when I can't tiptoe past Lucy's room without checking in on her. She is curled up on a smidge of the mattress her uncle isn't hogging, clutching her toy rabbit. She'd kept my thoughts far from her father during the first two hours of her return from the ice cream shop, but once bedtime arrived and Thane apologized for pushing me into the shit pile with a bottle of vodka, my emotions got swept away on me and I stupidly put my feelings before hers.

Did she have a nightmare? Is that why Thane is sleeping in her bed? If so, why was Brodie downstairs with me instead of with his daughter? She is meant to be his main priority. My placement was meant to ensure that.

It seems to be doing the opposite, and I need to stop it before I hurt her more than I already have.

With Amelia confident she could convince me to stay, it took me longer to pack than expected. Lucy and Thane are now awake. I can hear them chatting in the kitchen that for the first time in a week doesn't smell like a disaster in process.

"Henley!" Lucy shouts when she spots me by the door. She races around the island covered with an array of breakfast foods. "Daddy is making breakfast. His pancakes are better than mine..." Her words trail off to silence when she spots my suitcase. "You're leaving?" Before I can answer, she slings her head to her father and shouts, "I told you she would leave. You scared her away!"

Brodie stops flipping pancakes before he darts his eyes between my suitcase and me. He looks upset. Perhaps even a little devastated, but just like I couldn't, he can't get a word in between Lucy's shouts for him to fix his mistakes and to not let me leave.

"I begged for her. She is my wish, so you're not allowed to scare her away."

"Lucy, I—" She cuts me off by banding her arms around my thigh and hugging me tight.

"You're my wish. I wished for you on my birthday last year. You can't go. Please, Henley. I don't want you to go."

"This isn't your dad's fault. He didn't do anything wrong. This is on me." Careful not to hurt her since she's gripping me for dear life, I peel her off me before bobbing down to her height. My heart breaks when I see the tears streaming down her face, but my wish for her not to blame her father is my sole focus. "I wasn't meant to come—"

"Yes, you were. I wished for you." Her pigtail slaps me when she spins to face Brodie and Thane frozen on the other half of the kitchen. "Remember the shooting star? I had just blown out my candles, and it whizzed over our heads. You said I could make two wishes. I only made one." Her eyes are back on me, blinking and wet. "I wished for you, and you came. I just had to be patient."

"Honey, I..."

I'm lost for words, so Brodie steps in. "You can't force someone to stay when they don't want to, Lucy. That isn't how life works. They need to want to stay for themselves."

His words resonate with me more than I could ever express, but Lucy just hears excuses. "She wants to stay. You're just too stupid to tell her you like her more than Uncle Thane does!"

"Hey, Lulu, come on, calling people names isn't nice," Thane pipes up. "We talked about this last night."

"It isn't a name when it's true," Lucy fights back, her eyes hot and heavy on Brodie. "If she leaves, I'll never forgive you. I will hate you for eternity."

She doesn't quite get her last word out right, but it cuts through Brodie like a knife. The vein in his neck works overtime as his jaw stiffens, but he keeps a calm head—for the most part. "Go to your room."

Lucy balks in shock before folding her arms over her chest and standing her ground.

"Now, Lucy. And don't come down until you're ready to apologize." The threat in his tone doesn't budge her an inch until he locks his narrowed eyes with me and snarls, "And you..." He works his jaw side to side. "You can do the same."

"I beg your pardon?"

"Room. Now!" He shunts us away with a wave of his spatula.

"I'm not a child. You can't order me to my room."

The anguish on Lucy's face switches to excitement when Brodie steps closer to me while licking his lips. Remembering how delicious they taste instantly drops my defenses, not to mention what he says next. "You're hungover. She only got six hours." He points the spatula at Lucy during his second sentence. "So I'm not dealing with either of you until you go back to bed and wake up on the right fucking side."

"Hey!"

Brodie grabs his wallet off the bench and hands it to Lucy, his eyes never once leaving mine. They expose he isn't relieved about my wish to leave. He's angry. Real fucking angry.

After pulling two dollars from the bills section of his wallet and dumping it back onto the island, Lucy curls her empty hand around mine and guides me to the stairs.

In my shock that Brodie wants me to stay, I go with her.

19

BRODIE

I'm clutching the spatula so firmly, it takes Thane prying back two fingers from its handle to free it from my hold. His breathy chuckles fan my cheek when he replaces it with a wooden spoon. "It's a little more durable than the spatula, though I wouldn't recommend testing it out on Lucy. Supposedly, there are rules now about parents not spanking their kids." He laughs before plucking a strip of bacon from a plate and shrugging. "The occasional spank on my butt when I was being a brat didn't hurt me. It was probably the only thing that stopped me from joining Thorin on 'vacation.'" He air-quotes his last word.

Thorin is Lucy's second favorite uncle, so instead of telling her he's doing a stint in prison, Thane tells her he's on vacation. His extended leave creates fewer questions. Its value can't be calculated for a kid as inquisitive as Lucy.

"What do you think that's about?" As he uses the spatula to remove burned pancakes from the skillet, Thane nudges his head to Henley's suitcase.

"I don't know." I'm not being deceitful. I truly don't know.

Our conversation downstairs was lighter than the one we had upstairs, but I can't recall anything that would cause a knee-jerk reaction like Henley believing she had to leave to make things right.

Vomiting for hours isn't pleasant, but I've dealt with worse.

While shuddering off the image of my wife lying bloody and lifeless, I say, "Probably the email she thinks I sent."

Thane groans like he's not buying my suggestion. I understand why when he says, "She's known about that for days." He shifts on his feet to face me. "Did anything happen last night?"

I shoot daggers at him. "Are you seriously asking me that? She was drunk."

"And the original box of condoms in your bedside table went out of date before Lucy was born." His teeth crunch through a crispy strip of bacon. "You're welcome, by the way," he says through a mouthful of lard. "If I hadn't forced you to take the box, you might have had to pay for your baby mama to watch her own kid." When I glare at him, he barks out a laugh. "What? It's true, isn't it? You wouldn't have stopped even if you hadn't found a condom. *I sure wouldn't have.*"

I could have lived without his last four words.

"I haven't given it much thought."

I don't know why I bother trying to lie to Thane. He can read me like a book. "You did, hence why you moved the box from your bedside table to the drawer in your desk."

"You're a fucking snoop."

He shrugs but doesn't deny my claim.

Then he hits me where it hurts. "Maybe it's time to get a new mattress. Then it won't matter where the action happens."

"How the fuck do you know—" My eyes bulge when one revelation makes room for another. "Did Lucy see us?"

"What?" Thane looks as ill as I feel. "No!" He furrows his brows, then wets his lips. "Well, if she did, she hasn't mentioned anything to me."

"Then she didn't see anything," we say at the same time.

Lucy keeps nothing from Thane. Before Henley arrived, he was her only BFF.

"I saw how your cheeks whitened when you walked Henley toward your bed last night. You were white, man. Pasty the Fucking Ghost."

"It's Casper the Ghost."

He continues talking as if I never interrupted him. "Then I remembered the stuff I helped you move out of the house you shared with Caroline." I inconspicuously roll my eyes when he says, "She wouldn't be mad, you know. She only ever wanted you to be happy. That's why she was working so much. She was hoping maybe a big pay stub would convince you to switch roles."

"What?" That is as much as my overworked brain can handle.

He knows I heard him, so he doesn't clarify what he said. "She never mentioned wanting you to become a stay-at-home daddy?"

Hating that I must admit our relationship wasn't as rock solid as I make out, I pour a new batch of pancake batter onto the skillet before mumbling, "No. She never said anything."

He brushes off my moody comment as if it is a joke. "Communication will never be an Ashburn strong point."

I'm saved from replying by the doorbell ringing.

When my eyes shoot to Thane, he holds his hands in the air. "It ain't for me."

Huffing, I dump the skillet into the sink with the half-cooked pancakes, then head for the door.

I'm taken aback when I swing it open and find a former colleague on the other side.

"Agent Machini, to what do I owe the pleasure?"

She spins to face me, her smile picking up when she runs her eyes down my frame. "How many times do I have to tell you to call me Macy?" After hitting me with a wink, she asks, "Can I come in?"

She enters before I answer. Flirting and dominating are Macy's known traits. Steamrolling a perp into an admission of guilt is a close third.

"Is this visit personal or business?" I ask, mindful that twenty-four hours haven't passed since I assaulted two civilians in a location that would have been wired to the hilt with surveillance.

"A little of column A and a little of column B." Her mouth gapes when she enters the kitchen. "Wow. This is quite the spread." She dips her head in greeting to Thane before she pinches a strip of the bacon Thane almost demolished while I was answering the door. "I won't keep you long..." She stops, moans, then starts again. "This is *so* good."

"Wait until you try the pancakes. Heaven in an imperfect circle."

When her mouth salivates, Thane preps her a plate while we talk shop.

"What is this about?"

Macy accepts the plate from Thane before answering. "There was an incident last night at Aeros." I keep my expression calm and neutral. "A couple of thugs got taught a lesson." She talks around a mouthful of food. "Sup was ready to let it go until the fatalities started stacking up like..."

"Tin cans at a hurricane center," Thane fills in when she can't think of a saying.

"I might borrow that."

"You're more than welcome to it."

Thane sinks back to his half of the kitchen when I glare at him. Macy said fatalities, not accusers. That means the men I punched are dead.

"There was a paint graze at the victims' last known location." She balances her plate on one hand before pulling a notepad from the breast pocket of her blazer. "It is a unique color." After flipping a handful of pages, she hands her pad to me. "Ever heard of that color?"

Jesus. Fucking. Christ.

It is an exact match to the paint on my Harley. She even has the manufacturer's name jotted down.

Realizing it is better to tell the truth than lie, I say, "It's the custom paintwork of my Harley." I arch a brow before returning her stare. "But you already knew that since you worked that undercover op with me."

Mindful her ruse is busted, she shovels another forkful of eggs into her mouth before announcing the reason for her visit. "I need to check your bike. You won't hear from me again if it comes up clean and without a scratch." I barely groan for half a second. "It isn't me asking, Brodie. You know I wouldn't be here if it were my choice."

When she slants past me and waggles her fingers, I crank my neck back to the stairs.

"Back to bed, young lady," I grumble out when I spot a tiny pair of rosy cheeks at the top of the stairs. I'm not solely holding a grudge about the words she spoke to me earlier. I don't want her to witness my arrest when Agent Macy opens the internal door of the garage and spots the damage to my bike.

Our region of the bureau arrests first and asks questions later. They had no choice when a dozen of their agents were found to be rogue.

"What is the bureau's interest in this case?"

As Macy seeks the light switch next to the garage remote, she answers, "The victims were known felons. They hadn't been up this far in the country for years." She taps the side of her nose. "A certain someone had them on an extremely short leash." By 'certain someone,' she means Henry Gottle Sr., boss of all bosses.

Giving up on the light switch, she presses the roller door button on the remote, streaming sunlight into the dingy garage. When air whizzes from her nose, I follow the direction of her gaze. She isn't the only one shocked at the sight of my bike. It gleams as brightly as it did when I rode it off the showroom floor. There isn't a single scratch to be seen.

What the?

As Macy inspects my bike's perfect lines and over-the-top chrome accents, I sling my eyes to Thane.

He shrugs as if to say *it wasn't me.*

As a shadow above the stairs clears away, Macy says, "I'll let them know there's nothing to see here." She hands me her half-demolished plate along with a business card. "If you can think of anything I might need to know, you can reach me at this number." She sidesteps me, then enters the foyer of my home. "And either fix your landline or stop hoarding your cell phone number. I would have given you a heads-up that I was coming if I had access to either." Her eyes stray to the shelf in my garage before returning to my face. "But I guess someone already did."

After a second wink, she leaves as fast as she arrived.

20

HENLEY

"*C*alm the fuck down and take a breath." When I do as instructed, Amelia asks, "Did she see you?"

I shake my head so fast I feel sick. "But this is still bad. I royally fucked up by wanting to spread my wings a little."

"It could be worse." When I stare at her through my phone screen, she laughs. "Brodie could be sitting in a cell with you." She sounds amused. I have no clue why. "And when did you find the time between climbing down a rose bush and hurling up three ounces of vodka to buff out the scratches on his bike?" She clicks her fingers three times. "I also told you he gave off biker vibes. That man couldn't be sexier if he were paid to be."

Jealousy has me ignoring the last half of her reply. "I wouldn't have gone anywhere if you hadn't dared me." I plop my ass on my bed, then flop back. "And I don't remember buffing out the scratches. Everything is blank."

"I said you could get another bottle *if* you weren't scared to leave Brodie's house unaccompanied. It wasn't a dare."

I cock a brow. "I was well past tipsy. It sounded like a dare."

Amelia continues talking as if I never spoke. "And it isn't necessarily bad that you can't remember anything. You're a shit liar. A memory lapse means you don't have to fake forgetfulness."

"Amelia..."

"Don't Amelia me. I'm not the one causing all types of trouble hundreds of miles from home." She lowers her voice so much that I doubt she wants me to hear her next sentence. "Though I wouldn't mind a little more action. My life sucks." As quickly as her self-pity party arrives, it vanishes. "Does Thane look as hot as he sounds?"

"I plead the fifth." My voice is more playful than it has been all morning.

I glare at my phone screen when she murmurs, "I'll take that as a yes." She sits up. "Do you think you can take a sneaky pic for me?" Before I can deny her suggestion, she confesses, "I tried to convince him to FaceTime last night, but he said some crap about him sleeping in his niece's bed because he'd never get hard again if he had to sleep in the bed Ms. Mitchell masturbated on or the one Lucy was conceived on."

It's lucky my stomach is empty. I might have vomited if it wasn't. No one wants to imagine a sixty-seven-year-old lady masturbating.

"Hold on, how does Thane know Ms. Mitchell masturbated? Even at the start of her placement, she was old enough to be his grandmother."

"From what he said, she was a bit of an over-sharer. She also flirted a lot."

"He didn't..."—I make a rude gesture with my hand—"right?"

Amelia rolls her eyes. "No. But Brodie might have. From what I've heard, he has a bit of a hankering for nanny fucking."

If she were here, I'd strangle her. "You're disturbing."

"And you're overreacting, but that seems to be your go-to coping mechanism these days."

It hurts to hear, but she's right. "It's different this time. Lucy—"

"Is listening when she shouldn't be." My bedroom door pushes open before Lucy's tiny body fills a small portion of the gap. "I'm sorry."

"It's okay. Come here." I wave her into my room before focusing on my phone screen. "I'll call you later."

Amelia lifts her chin. "Just make sure it's after you take a picture of Tha—"

I disconnect our chat before she can horrify Lucy more than I already have.

I didn't think about my plan to leave thoroughly enough before attempting to implement it. I forgot she most likely has attachment issues like me. It is often the case when you lose a parent.

"I'm sorry I made you upset, Lucy-Lou. That was never my intention."

"I know." She sits on the end of my bed where I normally do her hair, so my fingers instinctively weave her glossy locks into two fishtail braids.

Once they're secured with ties, she twists to face me. Her expression isn't as hurt as it was earlier. "I shouldn't have said what I did to Daddy. I was just angry that he won't tell the truth. He likes you, Henley. He likes you a lot."

Her assurance warms my heart. "I like him too, but he isn't why I'm here."

"You're here for me?"

Her smile grows when I nod. "The day you went with your daddy to work, I saw you. You were walking through the courtyard, and your shoelace had come undone."

"And Daddy fixed it while talking to his work friend."

Again, I nod. "When he mentioned your new nanny, your face went really sad. You looked upset." I lift her downcast head with my hand. "That's when I heard your wish."

Her eyes bug as her mouth gapes. "You heard it?"

I nod. Since it isn't a lie, it doesn't present as one. "And I knew then that I had to help you." Her happiness has me struggling with my next words. "But I made a mistake, Lucy. I should have never come without asking your dad's permission first."

"He would have said yes." Her lie holds out for nearly a minute. "I think." She doubles down on her assurance by rolling her shoulders and repeating, "He would have said yes. He was making you breakfast. He doesn't do that for anyone. Only Mommy and you."

Not wanting to upset her, I pull back the baby hair still growing near her forehead and tuck it into the more established locks while asking, "You remember that?"

She shakes her head, but for the first time while talking about her mother, tears don't well in her eyes. "Daddy told me last night." Her feet stomp on the floorboards when she leaps down from my bed. "He said if I was a good girl and went straight to sleep, he'd make us breakfast."

"Us?"

"Uh-huh." Her head bob blurs my vision with its swiftness. "He said you'd want a greasy breakfast and that it would make you feel better." She licks her lips while rubbing her hands together. "I told him you also needed pancakes." I laugh. She loves pancakes so much she wants to eat them for breakfast, lunch, and dinner. "So after a story, he went down to check on you." My heart flutters in my neck when she looks up at me with big eyes. "Did you know Daddy met Mommy when she was still at school? She was really pretty but super shy, and that's why I must get my ten... ten..."

"Tenacity?" I suggest when she struggles to find the word.

Again, she nods. "Tenacity from him." Inquisitiveness crosses her face. "What's tenacity mean?"

Her answer comes from the last person I expected. "It means you're strong, stubborn, and persistent."

Brodie enters my room, not knocking. His expression isn't as confused as earlier, but the groove between his brows is deep.

"Persistent?" Lucy asks, going for the hardest word.

"It means you don't stop until you win," I inform her. "Not even when you should."

My reply is more for Brodie than Lucy, but she doesn't see it that way. "There's nothing wrong with winning. Hey, Daddy?" She cozies up to his thigh before peering up at him like she's on his side again. "As long as the better person wins."

"That's right," he answers, ruffling her hair. "Are you hungry?"

Lucy nods so fast her teeth clang together.

"All right, then you better head down before the pancakes go cold." Before Lucy can fire the plea we both see in her eyes, Brodie locks his with me and says, "*We* will join you in a minute."

She keeps her squeal locked up tight, but her fist bump can't be concealed. "I love you, Daddy," she declares while sprinting for the door. Before Brodie can announce that her feelings are mutual, she adds, "I love you too, Henley."

I melt into a puddle on the floor, and the mess worsens when Brodie pops out of my room for half a second before reentering. Not only does he look and smell divine after spending the night huddled at my side like a kinked pretzel, but there is something satisfyingly erotic about a brute of a man not taking no for an answer in the only way he knows how.

With dominance.

After rehanging my limited selection of clothing and stuffing my panties and bras into a drawer next to my single bed, he stores my brand-new suitcase on top of the freestanding closet, then nudges his head to the door. "If you think your stomach can handle pancakes, you better be quick. Lucy can eat Thane under the table when it comes to sugar."

His witty comment has a smile inching high on my face, but I can't just sweep my stupidity under the rug. I have done it for years, and it never ends well. "I—"

"Should save your energy," Brodie interrupts. "You're going to need it."

Forever curious, I blurt out the first thing that pops into my head. "For?"

My heart whacks my ribs when he says casually, "For the self-defense class I'm teaching this morning." He stares me dead in the eyes. "The one I'll teach every day until the only chipped teeth you have to worry about are the ones you're handing out."

He smiles at my shocked expression, once again warns me about a pancake shortage before leaving me shell-shocked and silent in my room.

21

BRODIE

*W*hen the creak of the kitchen door opening sounds through my ears, I completely drown out the story Thane is sharing and shift my eyes toward the noise. I take my time drinking in Henley's svelte frame and gorgeous face before looking past her.

I sigh in relief when I fail to spot the suitcase that had me on the back foot only an hour ago. It's hopefully still above the closet, where I plan for it to stay until long after I work out why Henley is as protective of Lucy as I am becoming of her.

Last night scared the shit out of me.

I just haven't had the chance to decipher why.

Things never moved this fast with Caroline. We courted for months before making it official, and we'd been together for over three years before she considered sharing a residence.

I've barely known Henley for a week and I'm already struggling to remember what our life was like before she arrived.

That is insane just to contemplate, but it is honest.

"Henley!" Lucy waves her over to the island we're using as a table. "I saved you a seat."

Of course, the seat she saved is wedged between Lucy and me. Thane lucked out and got the stool on the other side of the counter. He doesn't seem upset, though. He gets to take in Henley without any of the sneaky sideway glances I hit her with during the thirty minutes of breakfast.

Neither of us gets a word in. It is the Lucy and Thane Show the entire time, but once the food is demolished and there's nothing but dishes to clean, the kitchen is devoid of another word, and Thane and Lucy are out back playing a ball game.

Mercifully, Henley gives in to the tension first. "Last night—"

"If you're okay, it doesn't deserve mentioning."

She smiles before placing Thane's mug into the dishwasher. "I'm fine. A little embarrassed, but I doubt that requires a visit to the ER." After stacking another handful of dishes, she asks, "Did I...?" She waves her hand at my torso. "Did I spew on you?" Her face screws up when I don't immediately answer her. "At least tell me it wasn't on your good shirt." She balances her elbows on the counter and hides her face in her hands when I remain quiet. I've worn nothing but the shirts she and Lucy made the first three days of her placement. They're comfortable, but knowing that they made them for me would have me wearing them even if they weren't. "This is worse than I realized."

She cranks her neck and glares at me when I quote, "If it makes you feel any better, it isn't anything I haven't seen before." Uncharacteristically, I bring Caroline into our conversation. "Caroline was so sick the first few months of her pregnancy, even our dog heaved when he entered our bedroom."

I can see a hundred questions in her eyes, but Henley keeps to the easy stuff. "You had a dog?"

"Yeah." I smile while remembering his lopsided head and just as crooked smile. "Rex had air for brains, but he was a good dog. Fiercely protective of Caroline and Lucy."

My smile slips when she asks, "Where is Rex now?"

I could end our conversation, but how can I get my questions answered if I'm unwilling to answer any myself? "He's in the same spot as Caroline."

"Oh." Her shock is swift, but she holds it well. "I'm sorry."

I take a sip of my coffee to hide the quiver of my lips. "What have you got to be sorry about?"

She isn't given a chance to answer. Lucy sprints into the house from the backyard, uncaring that her boots are covered with mud. It stormed last night, which had me hopeful some of the evidence of my assault had washed away, but alas, I've never been lucky.

"You need to come outside. Uncle Thane found a frog."

"A frog?" Henley checks, her eyes popping.

"Uh-huh. It is big and slimy and so very beautiful!" Lucy locks her eyes with mine. "Can we keep it?" After slipping her hand into mine, she curls her other one around Henley's hand, making me realize how close we were standing while discussing a subject that usually demands a heap of space. "Uncle Thane could make it a house, and I could splat flies for it."

"But frogs like sleeping outside," Henley starts, saving me from breaking my daughter's heart for the second time today.

———

I slant my head to hide my smile when Henley enters the living room with a groan. Not only did Lucy win her debate about keeping a frog inside, citing that lots of people have amphibians as pets, but our first self-defense class ran over by two hours.

Get your mind out of the gutter. I'm already bordering on the cusp of being one of those dirty old men I regularly arrested in my rookie years. Still, my decision to continue had nothing to do with Henley's super-tight gym pants and everything to do with her eagerness to learn how to protect herself.

She listened to every bit of advice I gave and kept going until she perfected the move.

"Lucy is just finishing brushing her teeth, and then she'll be ready for her story."

I arch a brow when she plops onto the sofa beside me and rubs at her neck. I could offer to read Lucy a hundred stories, but she'd never pick one of mine over Henley's. She told me not to take it to heart, but "Henley does voices, and you just sound like you."

When Henley spots my shock, she smiles before saying, "She's hopeful you might tell a story similar to the one you told last night." She twists to face me. "She enjoyed hearing about how you and Caroline met, and as much as I want to elaborate on your story, I don't know enough about your wife to share." With silence still reigning supreme, my bewilderment more in response to how freely she can talk about Caroline without being jealous, she adds on quickly, "I'm happy to share what Thane's told me. I just think it would be better coming from you."

"I agree," I admit, shocking us both. I nudge my head to her shoulder, eager to change the course of our conversation but also desperate to make sure she's okay. "Are you all right? You have been rubbing the same side half the night."

I could punch myself for giving away that I've been watching her all night, but I can only smile when she replies, "Thane is as heavy as he looks."

"Yet you still tossed him around like a ragdoll."

Her smile matches mine. "I did, didn't I?" Her twinkling-with-amusement eyes dart around the living room. "Is that why he left?"

"Ah. No." Honesty is easy when you stop contemplating its effectiveness. "I asked him to give us the weekend."

"Oh." She wets her suddenly dry lips. It isn't from the tension that forever fires between us. Shit stirring is the only thing drying her mouth. "And he went willingly? That's a surprise." She rams her elbow into my ribs when I groan. "He's a bit of a flirt, but he doesn't mean anything by it. He's just being playful."

"I doubt that would be the case if I didn't ask him to step back," I blurt out before I can stop myself. Thane has been yanking my chain all day. I was close to punching him during our class, and he wasn't even grinding against Henley's backside. He asked her out on the guise that "everyone's gotta eat."

Henley blinks three times before asking, "You asked him to step back?" When I nod, she exhales. "From me or in general?"

She doesn't announce she's worried about Lucy, but her facial expression does.

"I won't go down that route again, especially not with Thane." When she exhales again, I add, "It was never my choice to go down that route to begin with."

"I know," Henley admits. "Thane gave me a bit of an update today." After sinking back, she folds her feet under her bottom and tilts her torso to me. "Chelsea is his big sis, but he's still mad at her." Her next admission isn't expected but much appreciated. "I stepped over the mark when I invited her to give Lucy dance lessons. I'll call and cancel them tomorrow."

"There's no need." Once again, I'm shocked. What Chelsea did was wrong, but she was young, and I was drowning in grief, so she did what she thought was best for Lucy. I can't fault her for that. "But since I'm paranoid as fuck, I'd rather they be scheduled for when I'm home."

"That's understandable. I'll add that to Lucy's schedule." She coughs to clear her throat before dropping her eyes to her hands. They're fiddling with the hem of her shirt as Thane would have anticipated. "Talking about schedules, I need to tell you—"

"Daddy, I finished brushing my teeth," Lucy interrupts, her voice bellowing down the stairwell. "Can we do a story now?"

When my eyes shoot back to Henley, she gestures for me to go. "We'll talk later. It's late, and we don't want to risk another rerun of this morning with another late night."

"Are you sure?"

She nods. "One hundred percent."

"All right."

I ruffle her hair, cuss at my stupidity, then climb the stairs two at a time.

Lucy's giggles lift the weight off my chest in an instant. "You're silly, Daddy."

"What are you talking about?" I scoop her into my arms and hang her upside down by her feet. "I'm the smartest man you know."

"You are," she agrees, giggling through the onslaught of my hand on her tummy. "But you're not supposed to mess up Henley's hair when you want to tell her you love her." Her giggles freeze along with my hand. Once I flip her back over and she brushes her hair out of her face, she cups her hand around my ear and murmurs, "You're meant to kiss her."

22

HENLEY

I bite my palm to lessen the leverage of my grin when Brodie tells Lucy she was born purple and screaming.

"Are you saying I'm an alien?"

"No..." Brodie's hearty chuckle hides my breathy laugh. "You were just screaming so tenaciously—"

"Stubbornly?" Lucy checks, forever seeking knowledge.

Brodie murmurs in agreement as I nod. "You refused to breathe until you were placed on your mother's chest." My heart faces its third stutter today. "Then you instantly stopped crying and looked at her in awe." His voice is loved up when he whispers, "It was love at first sight."

My back flattens against the wall outside Lucy's room when she asks, "Like you and Henley?"

This isn't the first time I've come up during their thirty-minute story session tonight, but it is the first time Brodie has taken his time to respond.

After a beat, he answers, "Kinda." Through the crack in her door, I watch him pull her head into his chest before running his fingers through her hair. "The love a child has for their parent differs from the love they have for their spouse."

My heart beats again when Lucy asks, "What's a spouse?"

"It is the person you choose to be with. Your girlfriend, wife—"

"My boyfriend?" Lucy pipes up, her little voice a roar.

"The boyfriend you'll meet *after* your thirtieth birthday." Upon noticing the slow blink of her eyes, he lowers his voice. "And even though nothing will change between us, you will love him differently from me."

"Because I chose to be with him?" Lucy asks between yawns.

"Uh-huh. And if you didn't, Daddy will bury him under six feet of dirt."

Lucy half laughs, half huffs. She's barely conscious enough to reply.

It has been a big day for all of us.

The reminder sees me standing and heading for the shower after collecting my robe and towel from my room. I'm drained of energy, which has nothing to do with my stupidity last night. Brodie's self-defense class was intense. It sweated the leftover alcohol out of my system and had me wanting to bend in two and heave, but I refused to give up. I want to know how to protect myself, but more than anything, I want to do everything I can to protect Lucy.

It dawns on me that my steps must be super sluggish when my track into the bathroom is interrupted by Brodie entering from his bedroom.

"Hey." The groove between his dirty-blond brows is nowhere near as prominent. "Good minds think alike," he says after noticing my belongings hanging over my arm. "You go first."

"Before you leave." He stops but doesn't turn around. "I still can't work out the faucet. I've been having cold showers all week."

A grin pulls at my lips when he murmurs, "You're not the only one."

The door lining the hallway is closed, so the space is even tighter than normal. Brodie's shoulder brushes past my chest when he steps past me to switch on the shower. It sends a zap of electricity rocketing down my spine and has my knees drawing together.

I am confident I'm not the only one feeling the current hissing between us, but Brodie tries to act ignorant to the rising hairs at his nape. "It's getting worse. I'll try to get a plumber in next week."

I can tell the exact moment he gets the temperature right, because the scent of his aftershave strengthens.

"If Caroline picked your aftershave, she had good taste."

He balks for the quickest second. However, he doesn't shut down our conversation. "It was too cheap for her palate." He looks at me through a sheet of hair that has fallen in front of his eyes. "But she grew to appreciate it." He wets his mouth and then nudges his head to the stream of water. "Is that okay?"

Brodie hisses when I lean across to check the temperature. "It's perfect. Thank you."

He nods to acknowledge my praise before moving back to his half of the bathroom. Although his movements are fast, I don't miss the quick inhalation he takes when his steps fluff up my hair. It's stinky and desperate for a wash, but he drinks it in as if it is liquid gold.

He almost makes it out the door before he suddenly stops and spins back around. I'm left a little lost when he mimics my praise. "Thank you."

"For?" My confusion can't be missed, even in the shortness of my reply.

His answer hitches my breath. "For saving me from making a mistake I couldn't take back." He peers through the door, picturing Lucy's room on the other side. "She deserves to know her mother, and I had no right to keep that from her."

Since I appreciate his honesty, I let him off the hook. "We all grieve in our own way." I swallow the lump in my throat before whispering, "I'm just glad you're still here to help her through it."

With my reply raising more questions, I smile before spinning away from him and unbuttoning my dress.

The door clanking shut trickles into my ear just before the cotton material slips off my shoulder.

———————

I curse to hell my stupidity of deciding on an early night when I notice the time. My brain couldn't comprehend my body's need to rest, so it figured I was just having a nap. It isn't even midnight.

I could cure my boredom by calling Amelia—she never crawls into bed before the rooster's crow—but with her flirty texts with Thane raising her curiosity, I wouldn't get anything more from her than a demand to sneakily snap his picture.

During our second self-defense class, I almost caved when Thane whipped off his shirt, but with Brodie having a near coronary and Lucy forcefully re-dressing her showboating uncle, it was more of a mental snapshot moment than a breach of privacy.

I also don't understand why she'd want to tease herself like that. FaceTime is great for keeping in contact, but you can't smell intoxicating scents like the one that keeps me awake at all hours of the night, or feel the heat of skin-to-skin contact. That can't be replicated no matter how much sex toy manufacturers wish it could be.

Giving up on sleep, I kick off the bedding and slip out of bed. Maybe a glass of warm milk will convince my brain that it's time to shut down. Overthinking hasn't done me any favors lately.

My already sluggish pace down the hallway slows even more when I notice new portraits on the wall. The originals are still on display, but a handful have been moved down the wall to allow space for some new yet old pictures.

A smile stretches across my face when I imagine how excited Lucy will be when she wakes. Even though she was too young to remember her, she will not doubt that she has her mother's eyes and golden hair. She can see it in every picture of them now adorning the walls.

When I detect I'm being watched, I slacken my smile before cranking my head to Brodie's open bedroom door. His shoulder is propped against the doorjamb, his pajama pants are low-hanging, and he isn't wearing a shirt.

"Can't sleep?" he asks when my eyes finally reach his face.

I shake my head. "I thought I might have a glass of milk." When he laughs, I ask, "What? It's good for shutting down your brain."

"Because it clogs it with sugar."

His laugh loudens when I stick out my tongue. It is an immature response, but I'm fighting not to drag it along the ridges in his midsection, so my tongue popped out before I could stop it.

"Come on. I've got the perfect remedy."

Goosebumps rise on my neck when he bands his arm around my shoulders and guides me down the hallway. Considering we're in the middle of July, I shouldn't feel as cold as I do when he frees me from his grasp as we reach the kitchen.

I watch him curiously when he removes a mug from the overhead cupboard and fills it with tap water.

"Water? Your solution for sleep deprivation is water?"

His grin makes my insides clench. "It's not just water. It's warm water."

"So, a hot chocolate minus *everything* that makes it good?"

God, I wish he'd stop smiling. The number of times I had to straddle his lap this afternoon already has my horniness at the highest level it's ever been. I don't know if I can handle another cheeky grin. "Quit whining and try it."

When I poke my tongue at him for the second time, I realize that the tension isn't one-sided. He adjusts his crotch while dropping his eyes to my mouth.

Desperate to dampen the fire raging through me from his hungry watch, I pick up the mug and gulp down half of its contents. "It doesn't really do anything. It's just..." A big yawn gobbles up my words. "What the hell?"

Brodie refills my mug before drinking from it himself. After wiping at his mouth with the back of his hand, he says, "Drinking hot water keeps you hydrated, eases congestion, improves digestion, and reduces stress so well your body thinks you just had a super long bath." The reason for the curve of his lips makes sense when he murmurs, "Most people get groggy in the tub."

Air whizzes from his nose when I sock him in the stomach. "And most people knock before entering."

"The door was open," he defends.

"Because I wanted to make sure I could hear Lucy."

His confession knocks me in a good way. "She's crazy about you."

"The feeling is mutual." I move closer as if we're not standing only inches from each other already. "I was wrong when I thought something was missing from her life. You're doing everything right. She is a well-adjusted, stable five—"

"Almost six," Brodie corrects as Lucy would have if she were here.

"*Almost* six-year-old." Our smiles match until I confess, "I was reflecting because it is easier to see other people's flaws than it is our own." I nervously tug on the hem of my shirt. "I—"

Brodie silences me by placing his hand under my chin and raising my head. His briefest touch switches the torment swirling in my stomach into something less debilitating. It reboots the confidence I only ever have around him and adds a playful touch to our exchange.

"Hasn't anyone ever told you it's rude to interrupt someone when they're talking?"

He accepts my gibe on the chin. "Hasn't anyone ever told you it's rude to listen in on other people's conversations?"

"I... When..." I give up. "I'm as fascinated by Caroline as Lucy is."

That wasn't what Brodie was expecting me to say. "Why?"

I shrug. "She makes up half of Lucy. What isn't there to love?"

He doesn't know how to respond. "It's... ah... late." He moves toward the door before retracing his steps. "I'm gonna go to bed." He leans in like he's going to kiss me, pats my head instead, freezes, cusses, and then turns back around. "Night."

Although disappointed, I almost lost the chance to interact with him earlier today, so I issue him the same farewell instead of pouting like a child. "Night."

He makes it five paces before he stops again. This time, he doesn't turn around. He remains facing the door, his chest rising and falling so erratically I grow worried he'll overwork his shoulder. "Are you okay?"

My question jumps him out of his stupor. "Yes. Goodnight."

He races through the swinging door so fast it is still flapping in the aftermath of his push when he tackles it for the second time, instead from the opposite direction.

"Did you forget something?" I ask, clueless about what has caused his angsty expression.

"Yes," he replies, rounding the island. "This."

Faster than I can blink, he weaves his fingers through my hair and seals his lips over mine.

He kisses me as if it is the only thing he was designed to do. It is a blinding embrace that releases a heap of pent-up frustrations while stacking more onto the pile. Our tongues clash over and over, but I need more. I'm desperate for more.

Thankfully, so is Brodie.

After clearing the island of every dish in sight, he lifts me to sit on the gleaming counter before wedging himself between my thighs.

My burns stopped stinging two days ago, but I am fond of how the silky fabric of my kimono-inspired dressing gown brushes against my bare skin, so I've continued wearing it sans panties for the past few days.

"Jesus fucking Christ," Brodie murmurs over my kiss-swollen lips when he realizes I'm without panties. He breaks our kiss and lowers his eyes to the dangerous split in my nightwear. "This is the exact reason I couldn't sleep. Knowing. Wondering." His Adam's apple bobs up and down. "Picturing. I couldn't get you out of my head."

His confession is shocking. I thought he couldn't sleep because he's reprimed his house with memories of his wife. I had no clue I was partly to blame for his restlessness.

I run my fingers through his hair, bringing his eyes back to mine before I kiss him again. I don't fumble and expose my nerves. I show him how confident he makes me feel and that everything happening is because I want it as much as he does.

Things move quickly after I've stolen the air from his lungs with a breathless embrace. In under a minute, Brodie kisses a trail from my neck to the apex of my pussy. Even quicker than that, he spreads me wide with his fingers, blows a hot breath over my slit, then drags his tongue up the lines running down the middle of my pussy.

A moan hums up my chest when his hairy chin scratches at my pussy as his tongue finds my clit, and then my eyes flutter shut.

"You have no idea how many times I've dreamed about doing this again."

I arch my back, as turned on by his confession as I am the rotations of his tongue over the sensitive bud between my legs. "Tell me."

"Morning."

Another lick.

"Noon."

And another.

"And night."

This time, he sucks my clit into his mouth, and when his teeth graze the hood, I combust.

My body shakes and shudders. I fall brutally and quickly, and I love every minute of it.

I can't breathe, and I'm almost sure the roof in the kitchen is full of stars, but before I can announce that it was the most powerful orgasm I've ever experienced, Brodie sprints to the edge of a frenzy all over again. He uses his fingers this time too, which are prodding and probing but mind-hazingly delicious.

It is a hurried pace but not frantic and out of control.

He takes his time and is surprisingly tender.

He makes love to my body with his mouth, and I surrender to every moan, whimper, and shudder he leisurely coerces out of me.

I've never been pleased in such a way. Beau was too selfish—*fuck you, Beau*—and anyone I was with before him I didn't trust enough to let them do this to me.

Being consumed like this is more unraveling than just having sex. It's more than a physical attraction. It involves trust and all that other scary shit months of disappointments start to discredit.

I distrusted everyone, even Amelia, and just as I was about to give up, I spotted Lucy.

I thought if I could fix her, I could fix myself.

I didn't factor her father into the equation until our first moment of eye contact settled the nerves my stomach hadn't been without for almost a year. I felt free. I could breathe again. Then I couldn't.

Brodie stole the ability when he wouldn't look at me the morning following our first rendezvous. He made me ashamed, and I felt like he was just another agent laughing while glaring down his nose at me.

I should hate him for it, but just like I couldn't blame my father for making me an orphan, I can't shift all of Brodie's hesitations solely onto his shoulders. He's trying to put his daughter first, and that is all I've wanted him to do since I first saw Lucy.

"Brodie," I murmur, my deliverance more a moan than an interruption. "We need..." I take a moment to relish how delightful the bump of his tongue running over my clit feels before continuing. "We should take this somewhere else. Lucy might..."

My back arches when his breaths are hot and heavy near my ear, as intimately close as his crotch is to my heated core. "Lucy is fast asleep. She could sleep through a hurricane."

He inches back and peers at me when I say, "Except when it comes to me being in pain." I grip his rock-hard erection through his pajama pants. "And there's no way I'll be able to take all that without whimpering."

"For fuck's sake, Henley."

He usually cusses when he's angry. I'm not getting the same vibe tonight. He loves that I crave him as much as he does me, and it makes him think he's invincible.

He lifts me from the counter without a single fetter of pain crossing his face before he heads for the office he hid in multiple times this week.

"Should you be carrying me? Your shoulder—"

"Will live if it gets hurt again." He lifts and locks his eyes with mine. "But I may not if I hurt you."

"Brodie, you didn't hurt me. I—" The rest of my reply is forced into the back of my throat when a second after he kicks closed his office door, he sits on the two-seater couch across from his desk. His cock is still encased in his pants, but the thin material leaves nothing to the imagination. I can feel every ridge, and my body is utterly thrilled at the chance to take it all in again.

The rough friction of the conjoined regions of our bodies sends a wave of cascading pleasure rolling through my body. It shimmers from the roots of my hair to the tips of my toes before clustering low in my stomach.

After exhaling an unsteady breath, Brodie raises me to my knees before tugging down his pants. I gasp in a sharp breath when his cock springs free. It's hard, glistening with pre-cum, and extended up past the bumps in his midsection.

Mistaking my expression, Brodie says, "We can stop right now. We don't have to go any further."

"No. I want this. I just..." I gulp again. "That thing is a monster."

He smiles, loving my praise, before he fists the base of his fat cock. Both sights are a rarity, and they make the tension between us so white hot sweat beads at my nape.

"Only take as much as you can." When he rubs the crown across the opening of my pussy, my worries vanish. I shudder as the throbbing of my clit overtakes the frantic beat of my heart. "We've got all night, Henley. We don't need to rush."

"Will you guide me?" I swivel my hips to loosen their firmness, causing him to groan. "I want it to feel good for you as well."

"It couldn't be bad with you, Henley. Everything you do is done with perfection."

I lose the chance to argue that I'm far from perfect when he notches the head of his cock into my pussy. There's no way I can have coherent thoughts while being fulfilled so well, not to mention how my arched position thrusts my breasts into Brodie's face.

He circles his tongue around the piqued bud of my nipple, loosening me up even more before encouraging me to sink down on him slowly.

"*Ohhh...*" I murmur, my moan barely a whisper.

"There's my good girl. Slow," he murmurs around my nipple, gripping me firm enough that I can't take more than an inch at a time. "Then, once I'm deep enough that you can't hold back for a second longer, you're going to give me the moans I deprived myself of the first time."

I cry out at the need in his voice, my knees buckling beneath me, but I don't sink further down his cock. Brodie won't let me. He refuses to hurt me physically because he's petrified of the emotional damage his earlier silence already caused.

The acknowledgment of that is more healing than anything he could say or do.

It also causes a pressure so blindingly bright I have no idea what it is until I'm pushed over the edge of orgasmic bliss.

I come—loudly.

Then Brodie's release chases mine several frantic minutes later.

23

HENLEY

The following morning, I wake up deliciously sore but happy. With the tension hot enough to scald, we were a little quick off the mark, but Brodie made up for our shortcomings on his desk, in the pantry, and in the shower where we were meant to wash off the sweat and sex smell clinging to our skin.

I was so spent I more wobbled to my room in the wee hours of this morning than strutted. It was the best walk of shame I've taken part in because not only did Brodie watch every staggered stride, but his lower lip also dropped a smidge when I slipped behind my bedroom door.

Last night was amazing, but I'd be a liar if I said I don't feel apprehensive about how things will go this morning. The last time we gave in to the tension, Brodie developed amnesia the following morning.

Although he appeared anxious about letting me go last night, I know how easily feelings change when distance is placed between people.

I thought my father was fine, but then I left for college, and the world crumbled beneath my feet for the second time.

With my mood not as ambient as earlier, I do a quick stretch before slipping out of bed and putting on some gym pants and a T-shirt. Brodie mentioned yesterday that our self-defense classes will run daily until he returns to work, and although I know I need to be honest with him about my placement before then, I need a couple more days to prove nothing I did was with ill intent.

My objective was never to upset or harm Lucy. I wanted to protect her from a hurt that almost swallowed me whole twice.

Talking about Lucy, the tiny patter of feet on wooden floorboards trickles into my room before a faint tap. "Henley, are you awake?"

I smile. She thinks she's whispering, but her voice is still as loud as a freight train. "I am." My grin grows when she pushes open my door, and her messy head pops into the crack. I'm clearly not the only one having a sleep-in. "Did you have a good sleep?" After taking in her messy hair for the second time and the pillow crease on her cheek, I say, "It sure looks like you did."

"I slept like a baby." She skips into my room, her rabbit closely following, before she leaps onto my bed. "Did you have a good sleep?" My giggles fan her face with hot air when she stands on my bed to ruffle my hair, which is as out of control as hers. "It looks like you did. You've got a big knot. Want me to brush it for you?"

"How about after breakfast?" Lucy is as sweet as pie, but my god, she has no clue how strong she is. I've lost more hair the past week than when I chopped off all my locks and dyed them black, hoping a new look would conceal me.

I was terribly wrong.

You can't stay hidden when you're forced out of hiding by the people meant to protect you.

After helping Lucy down from my bed, I ask, "Is Daddy awake?"

She half shrugs, half nods. "I think so. His bed is empty."

"Oh." When we walk hand in hand down the hallway, I can't help but peek into Brodie's room.

Lucy is right. His bed is empty. However, it appears as if it hasn't been slept in.

Brushing off my worry, I ask, "Do you have any big plans for breakfast today? I was thinking something light, and then we can do some crafts before Uncle Thane arrives for our self-defense class."

In the stupidity of my self-consciousness, I completely forgot about the new images in the hall that would stop any little girl in her tracks.

Lucy is staring up at the wall with her mouth gaping and tears flooding her eyes.

My heart thuds hard when she asks on a sob, "Is that my mommy?"

She doesn't wait for my answer.

She knows in her heart who she is staring at.

"She is so beautiful."

"Oh, honey, don't cry," I plead when tears splash her cheeks. "Daddy didn't put them up to make you sad."

"I'm not sad." She wipes her bunny across her face before using his floppy ear as a tissue. "I'm happy."

I bob down to her level. "Are you sure? You look a little upset, and it's okay if you are, as long as you know they're not there to make you sad. Your daddy loves you very much, and so does your mommy." I wave my hand at the photographs of them. "This proves that."

"How?" she asks, her little lip quivering.

"It's like when you can't find the right words, so you use gestures instead."

A memory of my father leaving a peanut butter and jelly sandwich on the piano in the great room every Tuesday afternoon flashes into my head as Lucy approaches me. "Like this."

I laugh when she noogies my head, which adds more knots to the mess her father's grip made when I went down on him in the shower.

"Yes, like that." I tug her into my chest. "We all have our own unique ways of showing people how much we love them. Some are silly. Some are annoying. And some you won't remember until it's too late."

Quickly, I brush my hand across my cheeks to ensure no tears have fallen before scooping Lucy into my arms and moving her closer to the wall of photographs to ensure she faces no issues taking in all the features she was gifted from her mother.

Her trip down memory lane warms my heart as well. My father wasn't the same after my mother was killed, but peering at a relationship similar to ours from the outside has me seeing things differently than I did when I was sixteen. I resented him for burying himself in work instead of giving him a reason to hold on, but he didn't hate me for that.

He loved me. His grief was just too intense for him to remember that when it mattered the most.

I press my lips to Lucy's temple and breathe in her scent when she praises her mother's beauty for the second time. "She is *sooo* pretty."

"She sure is." Confident she's had enough sentimental muckiness for one morning, I dip her until her piggy tails hit the floor, then attack her ribs. "Just like you."

She squeals during our gallop down the stairs and our race through the swinging kitchen door, and then she screams some more when she finds her father at the cooktop, flipping pancakes.

"You made pancakes two days in a row!" When she wiggles to be placed down, I oblige. "This has to be a miracle." She twists to face me. "He's never made pancakes two days in a row." Hunger blazes through her eyes as she licks her lips. "We need syrup. Lots and lots of syrup."

As she races for the walk-in pantry, I drift my eyes to Brodie. "Morning."

I hate my cracked tone, but my self-loathing only hangs around as long as it takes Brodie to reply, "Morning." After flipping a pancake, he checks the coast is clear before tugging me in and placing an impromptu kiss on the edge of my mouth.

His public display of affection is so unexpected I'm left a little gobsmacked. We agreed last night that anything we do after hours shouldn't affect Lucy, so I was half expecting another case of amnesia.

Grinning, Brodie closes my mouth before giving it a reason to gape again. "You don't deserve to be ignored. Neither back then nor now."

Tears prick my eyes, but with Lucy back at my side, looking up at me suspiciously, I don't have time to respond to them. Her pout is super cute and very dramatic.

"Are you okay?" I ask her like she's the one acting out of sorts.

"I can't find the syrup." Her devastated voice would have you convinced the world was about to end.

I arch a brow while spinning to face the pantry. "It should be on the shelf where we left it yesterday. Want me to help you?"

She nods so fast that she makes my head spin before she leads our charge to the pantry.

I'm taken aback when I notice the mess. Brodie and I were a little eager, but I had no clue the stickiness slicking my skin wasn't solely sweat until now.

My footprint is on the baker-size bag of flour on the pantry floor, and several tins and condiments are either sitting askew or on the floor.

I try to keep a straight face, but the fight becomes unbearable when Lucy folds her arms under her chest and says with a huff, "Daddy, I think we've got a raccoon im-fes-tation again!"

"What the fuck did you do with my uptight, 'I don't need anyone but my daughter in my life' brother-in-law? And where the fuck can I get some of that magic for myself?"

I laugh at Thane's hip thrust at the end of his sentence before jabbing my fists into his glove-covered hand. We're on day four of our intense self-defense class week, and I finally feel like I'm getting a handle on things. "I didn't do anything. I just—"

"Brought the life back into their eyes." When he nudges his head to Brodie and Lucy at the side of the makeshift gym, doing karate moves, I follow the direction of his gaze. "Lucy hasn't stopped smiling, and I haven't seen Brodie like this since..." He stops, swallows, then shifts his focus back to me. "I've *never* seen him like this."

"He loved your sister. He still does." *And our connection is more about sex than anything else, isn't it?*

Don't misconstrue what I'm saying. In between putting Lucy first and the extremely hectic schedule that will ensure that, we barely have time for anything else.

I don't mind. Sneaking around makes our exchanges more fire-sparking and adventurous. In the past four days, we've done it on almost every surface of his home *except* the place responsible for his guilt the morning following our first encounter.

We steer clear of Brodie's room because, as much as I want to believe what we have is more than lust, I have no basis for my claim.

We fuck, and then we maintain an amicable but flirty relationship during daylight hours.

Well, I thought we did. Thane is clearly seeing something we thought we were hiding.

"I'm not saying he didn't." I bob in just enough to miss Thane's sweep over my head with the pad on his hand to bring me back from my thoughts. "But he's different this time around."

"There's no 'this time.'" Even I can hear the deceit in my tone. The sex is out of this world. I've climaxed more times the past week than I have in my entire sexual existence, but moaning doesn't give much leeway to talking, and we have so much to discuss it should be the first item on our agenda when we're away from the prying eyes of an almost six-year-old. "I'm his daughter's nanny."

I stop swinging my fists when Thane murmurs, "And sucking the marrow from his bones every night." He drops his hands and glares at me when I cannot deny his claim. "Oh, fuck no. You do that too?" My squeal ripples through the basement when he unexpectedly bobs down and throws me over his shoulder. "You look like you *and* suck dick. You're coming home with me. Someone miswired you, so it's only right I try to bang out your kinks."

Brodie acts as if he didn't hear Thane's lewd comment. "Remember what you've been taught, Henley. No one can make you do anything you don't want to do. If you don't want to go with him, stop him."

"Yeah, Henley. Squeeze his head off until he runs away crying like Nathan Banks!" Lucy jumps in.

"Lulu! You're meant to be on my team," Thane says before I shorten his breaths by activating the maneuver I perfected earlier this week.

I can barely wrap my arm around Thane's thick neck, but the tightness of my hold, along with my feet making contact near his groin, sees me soon placed back onto my feet.

"Yes!" Lucy leaps up for a high five when Thane stumbles back while gasping in fast breaths.

"You suck!" He works his head side to side to make sure nothing is pinching before he locks his eyes with me. "And so do you." With his nose twisted up, he *pffts* at Brodie before making his way to the stairwell. "I hate you, man. Seriously, I loathe every fucking inch you've been working down her throat." He acts as if Brodie's glare has no heat whatsoever by spinning to face Lucy before asking her if she wants to help him lick his wounds with three rounds of dessert. "It's the least you can do after you tapped out on me. Your dad already got the girl. He didn't need to win this round too."

Lucy's excitement is palpable as she slings her eyes to her father. She isn't just excited about Thane's offer of a sweet treat. She's over the moon after his comment that her father won the girl.

Although I'll never tell Brodie this, Thane and Lucy spent most of our first self-defense class pondering ways to force us together. They had no clue my hurt ran deeper than being ditched after a one-night stand. Most of it centered around ghosts of my past.

Brodie holds out to Lucy's silent pleas for almost thirty seconds before telling her no amount of whining will have her skipping her vegetables tonight.

"I'll eat them all. I promise." She crosses her heart before waiting for the final head bob of approval from Brodie.

When she gets it, she practically flies into Thane's arms. "Let's make like geese and get the flock out of here."

"Thane—"

I snatch up Brodie's wrist before he can test Thane's self-defense skills for real. I'm not solely excited for a little bit of alone time in the middle of the afternoon, but Thane also shouldn't be blamed for something Lucy overheard Amelia say.

Brodie waits for them to vanish up the stairs before shifting on his feet to face me. "She said flock, right?"

Smiling, I nod. Lucy has a bit of a lisp, and I'm not one hundred percent confident in my reply, so I'd rather use a gesture than words.

My grin grows when he sighs in relief before nudging his head to the stairwell. "Hungry?"

Again, I nod. "Starving."

When I lick my lips, he groans. "Don't look at me like that, Henley. I'm trying to remember that you don't have to be naked every time we're alone. I might have years of a self-imposed sabbatical to compensate for, but I don't want you mistakenly believing I only want you for sex."

You have no idea how wild his statement makes me. Being desired is addictive, but realizing you are the sole reason someone ended an almost six-year abstinence from sex makes you feel worth your weight in gold.

"Henley..." Brodie groans while adjusting his crotch.

"We have thirty minutes tops. An hour if he takes her to the parlor on West Street. I can think of far better ways to use the time than pretending to act chivalrous." I graze my bottom lip with my teeth. "Like with your head between my legs." I take my time dragging my eyes up his body, my watch lingering on his thickening crotch. "Or perhaps mine between yo—"

He lunges for me before all my sentence leaves my mouth and fucks me hard and fast until Lucy is saved from eating vegetables by a tight schedule that demands the ordering of takeout.

24

BRODIE

"**H**ave you told her yet?" Lucy scrubs her back molars with her toothbrush for a few more seconds before spitting the froth into the sink and twisting to face me.

I wait for her to bare teeth so I can check her cleaning skills before asking, "Told her what?" I know who she's referencing without needing to ask. She hasn't stopped talking about Henley for the past five days. Almost every sentence starts with "Henley."

I don't mind. She's on my mind just as much. I simply hide it better.

After swishing water around her mouth and gargling it, Lucy disposes of it. "That you love her." I barely balk, but she's on me as much as Thane was for details after he took Lucy for pre-dinner dessert. "Don't deny it, Daddy. You can see it all over your face."

"You need to stop listening to Uncle Thane, and nothing is happening between Henley and me. We're friends." *Who are going to kill each other if we don't occasionally switch out sex for sleep.*

I thought the tension was extreme before I gave in to it.

I was dead fucking wrong.

The fireworks don't quit—not even in the middle of the day when they're being watched by an almost six-year-old.

Henley's beautiful face and cock-thickening body would have any man on the backfoot, but the way she always puts Lucy first and encourages her to speak about her mother as often as she does herself has me staring at her in awe more than I should.

I'm still too old for her, and a worry won't stop niggling in my gut, but one taste will never suffice.

If a death stare could kill, I'd be dead right now. "Grandma Stell was right. Boys are stupid." Lucy hops off her step, dries her face on the towel, then marches to her bedroom. "She said Henley could slap you in the face with a fish, and you'd still act stupid."

As I shadow her to her room, I ask, "What's with the name-calling today? That's the third time you've called me stupid."

She climbs on her bed before twisting to face me. Her expression is serious when she says, "It isn't a name if it's true."

"Hey..."

She holds firm for two seconds before her bottom lip drops. "I'm sorry. My hormones aren't playing nice. I think I have PSM."

"Do you mean PMS?"

Her brows furrow before she shakes her head. "Amelia said we get cranky from Putting Up With Men's Shit." She counts out the first letter of each of her last five words. "PUWMS."

Now she is as confused as me.

"I still think you mean PMS, but that's not something you have to worry about yet." I tug down her summer duvet before gesturing for her to slip under it. "Especially since you're not allowed a boyfriend until you're forty, so you don't have to put up with anyone's crap for a long time."

Her mouth gapes before it snaps closed just as fast. "Forty? You said I could have a boyfriend when I'm thirty!"

I shrug before tucking her in tight. "I changed my mind. It's my prerogative."

She's not happy, but curiosity will always reign supreme for her. "What's a per-per—"

"A prerogative is the right to change your mind."

She rolls over, ruining my superb burrito-wrapping skills, before tucking her hands under her cheek. "Like you did when you got scared?"

"Daddy doesn't get scared."

Lucy's clap backs are always fast and accurate. "Yes, you do. You get scared every time you leave me, and you were *really* scared the night you found Henley." She continues to prove she is far too wise for her years. "But you were way more scared the next day. You looked like you wanted to vomit when you saw her suitcase." Her face takes on a serious expression. "Did you want to vomit, Daddy? I wanted to vomit *so* bad."

After checking that the coast is clear, I gesture for her to scoot over before joining her in bed. "Can you keep a secret?"

She nods so fast I grow worried I'll need to take her for a CAT scan. "Uh-huh."

"I didn't just want to vomit. I did vomit." I tickle her ribs. "You should be glad Uncle Thane ate all the scrambled eggs before you went to the kitchen."

My laugh almost drowns out the faint giggle in the hallway when Lucy replies, "I told you eggs are vomit clouds." She gags like she's being forced to swallow a mouthful of the number one food on her hate list. "And they smell like fart. You're not supposed to eat farts."

I'm laughing so hard my words are chopped up when I try to move our exchange back to our usual bedtime routine. I will always love and cherish the time I get with my daughter, but it's been a long time since I've remembered I am a man as much as I am a father.

Henley gave me that.

"Do you have any story requests tonight?" My brow arches when she shakes her head. "You don't want a story?"

Through a yawn, Lucy replies, "Not tonight." A ghost-like grin spreads across her face when I fan my hand across her forehead to check her for a temperature. "I'm not sick, Daddy. I'm just tired."

"Okay. It's your prerogative if you don't want a story."

After slipping out of her bed, I lean down to kiss her forehead.

Lucy takes advantage of my closeness by gripping the collar of my shirt and whispering, "But you should tell Henley the thought of losing her by choice is way scarier than your worry someone will take her from you."

"Uncle Thane—"

"Not Uncle Thane," she interrupts, finally whispering as intended. "The bad people. Mommy didn't have a choice to leave. They made her go, but Henley has a choice, and it scares you that she might pick to leave."

She is spot on the money, but this isn't something she needs to worry about. My neuroses are mine. They don't belong on her shoulders.

"Luc—"

"Just tell her, okay? Then she'll stay. Please, Daddy?"

She is so worked up that I have no choice but to say, "Okay, I'll tell her."

You'd swear I handed her the keys to Disneyland when she squeals as she wraps her arms around my neck and hugs me tight. "I love you, Daddy."

"I love you too."

I already knew we had an eavesdropper, but Lucy gives Henley no choice but to announce her snooping ways when she says, "I love you too, Henley."

Never one to leave Lucy disappointed, Henley's nervous squeak escapes the hallway. "I love you too, Lucy-Lou."

Almost thirty minutes pass settling Lucy down from her euphoria of believing she's forced Henley and me together. By the time I return to the lower level of my home, Henley is seated on the couch, folding laundry and watching trash television.

"Hey."

She startles when I cough to clear my throat before she switches off the television. "Hey. I thought you must have fallen asleep with Lucy." The tension burns when she murmurs. "We've been burning the candle at both ends the past week, but now we have no choice but to rest."

She exhales so profoundly her shoulders sink before she cranks her neck to face me. The reason for her dour tone is revealed when I spot the bulky bulge at the front of her midsection. A hot water bottled is strapped around her waist, and pain medication is open on the coffee table.

"Now the PMS conversation makes sense."

Henley groans even with my comment being playful. "I'll try to limit how much time she spends with Amelia." Guilt flashes across her face. "I didn't realize she was in the room until she asked what PMS meant." She scratches at her neck, a telltale sign she's nervous, before murmuring, "Although if you want a cheat's way of explaining to her what fuck buddies entails, Amelia is the girl for the job."

"Is that what we are? Fuck buddies?" That hurt to ask more than I care to admit.

Feelings are developing.

Feelings that scare the shit out of me, and not all my fear derives from Henley's age.

I'm petrified of the same thing that happened to my wife happening to her.

Caroline didn't die of natural causes. She was killed by a man seeking revenge. He killed two dozen women in under a month, and the feds have nothing on him.

He is a ghost.

A myth.

The reason I've been so paranoid about letting anyone in.

He killed the partners of FBI agents to make them suffer as he did, yet we can't find a single connection between the families targeted. We didn't work in the same unit, never attended the same raids. Even the academies we studied at are different.

The attacks would appear random if it weren't for the messages he left at each scene.

You took my love, so I took yours.

But do you know what is even more concerning than that? Wondering if you're good enough for someone to make the sacrifice for a second time. Caroline knew the risks. She came into our relationship willingly, but with things not so great between us before she died, was she still happy with her decision in her final hours?

I want to say yes, but I'm not as confident as I used to be.

And then there's Henley—*beautiful, sweet, young Henley*—who hasn't had the chance to meet the man I was before I became a widow. I'm not fun anymore. I am not playful. I'm a damn grump, but Henley can't seem to get enough.

Even staring at me now, waiting for me to look at her so she can answer my question, her eyes drink me in like not all my good points died with Caroline. Like I still have so much to offer.

I do. I just need to get over my fear of losing—both in the not winning sense and loss.

I'm trying, but it is the equivalent of teaching an old dog new tricks.

Slow.

Once Henley's eyes return to my face and she realizes she has my attention, she answers, "I'm not exactly sure what we are. I... ah..." After a big breath, she rips off the Band-Aid in one quick motion. "Things changed the night I acted on impulse instead of fear, but I can't pinpoint what changed for you. I love Lucy, but she's a little off the mark on who she thinks was scared that night."

Her blonde brow shoots up high when I reply, "She wasn't. I was so scared about what I might stumble onto, you weren't shaking until you got on the bike with me." I intertwine my fingers together before lowering my eyes to them. With Henley's hormones out of whack, this probably isn't the best time for the conversation, but I can't hold back. "I was petrified I was going to be too late again." A ghost of a grin etches onto my mouth when I realize how smart my daughter is. "And that fear was just as strong the morning after when I learned you *wanted* to leave."

"I didn't want to leave, Brodie. But I had no right to stay. I wasn't assigned—" Her words halt when the landline buzzing into the room interrupts her.

For the first time in days, her expression turns fretful when it dawns on her what the noise is. She looks desperate to beat me to the phone, which only increases the length of my strides.

I want to protect her as fiercely as she's been protecting Lucy. That's why I didn't bring up the murders of the men who walked her out of Aeros. She doesn't remember much about that night, so I've kept the burden of their deaths on my shoulders.

It's the least I can do after she saved me from making mistakes that Lucy may have never forgiven me for.

"Hello—"

"Out of respect for your daughter, I'm calling to give you a common courtesy any agent should get."

"Who is this?" I ask, the voice familiar but not enough for me to make a guess. It is also muffled, like they don't want their identity exposed.

"It isn't the pope." Her next sentence gives her away. "Although he might be tempted to pop in to sample your breakfast spread." Agent Macy Machini gets back on track as quickly as she veered off it. "They have a suspect on the murders from last week. Things are being kept hush-hush, but when I make a promise, I don't care how much time passes between pledges. If I give you my word, you have it until one of us is in the ground."

I look at the time, the stairwell to make sure there aren't any little shadows, then over at Henley standing mute at my side, before asking, "What does this have to do with me?"

"They have a witness." She cups her phone, tells an agent I've not heard of before that she won't be a minute, then focuses back on me. "She verifies that the un-plated motorcycle we suspect was in the back alleyway of Aeros definitely was and gave a vivid description of the alleged assailant to a sketch artist." Ruffing papers sound down the line. "He looks a fuckton like you."

As I scrub at my jaw, I cuss under my breath, then turn my back on Henley to hide my confession behind my bulky frame. "I swear on my wife's grave, they walked away from our exchange breathing."

"Knowing you as well as I do, they would have more scampered away," Macy whispers with a sigh. "I don't blame your response, Brodie, especially when you learn what gang they're associated with, but I've presented as much evidence of your innocence as I can on your behalf. You need to come in to back me up or they'll come knocking with handcuffs."

A groove runs down the middle of my forehead as I ask, "They're coming here?"

"No." I breathe easy until she adds, "Not yet. I asked them to hold off until you deny my request for an official statement." Her sigh whistles in my ear. "I can probably stall them until the morning, but I figured you'd rather come in while Lucy is sleeping."

"I would," I agree, even with my stomach still twisted up in knots. "I'll be there in twenty. Ten if my bike will start."

"Having issues since the crash?" Macy keeps talking before I can remove my foot from my mouth. "I'll meet you at the west entrance."

When she hangs up, I dial Thane. I trust Henley with Lucy wholeheartedly; she will take care of her no matter what, but a niggle in my gut won't quit no matter how deeply I try to breathe it out.

"Hey, you've reached Thane. You know what to do. Except you, Christie. You still need practice."

I once found his voicemail message funny.

Now it is frustrating.

"Thane, it's me. I need to head out for an hour or two. Lucy is asleep, but I was wondering if you could keep Henley company while I'm gone. Maybe you could watch a movie or something?" Jealousy is solely responsible for my last sentence. Thane's antics have died down a lot over the past week, but he's quick to remind me I should consider myself lucky to smear the sheets with a woman as beautiful as Henley, and that plenty of men will happily take my place if I don't start proving I'm worthy of her. "I'll try the landline."

Riggs answers after one ring. "Ashburn residence."

"Riggs, It's Brodie. Is Thane in?"

"He is, but requested not to be disturbed."

The snideness of his comment tapers to silence when I say, "Tell him it's urgent."

Several long seconds later, a breathy response sounds down the line. "You want to have a good fucking excuse for interrupting me. Her mouth is like a hoover—"

"They've got a lead on the case I was telling you about the other night." His silence speaks volumes, as well as Henley's. I've never heard her so quiet. "I need to go in and assist with the investigation."

I hear the groan of a disappointed woman before Thane's promise. "I'll be there in five." When my breathy gripe adds to the female's frustration, he says, "I'm not The Flash. I can't move at the speed of light, but I promise I'll run every stop sign like you have pull with the local PD."

As the noise of his zipper sliding into place sounds down the line, I lower the phone from my ear and then collect my wallet and cell phone from the entryway. My wish to leave doubles when I spot a message from an unknown number. It shows the sketch Macy mentioned earlier. It is like looking in the mirror.

"I need to head out," I announce to Henley like she hasn't been eavesdropping on my conversation for the past couple of minutes. "I should be back no later than ten. Thane is—"

"Daddy..." When the patter of feet on the floorboards sounds through my ears, my eyes shoot in the direction of Lucy's groggy voice. "Can I have a glass of water?"

"Go back to bed, honey," Henley answers on my behalf. "I'll bring you a glass in a minute." She waits for Lucy's shadow to move from the landing of the stairs before shifting on her feet to face me. "What's going on? You've gone super serious." She tugs on the hem of her shirt. "Is it me? Was that call about me?"

"No. It has nothing to do with you." Lying is easy when it stops hurt. I wish I had remembered that six years ago. "I—"

"Can I have a cookie too, please?"

"Uh-huh," Henley replies, less ruffled by Lucy's second interruption than she is about my phone calls. She looks on the verge of hyperventilation, and my lie hasn't slackened the groove running down the middle of her forehead.

"And a story?"

Henley's breath fans my cheeks when she replies to Lucy's numerous demands. "As many as you want. I just need you to give me a minute, okay?"

"Okay," Lucy replies, her voice echoing down the stairwell.

We're interrupted again—by my cell phone this time.

It is another message from Macy. It is more daunting than the first.

UNKNOWN NUMBER:

> I can't stall until morning. They're gearing up to confront you, so if you want to tuck your daughter in tomorrow night, get your ass here now!

"I need to go."

"Brod—"

I snatch my leather jacket from the coatrack while replying, "If you want me to keep my promise to Lucy, I need to do this."

That instantly halts any further protest from Henley. She nods before shakingly gathering the key for my bike from a drawer in the entryway table I never use. "I found it in my room when I was packing." After wetting her lips, she confesses, "I don't remember much about what happened that night, but I'm reasonably sure I fixed your bike. My father and I—"

"Henley? Are you coming?"

Her smile at Lucy's impatience decreases the angst on her face. "Yes. I'm coming now." She squeezes my hand in silent moral support before twisting to face the stairwell.

I almost leave things there, but with my stomach refusing to stop flipping, I snatch up her wrist, tug her back to me, then seal my lips over hers before a single squeak can pop from her mouth.

I kiss her until the thuds of my heart overtake Lucy's screams of jubilation, and then I kiss her some more just for the hell of it.

25

HENLEY

"Into bed, young lady." I keep my voice stern, faking anger, but in reality my insides are dancing as much as Lucy's.

After kissing me breathless, Brodie noogied Lucy's head, promised he'd be back as soon as possible, then left us shuddering in the ripple of his motorcycle's healthy roar.

Once I've placed Lucy's water onto the bedside table, I bend the springs in her mattress by sitting on the edge before asking her what story she'd like to hear. They shifted from manufactured stories to real ones the past week. Usually, every one of them involves her mother, but occasionally, like earlier tonight, their focus shifts to me.

"Will you tell me what Daddy said?" Her red cheeks make her look like a little cherub. "Did he say he loves you, or did he noogie your head? I told him to kiss you, but Grandma Stell said he'd be too scared to do that." Her smile is even brighter than the gleam in her eyes. "He proved her wrong." She nuzzles into my thigh before peering up at me with wide, tired eyes. "I'm glad he's not scared anymore. The bad man who hurt Mommy made him afraid."

"Someone hurt your mommy?" I ask before I can stop myself, too shocked to hold back. I assumed Caroline died of cancer or a car accident. I had no clue she was murdered.

I hate my inquisitiveness when wetness pricks her eyes as she nods. "There was a big im-mesti-vigation, but they haven't found him yet." She looks as regretful as I feel. "That's why Daddy works so much. He wants to find the man who took Mommy from us when I was just a baby." Her head angles as her brow cocks. "Is that where he went? To help the people find the bad man?"

"Maybe," I reply, stumped for a better answer. "But how about we don't talk about that now? We're supposed to share happy stories before bed." *It creates less nightmares that way.* "Have you tried kissing Fernando yet?"

Lucy peers at her pet frog before shifting her focus back to me. "No." She looks unimpressed. "Why would anyone want to kiss a frog?"

"How else are you supposed to find out if he's a prince?"

When her eyes pop open, I realize she's never heard of *The Princess and the Frog.*

"A long time ago, in a land far, *far* away from here, there was a princess named..."

"And they lived happily ever after." My last two words are as faint as the tiny snores leaving Lucy's gaped mouth. She crashed not even halfway through the story, so I skipped the part about Princess Tiana kissing frogs that weren't princes and jumped straight to the happily ever after.

I love the time we spend together sharing stories and honing our crafting skills, but my stomach hasn't stopped churning since her confession that her mother was hurt by a bad man.

When I stood across from her two weeks ago, I saw a reflection of myself, just several years younger, but I had no clue how profoundly similar our lives are. My mother was also killed. She was murdered by a man seeking revenge on federal agents who he believed...

My thoughts trail off when a disturbing notion hits my stomach with a brutal blow.

Brodie is an agent, and his wife was murdered.

It could be a coincidence, but damn, that would be an extreme twist of fate.

As quickly as I can without waking Lucy, I race out of her room, stopping at the wall of photographs. I've scanned them a hundred times the past week, but this time, I look for any indication of the date the images were taken.

Most show Lucy as a newborn baby, but a handful are a couple of months later.

None with her mother go past the six-month one Brodie snapped of Caroline lying with Lucy on the measurement blanket they took photographs on to document her milestones.

It was snapped the week before my mother was killed.

"No..." I murmur, sickened. "This can't be true."

Desperate for answers, I yank my cell out of my pocket and dial a frequently called number.

Amelia's voicemail answers on her behalf. "You've reached Amelia—"

As I gallop down the stairs, I hang up and dial again.

It isn't even nine. There's no way she's already gone to bed.

When I reach her voicemail for the second time, I leave a message. "Call me. It's urgent."

Instincts direct me into Brodie's office. I've been in here multiple times the past two weeks, but I never paid the decor much attention until now. It is dark and moody, as morose as the fear making its way up my throat from my stomach.

Photographs of Lucy line one shelf, half a bottle of whiskey is hidden in the bottom drawer, and Brodie's laptop sits on top of a filing cabinet, but other than that, his office is a standard home office. Nothing gives away what happened to Caroline, and there isn't a single scrap of paper to appease my worry.

"Because everything is digital these days," I murmur while recalling Amelia saying the same thing to me only days ago. "Even someone as ancient as Hillary Seabourn would correspond electronically."

After sitting in Brodie's chair, I pull over his laptop and crack open the screen. I'm taken aback by an error message after I type in Caroline's name.

Assuming my shaking hands made me miss a key, I type it in slower this time.

The error message remains.

Determined, I go through the list Amelia and I worked through days ago.

I smile when his password is as simple as his daughter's given name.

My hand rattles when I scroll past the files on the desktop. My father never kept imperative files in plain sight. They were always hidden deep in the server, far from the prying eyes of his inquisitive daughter.

I stumble onto the jackpot when I find a locked file under a "budgets" tab. No one locks their budget files. The people rich enough to have anything to lose don't need a budget, and the rest of us have no shame displaying financial maturity.

I've had a budget since I saved up for my first Rise Up tickets.

Amelia will never have one.

With the file stating it hasn't been opened this month, I type Brodie's old passcode into the password field. It opens the file on an insurance claim that would make a bank clerk's eyes water if she was required to count each denomination by hand. The figure is excessive and displays Brodie could live as elaborately as the Ashburns when he cashes it in.

After closing down the seven-figure life insurance policy, I scroll through the files until I stumble onto one with a familiar keyword.

Case File: 70003417

I work my throat through a hardy swallow before flicking through the "victim profiles" in the file. I knew the diversity of the suspect's victims was wide-ranging, but I had no clue how many ethnicities were involved until it takes several clicks to reach the woman I'm searching for.

It isn't Caroline.

It is my mother.

Victim fourteen out of twenty-one—twenty-seven if you include the aftermath of the assailant's crimes.

Some couldn't continue after their loss.

Some died with their wives.

Then some were freed from the torment simply because children weren't a part of the madman's revenge.

I learn that Lucy was the latter when my sluggish click past my mother's profile has me stumbling onto a pair of dark-brown eyes, golden hair, and a smile identical to Lucy's in every way.

Caroline.

26

BRODIE

"Thanks for coming in." Macy holds open the west entrance door of our local HQ before gesturing her head to my cell phone I've just pulled out of my pocket. Thane called during my commute, but with a storm rolling in, I couldn't hear a word he spoke. "You'll need to check that." When I give her a look as if to say *are you serious?* she bobs her head. "There's been a handful of mishaps the past month. They're not taking any chances anymore."

"Such as?"

Before she can answer me, we're interrupted by another agent. "Brodie, it's been a while." Agent Grayson Rogers slaps my hand before clutching it for a firm shake. He's younger than me, a hundred times cockier, but a good agent. "This is bullshit, but we appreciate your willingness to help." He locks eyes with Macy. "Conference Room Three?"

I breathe a little easier when Macy nods.

If the accusation was serious, they wouldn't interrogate me in a conference room.

"Can I get you anything? Coffee? Soda? Water?"

"I'm good, thanks," I reply to Macy while following her and Grayson into the trenches I've not walked officially for a year and a half. "But if you could give me more details than you did over the phone, I'd appreciate it."

Again, she nods before gesturing for me to enter the conference room before them. "The murders were mafia hits." She dumps a folder thicker than my bicep onto the table, its slide exposing a handful of crime scene photos. "Clean headshots with unmarked bullets. Fingers were either removed or mangled to make identification hard." She spins a photograph of the man who stood at the back, barking orders. "He had most of his teeth removed."

"He was in charge."

"We figured as much," Grayson replies, propping his backside on the conference room table while gesturing for me to take a seat across from him. "Although we had little to go off, people talk when they fear they're next." Once I'm seated, he slides a mug shot of a man with blond hair, an angry snarl, and a neck tattoo across the table to me. "He said they were there to get his girl."

"Who is this?" I keep my tone neutral even with my back molars grinding together. The punk in the mug shot screams gangbanger. He's a bottom dweller, but even they're willing to risk charges for sex trafficking since most perps barely get a slap on the wrist these days.

Grayson folds his arms across his chest. "Beau Barichello."

"Beau?" I check before I can stop myself. I've heard that name before. Recently. And his description is a good fit for a low-ranking gangster who'd chip a woman's tooth for something as minor as letting off a bit of steam.

Grayson's eyes flick to Macy for the quickest second before he jerks up his chin. "Heard of him before?"

"Not that I can recall," I lie, but it is too late.

Something has given me away.

"What about her?" This question didn't come from Macy or

Grayson. It came from a man standing outside the conference room. He's tall, overweight, and holds so much arrogance on his face that he appears older than Grayson and me combined.

When he enters the room, Macy slips behind Grayson before saying, "Marshal Levalley, I thought you wanted us to head this interrogation?"

"And waste valuable time? You're giving him more intel than he's giving you." He nudges his head to the frosted wall behind my chair. "I also struggled to hear anything through the glass pane. It's not built the same as the windows in interrogation rooms."

"Making the perp believe you're on the same team is a proven tactic for disarming them." Grayson doesn't like this man any more than Macy, but he does a better job hiding it. "But if you think you can do better, go ahead. I still believe you're fishing in the wrong pond with fake worms instead of real ones."

He moves off the desk, giving Marshal Levalley center stage, but when his focus remains on him more than me, it announces who he thinks the real criminal is.

"Marshal Levalley," the man introduces, flashing his credential too fast for me to see. "United States Marshal Services."

"USMS?" I query, my eyes bouncing between Grayson and Macy. "I thought this was about a triple homicide?"

"It is," the marshal answers on their behalf. "And her."

He sets down a photo in front of me. It isn't a mug shot, but I'd never forget her snow-colored hair, cornflower-blue eyes, and tiny freckles that adorn her nose.

"Who is this?" I ask like I don't know the answer.

"Henley"—I sigh in relief until Marshal Levalley finishes— "Elsher."

Before I can overcome my shock that Henley gave me an alias, Macy hits me with a fact so damn firm, I'm almost knocked from my chair. "Henley is a witness who skipped her watch the day you arrived for your meeting with a supervisory special agent."

"Skipped? Or coerced to go?" Marshal Levalley snaps out, glaring at me in suspicion.

"You think I took her?" I ask, reading between the lines he's drawing in the sand.

When he looks at me smugly, I toss down Henley's photograph before pushing back from the table with a laugh. "Why would I do that?"

I choke on my laughter when Grayson answers on Marshal Levalley's behalf. "Because she's the only person capable of identifying your wife's killer."

"Allegedly," Marshal Levalley snaps out before he drops his eyes to me. "You might not have walked these gallows for over a year, but you've been here in spirit the entire time. You know everything happening, especially if it involves your wife's investigation."

"As I should," I bite back, pissed as fuck.

He continues as if I didn't speak. "So when you heard we had a witness, you scheduled a meeting for the same day as her arrival because you don't want him arrested. You want him dead."

Since I can't deny his claims, I keep my mouth shut.

My silence bothers the marshal more than Grayson and Macy. His jaw ticks as his hand on the table balls into a fist. "Are you so set for revenge you don't care who you take down to get it? Hasn't she been through enough?"

He pushes over a photograph similar to the scene I arrived at after my wife rang me sobbing and scared. Except this woman's hair is more snow white than golden, and tiny freckles adorn her nose, making her appear more youthful than she is.

"Who is this?"

"Henley's mother," Grayson answers against Marshal Levalley's wish for him to remain quiet. "She was the Night Killer's fourteenth victim."

As I scrub my hand over my head, I recall the horrifying scene I faced almost six years ago. I had just started my shift when Caroline called. Since I was feeling guilty about the way I left, I slipped out of a meeting to take her call.

Through a barrage of painful groans, she told me she loved me before making me promise I'd take care of Lucy.

I begged her to tell me what was happening, but the line went dead.

Reports state the killer slit her throat after disconnecting our call. I found her tied to a dining room chair in the living room, beaten, bruised, and unresponsive. Lucy was crying in her bouncer at her side. Her golden hair looked red since it was coated in blood. She wasn't injured. Caroline's killer smeared blood over her when he moved her from her crib to the bouncer.

He didn't kill children or the agents responsible for the death of his "one true love." He took what he believes we took from him. He stole the loves of our lives.

And he's gotten away with it since no one knows who he is. He's evaded capture for years because despite his victims being the wives and husbands of federal agents, our cases aren't linked. Nothing connects us... except...

"What is it?" Macy asks when my inner monologue freezes me.

I lift and lock my eyes with her remorseful pair. "Why did Henley leave witness protection? If she knows who killed her mother, she'd want him dead as much as the rest of us, so why would she skip her detail? Also..." I pause to ease the anger roaring through me. "Why hasn't a suspect been arrested?" Macy isn't as good at schooling her features as Grayson is. "You still don't know who he is." I stand from my chair so fast it smacks into the frosted glass wall behind me. "You said she could identify him!"

"She can," Grayson defends. His voice drops a decibel before he murmurs, "We just need her to go under again one more time."

"Go under? What the fuck do you mean go under? She isn't an agent."

"Henley wasn't meant to be home the night her mother was killed," Macy explains. "She was at a sleepover with a friend, but when they got caught by a local unit for underage drinking and he recognized her last name, he did her father a favor." She breathes out heavily. "His patrol car pulling into the driveway startled the perp. He pushed past Henley as she snuck in via the basement. Her backside shattered the glass pane opening as she fell, and a wayward shard wedged into the killer's wrist. When he dug it out, she spotted his tattoo. It was a symbol with text written in Latin."

"Allegedly," Marshal Levalley says again. "None of this is official."

Grayson is back up in his face quicker than I can snap my fingers. "Because your unit was too incompetent to write it up."

It takes me a few moments to respond, but when I do, it is shouted and aggressive. "Why the fuck wasn't any of this written up? It is an identifiable feature of a man we have nothing on, yet you left it off official reports!"

"Because we didn't know of its existence until we gained access to Agent Moses's personal files."

"Agent Moses?" I check. "The rogue agent who was killed by a fellow agent?"

Macy swallows but remains quiet, leaving the talking to Grayson. "Yes. He was the lead agent on Mrs. Elsher's investigation and Henley's handler."

"Handler? Once again, why are you treating her like an informant instead of a witness?"

I sling my eyes to Macy when she jumps back into the conversation. "Henley tried to move on from her loss when her father committed suicide on the second anniversary of her mother's death. She went to college in Florida and started dating."

"Beau?" I'm shocked I can speak. My throat is tight with anger, and my hands are balled so firmly, my clipped nails are digging into my palm.

Grayson nods. "One morning when she woke up groggy and confused in his bed, she witnessed an exchange between Beau and a man she described as being approximately six three, with dark hair, tanned skin, and an emblem in a foreign language on his left wrist," Grayson adds. "She was adamant it was the same man who barged past her the night her mother was killed"

"But Agent Moses told her she was confused." Macy rolls her eyes. "Since there was GHB in her system, the lead field agent of his unit agreed with him."

My back molars are already being gnawed to nubs, but they're wholly obliterated when Grayson confesses, "We tried to put her back in a handful of times to see if she could identify him again, but we never got close."

"We?" I ask, sure as fuck not letting him pin any of this shit on me.

Henley is a victim. She should have never been a part of the operation to secure the man who murdered her mother.

"The bureau," Grayson answers, like he can't spot my fisted hands and tight jaw. "When Agent Moses's erroneous mistakes were unearthed, I had Henley transferred to our division."

"She was only meant to be placed into witness protection," Macy assures me. "But when details emerged of a similar sanction to the one Beau operates in Miami forming here—"

"You asked her to go under again?" I interrupt.

"Not me," Macy fires back, as disgusted as I am at the possibility of Henley being so poorly mishandled. "I told them it was a bad idea, but they wouldn't listen to me."

"For just reasons," Marshal Levalley mutters, angering her more.

"But enough of the small talk. I'm not here for he said she said." He shifts his eyes to me. They're as murky as the blood circulating in my veins. "Either give up her location or take the fall for her murders."

I laugh at his belief Henley is capable of murder.

He nips it in the bud quick smart. "Whoever removed all traces of your involvement digitally forgot that DNA is the slam dunk of every case." He slaps down a photo of a boot imprint bruise on the chest of one of the victims before a soil sample report. "Soil-borne pathogenic organisms are distinct in this region. It isn't hard to pinpoint where you've been. Then there's this." A second report. This time, it is the DNA results for a nail scraping. "Your boot, her blood."

"My *alleged* boot imprint, and an *alleged* DNA sample for an unidentified female." I eat my words when Marshal Levalley pulls across the sheet hiding the sampler's details. "She is in witness protection! You can't put her name on an official document." Bile burns my throat for the second time when another horrifying fact smacks into me. "Tell me you weren't so stupid to write her up as a suspect?"

Grayson reacts to the guilt in Marshal Levalley's eyes before I can. "You fucking idiot. I'll have your badge for this."

"Her DNA was found on a victim," he defends. "She—"

I barge Grayson out of the way so I can glare into the eyes of the man who just signed Henley's death certificate. "Because he dug his fat fingers into her arm too deeply when he was forcefully walking her out of Aeros against her will after most likely spiking her drink." I shake him so hard his brain rattles against his skull. "You just gave away a witness's details to someone so knowledgeable of law enforcement he's killed several agents' partners and not left a shred of evidence!" Terror rains down on me. "He could have her details now."

I want to punch him. I want to distribute some of the fear tearing me in two to him, but getting to Henley and Lucy before the man who killed my wife far outweighs my wish for revenge.

"If you walk out that door, it could be seen as an admission of guilt," Marshal Levalley warns as I race through it.

I sprint down the hallway so fast I barely register Agent Macy calling in a possible incident at my residence for the second time in her career.

27

HENLEY

I drop the pen Lucy gifted Brodie on Father's Day last year when an annoying trill breaks the silence. I've been sitting in Brodie's office for the past twenty minutes, striving to work up the courage to tell him about our connection. I don't want him to think I sought him out.

My father's inability to let go of the details surrounding the cases was the final nail in his coffin. I didn't want to go down the same route, so I acted as if my parents were still alive while I forged a new life in Florida. Amelia could have made me anyone, but since Henley was my mother's middle name, I kept it while rotating my surnames to fit the situation.

For the first few months of my new life, I was of Finnish descent.

I could only pull off Italian for about a week.

Henley Seabourn was founded solely because of Lucy's true nanny's identity.

Hillary was peeved as hell when I met her at the train station with a hundred apologies from the nanny agency. I told her there was a huge mistake and that she was meant to be nannying for a couple on the West Coast.

She was frustrated, but when Amelia disclosed she had grandchildren in Seattle, her placement with a recent signup at the nanny agency saw her practically skipping to the ticket booth to purchase a one-way ticket to Kirkland.

The rest of my ruse was relatively simple.

Well, it would have been if Brodie hadn't been so opposed to a young nanny.

Hillary's full head of gray hair, her wrinkled face, and her aged body should have hinted at Brodie's dislike of a young placement in his house, but I figured his comment—that he had to accept a placement from across the country because he'd gone through every local nanny—as he walked through the courtyard Agent Macy Machini had taken me to for a breather was because he overstepped the mark with his prior nannies.

I'd had no clue he only hired nannies older than dirt.

I remember the reason for my near coronary when the cordless landline phone on Brodie's desk commences ringing again a second after it stops.

"Hello," I answer, my voice aged.

It is almost nine, so I doubt the nanny agency is calling now, but I need to be cautious. I don't want anyone spilling the beans to Brodie before I do.

"Henley?"

Since the voice is echoing and surrounded by sirens, I continue with my ruse that I'm ancient. "Did you say Hillary?"

"It's Brodie."

I breathe out in relief. "Hey. Ah..." I can't have this conversation over the phone. I need to tell him in person. "Lucy is sleeping peacefully."

His sigh matches the one I released when he announced himself. "And Thane?"

"MIA," I answer before scanning the time on Brodie's laptop. Thane should have arrived thirty minutes ago. "Did you ask him to stay outside?"

I move closer to the lace curtain covering a window that faces the front of his property. His house has a long frontage, so there's plenty of room for Thane to park behind Brodie's truck, though it appears he went a different route today.

"I think his car is parked across the street. Do you want me to check? He might—"

I stop talking when Brodie shouts, "Don't go outside!"

"Okay." I step back from the window, frightened by the fear in his voice. "After turning off the lights, I need you to get Lucy and go to the basement." Even though he can't see me, I nod when he asks, "Do you remember the wine cellar I showed you?" He must hear my head's whooshes. "It's not a wine cellar. It's a panic room. The lock code is Lucy's birthdate." It's hard to hear him over my swallows. "Take Lucy in there and close the door. You can't come out for anyone, okay?"

I continue nodding while climbing the stairs two at a time.

Our sneaking around the past week pays dividends when I make it to Lucy's room without bumping into a single object.

"It's okay, honey," I whisper to Lucy when she grumbles about me lifting her into my arms. "We need to go on an adventure, but it's okay if you want to stay asleep. Rest your head on my shoulder."

"Mr. Bunny," she murmurs, reaching for her stuffed rabbit on her bed.

While juggling the cordless landline between my shoulder and ear, I scoop up Mr. Bunny and stuff it between Lucy and me before heading back toward the pitch-black hallway.

As I walk through Lucy's bedroom door, I freeze.

A creak sounds from downstairs. It is closely followed by a grumble.

"Brodie?" I murmur, my voice as fearful as his breaths but barely a whisper.

"Yeah?"

I have to force my reply past the lump in my throat. "There's someone downstairs. I heard a creak." I step back from the opening of the stairwell in just enough time. The shadow at the bottom cranks his head up a second after I hide Lucy and me in the blackness of the dark hallway. "He's at the bottom of the stairs."

"Go to the furthest room from him and lock yourself inside. Help is on the way." Brodie's voice is surprisingly calm for how shaky his breaths are. I realize why when he murmurs, "Keep as calm as possible for Lucy. She'll think you're playing hide-and-seek if she doesn't spot your fear."

Again, I nod before cranking my head to the stairs.

I recognize the next set of creaks.

"He's climbing the stairs."

I couldn't be more scared until the mocking call of a stranger jingles in my ear. "Henley... come out come out wherever you are." His voice is chilling, and it flashes up memories of the first time I left Beau. He tried to make out it wasn't him who spiked my drink, but he was so paranoid about me associating with anyone who wasn't him that he never let me leave his side even while supplying my drinks.

This voice doesn't belong to Beau, though. It's too deep and manly.

"It's okay, baby. You're okay," I promise Lucy as I stuff her into the freestanding closet in my room. "We're just hiding in here, so Uncle Thane won't find us. You don't want to lose, do you?"

She doesn't believe me that the man searching for us in her room is Thane, but she's too scared to argue. "Uncle Thane?"

"Uh-huh. Remember Daddy asked him to come over before he kissed me? You were listening then, weren't you?"

"Yes." Her lip quivers as she peers out the crack in the warped wood. "I'm sorry."

"It's okay, you have nothing to be sorry for. I just need you to be really quiet so we're not found. Can you do that for me?"

When she nods again, I lift the phone to my ear and say, "We're in the closet."

Before Brodie can reply, the intruder I only know as the Night Killer taunts me again. "You know this would be much easier if you just came out. I'm not going to hurt you. I just want to talk."

When my silence angers him, he takes something to the wall of photographs. Glass splintering booms into the closet, hardening Lucy's whimpers to sobs.

"Don't listen to him," Brodie pleads when the Night Killer tries to convince me to come out by promising not to hurt Lucy. "You can't trust anything he says."

"If you don't, I'll gut her like I did her mother." His steps get closer as he continues to taunt. "Did he tell you that, Lucy? Did he mention how he found you surrounded by your mother's insides?"

"Cup your ears really tight, baby. Then you'll be able to hear your heartbeats." I tighten Lucy's grip around her ears before asking, "Can you hear them?"

When she nods, I fight not to sob.

She's so damn brave.

Unlike me.

I swore if I had the chance to confront the man who killed my mother so inhumanely that I would terrorize him as he had her. Yet here I am, hiding in a closet with a little girl who would still have her mother if a high alcohol reading hadn't hindered my ability to be a witness.

Agent Moses laughed in my face when I told him I could sketch the assailant.

"He was wearing all black clothes, a hoodie, a full facemask, and sunglasses. You didn't see anything but a black blob," he shouted that day.

"I saw his tattoo," I fought back. "And his—"

The words had barely left my mouth when my father arrived out of nowhere and declared Agent Moses's interview over. "She saw nothing," he agreed with him, shocking me.

I thought he was calling me a liar until he asked me to describe the tattoo the following morning. His sketch was so perfect, I hoped he would be the key to finding my mother's killer, but years went by before it was mentioned again, and I was the person bringing it up while shouting at Agent Moses that my mother's killer was at my boyfriend's home earlier that day.

He said he believed me, but he needed more, that we'd never get a conviction without at least a name to go off. He convinced me the easiest way to do that was to go "undercover" as Beau's girlfriend.

I only learned there were no official details of my "stings" when Agent Moses was killed by a fellow agent. I'd felt like an idiot, and I do now as well.

"I have to go out there," I whisper to Brodie when the bang of the bathroom door hitting the tub from being opened too quickly sounds through my ears. "He's here because of me. I didn't know. I swear to you I didn't know who you were when I sent your nanny away. I just saw Lucy and I wanted to help her. I wouldn't have come if I had known."

It takes Brodie three goes for me to realize he's shouting my name, but my mind is made up, so there's only one way for me to respond. "I'm sorry."

28

BRODIE

"*H*enley... *Henley!*"

The silence is deafening and heartbreaking.

Even more so when it is ended with the soft sob of my daughter. "Daddy..."

"Hey, honey." The relief in my tone can't be missed, and neither can the fret. "Is Henley with you?"

Her sobs louden. "No, she's with the bad man." A crash sounds down the line before Lucy's loud whimper. "He's hurting her, Daddy. I need to help her—"

"No, baby, no. Stay where you are." I whizz my motorcycle down a side street so fast that I startle a homeless man pushing a shopping cart. He cusses at me in a manner I assume Grayson does when the black SUV he's tailing me with can't fit down the sidewalk I take at a million miles an hour.

My bike only just fits, the handlebars inches from the brickwork of multiple recent developments.

"Daddy is on his way. I'm just around the corner. But I need you to stay in the closet—"

The clang of our call disconnecting sounds through my ears a second too late.

It came after Lucy's frantic squeal bellowed through my helmet speaker.

"Lucy... Luc?"

Silence.

Heartbreaking silence.

As I thrash the living hell out of my bike, I say, "Siri, call my home number."

More silence.

It doesn't even ring.

When I arrive at the front of my house, I dismount my bike as I did at Aeros' back entrance. It skids to a stop under a black SUV with a tint not dark enough to hide the slit in the throat of the man seated behind the steering wheel.

"Henley?" I call out after pushing open the front door that was partially ajar.

The house is eerily quiet. It is also in ruins.

Not a single inch of the floor plan is untouched.

After removing a gun taped under the upturned entryway table, I slowly make my way to the living room. The muted television flickers light into the room, but it is thankfully void of the horror scene I faced the last time my heart thudded this fast.

The living room is empty. Nothing but slashed couches fill the space.

With my pulse ringing in my ears, I clear the dining room and kitchen before going to the stairs.

The silence is killing me. It is gripping my throat so firmly that I can hardly breathe, and the situation worsens when I enter the hallway at the top of the stairs. The wall of photos is damaged beyond repair, and several shards of the cracked glass left in the frames are splattered with blood and pieces of snow-white hair.

I move down the hallway so fast that the creak of the floorboards under my boots gives away my approach, but I don't give a shit.

The further I travel, the direr the situation becomes. Blood splatter coats the walls, and it is obvious someone has endured the fight of their life.

"Fuck," I breathe out when I enter Henley's room, like death and despair aren't common in my field of work.

Seeing Henley sitting propped up against the freestanding closet, battered and bruised, has my memories jumping back almost six years ago, but before they can bombard me with grief, a flurry of black at the side captures my attention.

I fire before issuing a warning, then count the steps of my approach to the open bedroom window with bullets. I discharge my weapon until there's no ammunition left to disperse, then sling my gun to the door when I hear someone approaching me from behind.

There have been a handful of mock scenarios that hinted at multiple perps.

"Assailant escaped out the window," Macy shouts into her phone before joining me at the window. "He's been hit," she announces while dabbing at the fresh blood pool on the windowsill. "Possibly multiple times." Her face whitens when her eyes sling to the other side of the room. "Send up EMTs. Now!" In shock, I watch her cautiously approach Henley to check her for a pulse. "She's still breathing."

"She is?"

Macy nods like my stupidity is understandable before demanding I help lay Henley down. "We need to stop the bleeding before she bleeds out." When a creak sounds over Henley's painful groan, Macy shouts, "Last room on the right!"

"Lu... Lu..." Henley stutters between low, weak breaths, peering up at me with eyes filled with pain. "Bir-Birt—"

"We've got men looking for her," Macy assures her while pushing down on a large cut in Henley's stomach before gesturing for me to do the same to a thinner slash across her throat. "We'll find her, but for now, you need to keep fighting. You did so well, but you can't stop yet."

EMTs enter the room just as the closed closet door pops open.

As I struggle to stop the blood gushing from the wound in Henley's neck, my eyes dart around the almost empty space.

There are no signs Lucy was in the closet during Henley's brutal battle. Not a single mark or droplet of blood—thank God.

"Lu... Lu... Bir..." Henley tries again, her bloody hand rising. "Hi-hide."

"We've got you," one of the EMTs assures her, grabbing her hand and pulling it down.

His oath doesn't hold true for even a second. Henley starts convulsing long before he pricks a needle into her arm. Her eyes roll into the back of her head, and her back arches.

"We need to move her now. She's crashing."

Quicker than I can blink, they lift her onto a crash cart and wheel her out of the room.

"I'll go with her," Macy says, easing my guilt when my steps toward the door are slower and more weighed down than hers. "She'd want you to find Lucy."

Silence falls around me for the second time tonight when she follows the EMTs out of the room.

Lucy could be hiding anywhere, but my intuition is telling me she's close by.

I can feel it in my bones.

"Lucy..." I call out, my voice barely a squeak. I'm shaking so much that my body is aching, and my breaths are shallow and ineffective. "It's time to come out now."

Desperate, I shout, "Lucy! Come out this minute. This isn't funny!"

I am fucking petrified and living my nightmare for the second time in my life.

"You're scaring me, Luc—"

My shout of her name is cut short by a faint whimper. It is scarcely louder than the thumping of my heart but distinct enough for any father to understand.

My daughter is as terrified as me.

"Lucy..." I spin in a circle, confident the whimper came from Henley's room.

I have no clue why. I've searched under the bed and in the closet.

There's nowhere left to check.

"Except there," I murmur when I spot Henley's suitcase above the closet where I left it a week ago.

Baby pink fur is stuck in the case's zipper I stripped as bare as Henley made me feel the first time I stood across from her. It appears as if someone zipped it closed in a hurry.

"Lucy," I murmur again when I recognize the woolly material.

It is the color of Mr. Bunny's fur—the toy rabbit Lucy is never without once the sun goes down.

The heaviness of the case when I yank it down fills me with relief, but nothing will ease the shake of my hands when I spot the combination lock on the zipper.

It could take me hours to work out the four-digit combination.

My breath catches in my throat when I remember Henley's fight before she was lifted on a gurney. *"Lu... Lu... Bir..."*

"Lucy's birthdate."

My hands should be too big for the lock. I should fumble while placing in Lucy's date of birth, but in less than three seconds, the lock pops open, and I drag apart the zippers keeping my daughter hostage.

The sobs Lucy can't contain tell me she's alive, but the amount of blood on the outside of the suitcase Henley hid her from a madman in means I can't issue the guarantee for Henley.

"Lucy..." This time, nothing but relief fills my brief murmur. She's huddled in the middle of Henley's suitcase, clutching her rabbit, but ultimately uninjured.

"Daddy," she whimpers when she realizes who's hovering above her. She leaps into my arms, my shoulder knocking off the noise-canceling headphones far too big for her ears. "You came." Her breaths quiver in my ear as I pull her in close. "He-Henley said you would. She said you'd find me."

When she goes to peer in the direction Henley was last seen, I cup my hand over her eyes and then exit the room at the speed of a rocket.

She doesn't need to see that.

Hell, I don't want to see it either.

There's only one person I need to see. She's currently being pushed into the back of an ambulance at the front of the property I'll no longer call home.

"Where are they taking her?"

When Macy spots Lucy in my arms, she sighs so heavily that it flaps Lucy's hair into my face. "Mercer. Do you want a lift?"

I nod just as Thane comes to a stop at my side. "What the fuck?" he murmurs, his hand shooting into his hair as he takes in the scene. "What did I miss?"

"Where the fuck were you?" He doesn't deserve my anger. Nothing happening is his fault, but when you're drowning in grief, you take it out on anyone but yourself.

Thane's hand drops from his hair to Lucy's as he explains, "You called right on the end of the game. The streets were flooded with Red Sox fans. I called you. Numerous times. Traffic was gridlocked." After dragging his eyes over every inch of Lucy to make sure she's okay, he peers past her to the ambulance whizzing down the street lined with federal-plated cars. "Is she...?" He can't say the words any more than I can.

"It's touch and go," Macy answers on my behalf, doubling my guilt. "They're taking her to Mercer. You can follow us there."

I adjust Lucy from my bad shoulder to my good as Macy slowly paces back into the waiting room of Mercer ER. Lucy isn't asleep, but she is as unwilling to let me go as I am her. She hasn't left my sight for a second. Not even during our somber trip to the hospital.

It was done in the back of an ambulance. She has no physical injuries, but since she wouldn't quit shaking, Macy said it would ease her mind if we had her checked out by an EMT.

Shock was the diagnosis.

"Any news?" I ask, too impatient for Macy to make the final few steps.

Her brows furrow before she murmurs, "She isn't here. The nurse at the station said Lucy's ambulance was the only one directed here tonight."

"What?" Surprise echoes in my tone. "You said they were bringing her here!"

With my temper rising, Thane moseys closer but remains quiet.

"Because that's what they told me." Macy's eyes pop. She cusses, then yanks out her phone. "Have you got eyes on Marshal Levalley?" she barks down her cell once her call is connected. "Henley hasn't arrived at Mercer. He told me this was where they were bringing her." She flicks her eyes up to mine before shaking her head. "I told you I had a bad feeling about him." After wetting her lips to loosen up her words, she asks, "What about the perp?"

She puts her call on speaker so we can hear Grayson's reply. "Sniffer dogs tracked him for over half a mile but lost the scent near Daniels Avenue. It looks like someone picked him up."

"So you know fucking nothing?"

I wait for Lucy to reprimand me for swearing, but all she does is huddle in closer. Her tremors expose that now isn't the time for me to fight, but my god, it takes everything I have to walk away.

"We will find her, Brodie," Macy assures me, conscious of where my fear stems from as she stalks my brisk exit.

"You wanna hope it's before me." I stop just outside the double exit doors before spinning back around. "Because I won't let her anywhere near any of you if I find her first."

29

BRODIE

"*No!*" Lucy's scream pierces my ears, and her nails dig into my thigh. "I don't want you to go!" Her tears drench my jeans. "Please, Daddy. I want to stay with you."

After gesturing for Stella to stay back, I carefully pry Lucy from my leg before bobbing down to her level. Tears flood her cheeks so hard and fast my thumbs can't keep up with them. Every drop breaks my heart, but I know her heartache will be ten times worse if I don't do this.

"I know you're hurting and scared, but if I don't go, I won't find Henley." One name and her tears switch from a deluge to a trickle. "You want me to find Henley, don't you, baby?"

She nods through a hiccup.

"Then I need you to stay here with Grandma Stell." I run my hand down her hair, which is sticky with sweat. It was humid in the suitcase, but that isn't the cause of her sweaty head. It is the fight she put up when I removed her from Thane's car and carried her up the stairs of the Ashburn residence. "I can't take care of you and Henley at the same time." That sucks to admit, but it is true. "One must sacrifice for the other. Henley did it for you tonight, so now you must do the same for her, okay?"

Her lips quiver when she replies, "Okay, Daddy."

Tears prick my eyes when she throws her arms around my neck and hugs me tight. She's struggling as much as me, but just like I know I'd never forgive myself if I don't find Henley, she also does.

"Take Mr. Bunny," she whispers as she inches back. "He will keep you safe."

She doesn't give me the opportunity to tell her Mr. Bunny is her guardian. She thrusts him into my chest before racing into her grandmother's arms.

Stella cradles her in close before mouthing to me that she'll be waiting for me when I return.

For the first time in a long time, I trust her words.

"What are you doing?" I ask when Thane shadows my walk down the stairs of his family home.

Ignoring me, he slips into the passenger seat of his car before tossing me the keys.

"I can't guarantee my actions tonight won't find you in a cell next to Thorin," I warn him.

He shrugs before pulling on his seat belt. "It'll be worth it." He drags his teeth over his bottom lip before locking his eyes with mine. "I just have one request." I jerk up my chin, permitting him to speak. "We focus on Henley first."

I stab the key into the ignition and fire up the engine of his fancy sports car. "I wouldn't have it any other way."

"Who the fuck are you? And what are you doing in my office?"

My home is swarming with feds, but this room isn't lit up like a Christmas tree. The assailant ruffling through my now-open filing cabinet is doing it in the dark—a clear sign that their activity is illegal.

Thane's Adam's apple bobs when I flick on the light before he steps between me and the female with black curls sprouting from the top of her head. "Brodie, meet Amelia. Amelia, Brodie."

Amelia snaps shut the folder containing my home and contents insurance policy before asking, "Do you know that after the sixth Night Killer death, the deeds of federal agents were placed under aliases?" She rounds my desk to size me up. "They thought that was how he'd gained access to agents' personal information." Since she's a good foot shorter than me, she has to crane her neck to look me in the eyes. "It wasn't. The three deaths following the first six were conducted in rental properties. Another four after that were—"

"Houses purchased under trust funds."

Nothing she is telling me is new. I studied the case files of these murders even before Caroline was killed. I know them inside and out.

She smiles as if pleased by my response. "With deeds under aliases, it made it much harder for IA to track fraudulent activity." That piques my interest. "Rogue agents greatly benefited from their colleagues' paranoia." She nudges her head to my open laptop screen. "Him more than anyone." It displays Agent Moses's identification and badge number. "Most of his purchases are centralized to the Florida area—"

"Except one."

Thane, Amelia, and I turn to my office door in sync.

Satisfied she has our attention, Agent Macy finalizes her statement, her words more for Amelia than Thane and me. "If you're going to hack a government database, you shouldn't use an active crime scene's IP address."

Thane coughs to hide his laugh when Amelia replies, "It worked, didn't it? You're here."

Macy's eyes zoom to Amelia. "Not in an official capacity." Her eyes are back on me, hot and remorseful. "Marshal Levalley has the sup convinced there's no investigation into the disappearance of Henley Elsher. He's adamant her location is being kept under wraps for her safety."

"And you believed him?"

Macy huffs. "No. But if you go off the intel they're feeding you, you'll spend the rest of the week in an interrogation room. A BOLO is going out for you by the end of the hour."

Cussing under her breath, Amelia yanks out the cords attached to my laptop before throwing it to the floor so firmly it cracks.

"Hey!"

She blows a curl out of her eye, puffed from the strength of her throw. "I'm sure you can afford a new one. You just need to cash in that massive insurance policy you're hoarding as if it's fake first."

Thane arches a brow in interest, but before he can ask what she's referencing, Macy says, "Levalley would be stupid to do anything now. IA is breathing hard down his division's neck. He'll have Henley in a safe location." I'm about to *pfft* her until she adds, "So we need to be more selective about how we search the database for her details."

"Her name is out there, so they won't use that."

Amelia nods, agreeing with me. "But DNA is long and costly." She rolls her eyes when Macy scoffs at her like she's out of her league and far too young to be included in our conversation. "You get paid fifty grand a year tops to chase serial killers. Who's the idiot here?"

"What about fingerprints?" Thane asks, joining the conversation for the first time tonight before an all-out brawl starts.

"No good. We don't have a sample to compare." Amelia shoots her eyes to me. "When they showed up to collect her"—she nudges her head at Macy during the "they" part of her reply—"I tried to get her out. USMS servers are impossible to crack."

"Because they're technically illegal," Macy interrupts, unexpectedly smiling. "Let me make some calls. I'm owed a favor by the man who built the system." She pulls her cell from her pocket and enters the hallway. "Hunter..."

As her greeting merges with the noises of forensic officers scanning my home for evidence, I do what I came to my office to do.

I reload my gun.

When I open the bottom drawer where my bullets are located, the wobble of my yank wiggles the pen Lucy purchased me for Father's Day last year. Instinctively, I pick it up to flip it between my thumb and forefinger. It has been my go-to stress reliever tool for months, and it isn't any different today. The "woo" of the whistle inside the barrel always makes me smile, but today it comes with a drawing.

An oddly detailed drawing.

"What is that?" Thane asks, stepping closer. "It looks kind of satanic."

"The sigil of Baphomet?" Amelia asks before spinning around the pad on my desk to face her. "It is the official insignia of the Church of Satan." When Thane stares at her with his mouth gaping, she closes it for him. "I did a brief stint of pentagram studies for two semesters." Her brows furrow. "Except those aren't Hebrew letters on the pentagram points. They're—"

"Latin?" Thane either guesses or confirms. I can't quite tell. His tone is off.

"Allegedly," I murmur while recalling a conversation from earlier tonight. "Henley saw a tattoo on the killer's wrist. It was a symbol with Latin writing."

"She saw her mother's killer?" Amelia asks, her tone finally matching her youthful face.

"You didn't know?"

She flops onto the couch Henley and I fooled around on numerous times this week before shaking her head. "I didn't meet her until after her parents died, and she was striving so hard not to get snowed under like her dad, I didn't push her for info. Fuck." She looks up at Thane, her eyes wet. "Does that make me a shit friend?"

"No," Macy answers on his behalf. "She probably didn't tell you because she wanted to protect you." Her eyes lower to the sketch before she confesses, "The last time I saw a pentagram similar to that was the afternoon of Agent Elsher's suicide." Guilt hardens her features. "It was scribbled on the suicide note that never made it to evidence." Her words are barely whispers when she warns, "You can't put that through the system." Her suspicions are finally where mine have been since day one. "We've suspected for a long time that Moses wasn't working alone."

"Then what do we do?" Amelia asks, as eager to find Henley as I am. "We can't just fucking sit here and wait for the devil worshipper to find her first."

Macy's shrug only lifts her shoulders to the shell of her ear before they sink again. She fumbles while removing her phone again before her voice is as smooth as milk when she says, "Hunter, I'm calling in that favor for real this time. I need to know everyone who handled the files of a suicide three years ago..."

30

BRODIE

"lear."
"Clear."
"Clear."
"Clear."

The repeated words break through my earpiece while we raid a derelict property on the outskirts of New Jersey.

Macy's hacker friend Hunter advised that the only heat source he found via satellite surveillance was in a nonhuman form, but voiced caution because of the content he found online.

The symbol Henley sketched on the notepad in my office was the break in the Night Killer's case we've been seeking for the last five years. It led us to a satanic cult running on the east coast. The members' identities are locked up tighter than the details of witness protection clients the feds are meant to protect.

I'm reminded that I'm wearing a body cam when the gravelly voice in my ear asks, "Can you pull anything out of the flames?" I'm standing next to a lit trash can filled with computer equipment. "Most of the mainframes appear melted but could still be useable."

When the raging inferno melts the glove covering my hand, I kick over the trash can before separating the melting bits of plastic and steel with my boot. Even with surveillance announcing the property was empty, we entered in full riot gear. The stuff Hunter unearthed about this cult made even the most seasoned agents' stomachs revolt.

"Which piece?" Macy asks, joining me near the debris.

Hunter's reply comes through both our earpieces. "The green one on the right."

Macy picks up the flat disc-looking object, dusts it off, then moves to the counter that most likely housed all the equipment the criminal entity disposed of before abandoning their hideout.

"There's a cable in your backpack. Second pocket from the front. It's around three inches long."

"This one?" Macy asks after rummaging through the backpack supplied to us by a known mafia source.

"Yes. Plug it into the right quadrant of the driver, then into the laptop in the bag."

I stop watching when a familiar voice calls my name. "We've got something near the scene."

"Go," Macy suggests. "I've got things covered here."

Trust does not come easily to me, but since Macy and Grayson brought me in on the investigation instead of demanding I sit and twiddle my thumbs like the head of our unit did, I jerk up my chin before hotfooting in the direction Grayson is standing.

"Dogs followed a scent through the back streets. It initially led us to a dead end, but a civilian called in about a dark sedan crashed into a power pole two miles from your house. The occupant is refusing to surrender to local authorities until he speaks to you." The stomps of our boots chop up his last words as we race to an empty SUV.

"Prepare yourself," Grayson warns during the commute. "This is worse than we realized."

My skyrocketing heart rate reduces to a sluggish thump when the plates on the sedan we're approaching register as familiar.

They're government-issued plates.

As I cautiously approach the sedan from the back, Grayson provides backup by moving in a circular pattern around the vehicle. Grayson will take him down if the driver moves his hands an inch off the steering wheel.

The reason for the driver mounting the curb and crashing into the pole becomes apparent when I spot the blood coating his clothes. I hit him as suspected. There's an exit bullet wound in the upper left quadrant of his stomach and a second one in his shoulder.

Blood splatters on the cracked windshield when the man says, "I ca-can't believe you shot me." He smears his teeth with blood when he runs his tongue along them to loosen up his next set of words. "I-I thought we were friends?"

His words are barely audible since he's in a world of pain, but his hitched-at-one-side smile gives him away.

"Leroy?"

He smiles again before pulling off the balaclava and glasses keeping his face hidden. He knows he's minutes from death, so there's no need to continue hiding.

"How have you be-been, man?" He coughs through the blood gargling in his throat. "It's been a long time si-since you've looked me in the eyes. Was it at Caroline's wake?"

We lost touch after Caroline's death. I didn't want to associate with anyone, family or friends. When I returned to work after a six-month absence, I was pulled off the investigation of the Night Killer, and Leroy was promoted to it. I used protocol as a reason not to associate with him, but in reality I resented him for putting more hours into his other cases instead of Caroline's.

He was lazy and mishandled everything, so the distance Caroline's death placed between us grew further and further with each passing day.

I lose everything I know about myself when Leroy says, "I'm no-not surprised you went for a closed casket. She was messed up." His bite backs a bloodstained grin. "I fucked her over good."

"You fucking son of a bitch." I'm grabbed at the feet when I lurch into Leroy's car, so I can only get in a handful of hits before I'm pulled back out. "You were my partner, the godfather of my daughter. Why would you kill my wife?"

"She wanted you to leave, to be on da-daddy duty." I don't think he means to spit, but the amount of blood in his mouth leaves him no choice. "That's not how things work. We were partners before you met her. We'd been through thick and thin—"

"She was my fucking wife!"

"Who made you soft," Leroy roars back, his voice shockingly firm. I fight like hell to get out of the agent's hold when he says with a snarl, "Just like she would have. You ha-hardly knew her, but you were fawning over her at the barbecue because you didn't want anyone seeing her skin but you."

I've hardly seen him over the past five and a bit years, but it makes sense he'd attend the Ashburn Fourth of July barbecue. He is Lucy's godfather, and Stella invites everyone associated with her to major family events.

"But I had no clue how snowed under yo-you were until your heroic act of machoism at Aeros." Leroy sucks in a wheezy breath. "Your interest in her could ha-have seen you going down for murder, but you still defended her when the bureau paid you a visit." Blood splatter flies in the air when he *pffts* at me. "You're a fucking fool."

He's never understood the depths to which a man will go to protect someone he cares about. He's always been the single one of the pack, the loner with no true friends, hence Caroline suggesting him as one of Lucy's godfathers. She thought the role would mature him a bit.

We couldn't have picked worse.

"I trusted you."

His reply is barely audible. "But not as much as you trusted her." He licks his lips, glossing them up with more blood. "You told Caroline more about the Night Killer case than you shared with me, I had to improvise so she wouldn't know what was coming next." More blood splatters on his lips when he coughs out a laugh. "Kinda like now..."

Everything freezes when he removes his hands from the steering wheel. Grayson warns him to keep them in view, but he has no choice but to fire when he drops them to the gun in his lap.

"No," I scream before finally breaking free from the agent's hold.

My race to Leroy is in slow motion, but in less than a minute, I drag him out of the car, lay him on the asphalt, then push down on the new bullet wound in his chest.

"Tell me why you killed them. Give their families closure."

"I... I... I..." His eyes close during his final stumbled word.

"Leroy...." I shake him so hard that his hands flop to his sides.

He's dead, but even more shocking than that is the lack of a tattoo on his left wrist.

As the EMTs load Leroy into the back of a coroner's van, Grayson sits beside me. I'm sitting in the trunk of Leroy's car, trying to wrap my head around what the fuck just happened. My mind is reeling, overloaded with information. I had enough guilt knowing the lengths to which Henley went to protect a little girl who doesn't share an ounce of her blood, but to learn her injuries had nothing to do with her ability to identify her mother's killer makes it ten times worse.

Leroy wasn't the Night Killer. He was a copycat. He took what was unearthed during the investigation of earlier murders and used it to kill my wife. And for what? A troublesome duo that I would have outgrown not long after leaving the academy.

Leroy and I met during the recruitment process. He was a freshman, and I was a sophomore. Caroline didn't enter the picture until a month before Leroy graduated from the academy. He was always jealous of her and the attention I gave her, but I never thought it would come to this.

Not in a million years.

I shake my head when Grayson thrusts a water bottle under my chin.

He's about to lecture me about staying hydrated during long raids, but Macy arrives out of nowhere before he can. "We've found something." As we follow her into a van that smells like burning plastic, she explains. "Leroy might not have been the Night Killer, but he knew the real killers' identities."

"Killers?" I check, noting her last two words.

She nods. "Most of the files were destroyed, but Hunter lifted some information from the hard drive we pulled from the trash can." She clicks open a file on the laptop.

"They're federal badge numbers," Grayson jumps in.

Again, Macy nods. "But they don't belong to the victims."

"Potential victims?" I ask.

This time, she shakes her head. "They're current bureau members with a known association with each of the victims' partners." She opens up a mug shot. "Agent Mahone was overlooked for a promotion three times in the two years before his ex-partner's spouse's death." Another image. "Agent Sylvian forever excelled further than the agents who graduated with her."

"So you're telling me they committed murder for a petty thing like a colleague getting a promotion before them?"

I'm taken aback when Macy hums in agreement.

"Why not kill the agents? Why their partners?"

I get my questions answered by the laptop speaker. "Because in some satanic cults, sacrificial scapegoats are usually the more innocent of the group. Wives. Children. Virgins." Amelia huffs before murmuring, "Hence me losing my purity early." When Macy groans, Amelia gets back on track. "And by sacrificing the cause of someone's purity, the intended target's rejuvenation under the Church of Satan will occur more rapidly."

Macy clicks open a barrage of disciplinary action forms usually concealed from any agent who isn't IA. Every name on the top of the document belongs to an agent who lost a partner at the Night Killer's hands.

"There's no quicker way for a man to dance in hell than to make him dead set on revenge first."

Amelia's comment makes sense until I recall Leroy's reason for attacking Henley. "Leroy didn't like that I went against protocol to protect Henley. Shouldn't that have been his objective?"

"Things with Leroy were a little different." My stomach twists when image after image after image of me in various poses pop up on the laptop screen.

"And you wonder why I still have a landline," I mutter under my breath when it is obvious some images were bounced off my cell phone camera. "Am I naked in that shot?"

"And regrettably lying on your stomach with the sheet around your waist? Yes, you are." Amelia giggles at my huff before firming my anger. "That's just what I found on his work computer."

"There are thousands more in his private home files," Hunter adds on, groaning.

Confident I've gotten the point, Macy commences closing down the hundreds of images.

The mouse clicker icon freezes partway across the screen, and when Macy's eyes flick to Grayson, they have a private conversation.

"What is it?" I ask, not as coached on reading silent words.

Macy isn't a book I'll ever be able to read.

"This number is different." Macy highlights a number at the bottom of the stack before cranking her neck to me. "It is a USMS badge number."

I twist the laptop screen to face me. "For Marshal Levalley?"

She shakes her head. "No. For an ex-partner he left behind when he was promoted to supervisor."

31

BRODIE

"*D*rop the weapon."

The perp standing across from agents wearing the same riot gear my unit wore while raiding a property on the outskirts of New Jersey doesn't heed the agent's warning. He dives for Marshal Levalley's wife, who is bound and gagged on a chair in the living room of their home in Ravenshoe, Florida, leaving the agent no choice but to fire.

Since his aim isn't hindered by a steering wheel and the body of a mangled car, he shoots the assailant in the knee and shoulder, bringing him down along with the knife he intended to slit across Lania's throat.

"The perp has been contained," Macy says down her cell phone, twisting away from the monitor displaying the action occurring hundreds of miles away. "Your wife is rattled but okay…"

Her voice drowns out when Alex Rogers, Grayson's brother, yanks the balaclava down the killer's face.

"Jesus Christ," I murmur, matching Grayson's sentiments to a T when the assailant is exposed as female. It is the rookie recruitment officer Marshal Levalley took under his wing at his last placement. She looks barely over the age of twenty-five.

"Organize secure transport. I want her here *and* alive."

The cult membership numbers are in the thousands, but we only have a few dozen names on our list, so if we want any chance of narrowing it down, we need her alive and capable of speaking.

"I'm not bringing her to you." Alex snarls at his reflection in the entryway mirror of Marshal Levalley's family home. "If you want to talk to her, you can come here."

"She's my fucking target," Grayson shouts.

"Who was caught in my jurisdiction," Alex fires back.

While the brothers continue arguing, Macy stores away her cell before twisting to face me. Her smile isn't one I expected to see today, but it makes sense when she says, "We've found her. Henley is alive and well. In his relief, Marshal Levalley gave up her location. She is in a hospital in Newark." She tosses me a set of keys. "That's Grayson's baby, so if you get a scratch on it, he will kill you."

I'm out the door before half her threat leaves her mouth.

When I encroach a bed in the middle of an intensive care unit, I'm confident the officers standing guard outside the unit told me the wrong bed number. The woman in the bed looks nothing like Henley. Her hair is dark and stormy, sitting just above the bandage hiding a horrific knife wound on her neck. A mottling of bruises and cuts obscures her freckles, and her hospital gown and the bedding keeping her warm from the AC hide her sweltering curves.

She looks so different. Even if the man who killed her mother stood across from her, he wouldn't recognize her.

The man who startles me should be grateful I removed my gun before entering the hospital. "We had to change her look to hide her identity." Marshal Levalley steps closer to the machines keeping Henley alive. He looks as tired as me, his eyes just as wet. "It is all reversible, but from what I'm hearing, we won't be able to do that for a little while."

My eyes shoot to him in silent questioning.

Mercifully, he can read me better than I can Macy.

"She is the only person who can identify her mother's killer."

"By a tattoo potentially thousands of people have."

I'm knocked back two spaces when he confesses, "She saw his eyes too." He licks his lips that appear as if they won't stop quivering for days. "I left it out of the report. I didn't know why at the time. I just knew I had to."

"Then why did you write her up? If you had kept her name out of all reports, she wouldn't be here, fighting for her life."

That's a lie. Leroy would have still come because he knew what I was too scared to admit.

Henley had crawled under my skin. She had imprinted herself on me. But now I might lose her, and I'm the most scared I've ever been.

Shame flares through Levalley's eyes. It is quick, but it exposes everything.

"What does he have on you?"

"She," he corrects, too scared to continue lying while reminding me we hardly know anything about the cult running rampant through the bureau. "She knew about my affair with one of the witnesses under my watch. She threatened to tell my wife if I didn't bring you in for questioning and place her name on official reports." He looks at Henley when he says "her."

"Your partner?" I query, certain I'm wrong. Their taunt is to have us walking a tightrope above hell, so why would she punish him for the most godawful act a married man can do?

He shakes his head, a tear in his eye almost falling. "This goes far higher than a handful of law enforcement officers missing a promotion." We're interrupted by a blonde in a stiff black suit, an angry snarl on her face as she waves Marshal Levalley over. "I have to go." He angles his head to hide his lips from the officers in the hallway. "If you want her to stay alive, trust no one." He backtracks on his warning almost immediately. "Except perhaps her." He nudges his head to Macy, who's barging through the procession of IA officers like they're below her. "She'll never admit it, but I know she knew all along that Henley was with you. She is a good agent, but she is a shit liar."

After a final remorseful stare at Henley, he dips his head in farewell, then approaches the agents waiting to handcuff him.

32

HENLEY

*a*n argument wakes me.

"Is it true? Did you know Henley was fronting as my nanny the entire time?"

Oh no.

I fight my eyes to open, to bring me out of the stupor hurting every inch of my body, but no matter how hard I fight, my eyes remain shut.

"Not the entire time." I recognize the voice of the woman replying to Brodie's question. We only spoke for a few minutes, but when I freaked out about possibly going undercover with Beau's crew again, she took me to the courtyard for a breather.

Apart from Brodie, Macy was the only agent who didn't look down her nose at me. She was nice. Almost too nice. If she hadn't trusted me, I probably would have been waking up with a thumping head in Beau's bed for the hundredth time this year.

"I saw her looking at you, but everyone was." My lips wrangle into a grin when Macy says, "You're a single dad, for crying out loud, and you look like that. Of course she'd look!"

"Then why did Levalley say you knew she was with me?" Brodie's voice isn't as angst-filled as it was only seconds ago. More relieved.

A faint memory trickles into my head when Macy replies, "I pinched a buffer disc when you weren't looking the morning I visited your home." Feet scuffling on the ground sounds through my water-logged ears. "Her father wasn't just a brilliant agent. He could turn a pile of junk into a showroom piece." My smile doesn't hurt as much this time around. "Henley must have learned some skills from him, because your bike was in showroom condition." I imagine her plonking onto her seat and resting her head in her hands with a flop, which is quickly followed by mumbled words. "I knew Levalley was hiding something, so I thought it would be best to leave Henley with you until I found out what it was. She was safer with you than with him."

"Lucy—"

My heart breaks at the mention of her name. I doubt she'll ever forgive me for how I shoved her into my suitcase and fixed the zipper and lock into place. I had to do something to make her stay.

The first time I left the closet, she followed me out. She said since she had wished for me, it was her job to protect me and that she loved me too much to watch me get hurt.

I assured her I'd be fine, that her daddy and uncle had taught me how to defend myself, and that they were good teachers.

That kept her in the closet until the killer threw me down the stairs.

Lucy whacked and kicked into him with everything she had, so much so that he soon joined me on the landing.

He looked up at her like he hated her and snarled about her being just like her mother.

That's when I realized he was going to kill her too.

I had to move quickly to find Lucy a safe hiding place. It wasn't the most practical location, but I figured with my headphones over her ears, blasting her favorite tunes, she might stay still enough during my fightback to keep the killer's focus on me.

I'd only just hoisted the suitcase on top of the closet when he kicked down the door. I'm not exactly sure how long I held him off. Things began blurring when he stabbed me in the stomach.

He was searching for Lucy when I heard Brodie call my name, but the gash in my throat didn't allow me to warn him.

Mercifully, he found us before the killer found Lucy.

"Lucy was never in any danger, Brodie," Macy pushes out, hearing the torment in Brodie's voice as well as I am. "I had an agent at your place the entire time."

Brodie's roar bounces around the room. "An agent who died!"

"Because this case was never about Henley."

What? How isn't this about me? I brought the Night Killer back into Brodie's life. I risked his daughter's life because I was sick of being pushed around by snobby agents with misguided agendas.

This is my fault. Isn't it?

"Leroy..." A growl completes Brodie's sentence, but I miss the rest of what he says since I'm repeating the name he spoke in my head.

I swear that was the name of the man at the barbecue. The man Lucy didn't like. Since he gave off creeper vibes, I didn't reprimand Lucy for being short with him when he tried to stop her from charging up the footpath after Nathan Banks told her she looked fat. I told him it was girls' business before closing the pool room door in his face and comforting a teary-eyed almost-six-year-old.

"Leroy is only the surface of this investigation, Brodie. We still have a mountain of evidence to go through." Macy breathes out heavily before the pad of her feet inching toward my bed quickens my pulse. "But before that, we need to get her somewhere safe." There's a slight pause before, "I know somewhere I can take her."

My eyes are still refusing to open, so I can't see Brodie, but I picture his head shaking when the scent of his aftershave filters in the air. "She can stay with me."

"That isn't possible, Brodie. These people are trained operatives across the board in our industry. They'll find her fast, which means they will also find Lucy."

"Then we will go into WP with her."

I smile at Lucy's inclusion in his "we," but it only lasts as long as I take to recall how lonely witness protection is. There's no life in witness protection. No laughter. The light that has only just been relit in Brodie's and Lucy's eyes would be snuffed instantly.

"No..." I think that comes out of my mouth. It might sound more like a groan than a stern denial, but a squeak is better than silence.

"Henley." Brodie's body temperature is so skyrocketing when he curls his hand over mine fisted at my side that the zap it sparks up my arm is intense.

As I fight my eyes to open, Brodie instructs, "Grab a nurse." The door opens and closes before he demands, "Don't overexert yourself. You fought enough. It's time for you to rest now."

I blink and blink and blink until my vision finally clears, and I spot Brodie leaning over me. His hair is pulled back in a mannish bun, and his beard is more scraggily than usual, but he is still devastatingly gorgeous.

"Hey." He pushes back a dark strand of hair hindering my vision, his hand shaky but unable to take away from the relief in his eyes, before he asks, "Is that better?"

I nod, and it hurts like hell.

Hold on... a dark strand of hair?

When my eyes shoot up to the hairs tickling my brows, Brodie announces, "They cut and colored your hair. I hope you like bangs." His laugh is as fake as his pledge. "They suit you."

Although peeved they cut my hair without permission, I'll be more annoyed if they steal Lucy's childhood from her like they stole my formative adult years from me.

"You..." That burned more than you can imagine.

"Can she have water?"

I sling my eyes to the side of the room when Brodie projects his question that way.

A nurse in scrubs jerks up her chin before moving to the bedside to fill a cup. "Slow slips."

Pure. Heaven.

Once I have enough wetness in my throat to speak, I lock eyes with Brodie and say, "You can't co-come with me. Lucy—"

"Is already angry at me," he interrupts. "She wanted to come see you." His eyes bounce around my face. "I didn't think you would want her to see you like this, so I made her stay with Thane and Amelia."

Knowing Amelia is here makes me smile, but it doesn't alter the facts. He's right. I don't want Lucy to see me like this. The last image I have of her is her tear-stained face, but I'd pick it over the image reflecting in Brodie's massively dilated eyes now.

I look wretched.

"Sh-she needs her family as much as th-they need her." Since he can't deny my claims, he remains quiet. "My father hid us away so well I didn't have anyone to fall back on when he passed. They showed up at his funeral, then just left. I had no one." A ghost-like grin spreads across my face. "Until I met Amelia and then eventually you." My brows furrow as my confusion clears. "I always thought it was Lucy I was drawn to that day, but it wasn't." The remorse clouding his eyes clears away a smidge when I whisper, "It was you. But you wouldn't be half the man you are without Lucy, and she wouldn't be half who she is without Caroline's family." He grips my hand harder when I say, "She needs them in her life, Brodie, and I need to make this right."

"It's not your job."

"It is," I deny. "I should have fought harder. I should have kept shouting until someone listened to me."

"You were a child."

"Then," I reply. "I'm not anymore. I am a grown woman who can make her own decisions." The tension shifts from angsty to lusty when the remembrance of me saying that to him when he told me I was too young to fuck a thirty-seven-year-old man pops into my head. "And I'm choosing to do this. I'm choosing to use my voice as you have for the victims over the past sixteen years." When he scoffs, I murmur, "Don't let one batch of rotten apples ruin it for the rest of them. There are more good agents than bad."

Brodie's surprised eyes dance between mine. "You know he was an agent?"

I nod. It doesn't hurt as much this time around. "Curtains offer as little privacy as a two-way bathroom." When I laugh, everywhere hurts. "I'm sorry."

"For laughing?" Brodie asks as he watches a doctor check that my pain medication is being adequately distributed through my IV drip.

His eyes snap back to mine when I murmur, "For lying. I-I—"

"It's okay," Brodie interrupts, uncaring of my reason. "We all make mistakes."

"Is-is that what I was? A mistake?"

"No," he answers immediately, taking my pain away better than the needle the doctor jabs into my IV. "Was I to you?"

Macy's giggle fills the room when I say, "Maybe."

I'm a liar, but sometimes lies are needed when you're trying to ease a man's guilt.

The past two weeks were some of the best of my life, but Brodie and I hardly know each other, so I refuse to let his guilt force him to accept the blame for something he didn't do.

The pain relief the doctor inserts into my IV makes my words groggy, so I have no choice but to move quickly. "Will you do something for me?"

Brodie's immediate answer exposes that my worry about guilt fueling his responses was accurate. "Anything."

"Will you call Lucy for me?" His hand freezes halfway into his jeans pocket when I whisper, "I don't want to leave without saying goodbye."

EPILOGUE
BRODIE

Four months later...

*W*hen I peer at Lucy to gauge her response about our last candidate, she rolls her eyes. "Her breath smelled like tuna, and her feet were gross. Has she never heard of a pedicure?" She stumbles on her last word. "It's a no from me."

I look at Thane, who is just as invested as Lucy in finding Henley's replacement. I'm hoping he will help me outvote Lucy two to one, but instead, he shakes his head.

While grumbling under my breath, I cross out the name of the nanny we had just interviewed. She was candidate number eight. "At this rate, we're going to run out of candidates."

Lucy smiles, pleased by my response.

I swipe her happiness out from beneath her. "If you want Henley to ever return, we need to do this. I thought we agreed on that?"

It's been four months, but Lucy still can't help but immediately respond when Henley enters the conversation. She cried enough tears to fill a river when Henley told her she had to leave, but for once, I cherished her stubbornness when she refused to let Henley off the hook until she made her promise she wouldn't be gone forever.

"Promise me you will come back," she begged that morning. "You're my wish. I wished for you, so you cannot leave unless you promise to return. Promise me, Henley. *Please.*"

The darkness that ran through me when the doctors listed Henley's extensive injuries lightened a smidge when Henley murmured, "I promise."

"What time is the next candidate arriving?" I ask Thane, exhausted.

I've been burning the candle at both ends for the past few months. Lucy hasn't slept through the night since the incident that had her reliving her mother's death, even with her not being old enough to remember it. I work a minimum of twelve hours a day, usually at night with Lucy snuggled on the couch in my office, on the case files Macy keeps me updated on even though I'm not officially under the FBI banner anymore.

I've gone private, but there is only one case I am working on right now.

The one that will allow Henley to keep her promise to Lucy.

The one that will bring her home.

Twenty-three arrests have been made in the past four months. It is predicted that there will be another dozen by the end of the year. The end is in sight, but it still seems so far away.

Thane checks his clipboard like any good PA would before reminding me I was stupid to hire him to help me get my new business off the ground while endeavoring to be a hands-on father. "I forgot to write down what time she said." He shrugs. "My bad?"

He's shit at timekeeping and anything to do with a computer. If I were smart, I would have hired him as Lucy's nanny instead of my assistant. He is the only reason I haven't burned out the past few months. He keeps Lucy occupied while I get a couple of hours of shuteye during the day, but I can't keep going like this or I'll end up in a grave.

"I already told you no," Thane says, spotting my arched brow. "I love you, Lulu, and I'm proud you can wipe your own butt, but you've not yet learned that towels are not tissues."

Lucy giggles at her uncle's comment while shadowing him out of my home office. We moved again, the two weeks of memories at the last house not enough to overtake the image of Henley propped up lifelessly on the closet in her room.

Our new home is bigger than the last. It has five bedrooms and two detached bathrooms, and the main room has an ensuite and a brand-new king-size bed. We went for a recently revamped old house since the creak of floorboards can be the difference between life and death.

I purchased it with the money I got from the life insurance policy Caroline took out in her name. Since she believed my job would take me away from our family before her, the payout figure was far less than what Lucy will be awarded in the event of my death.

It was still plenty, but not close to what we lost when Leroy killed her.

My thoughts are dragged back to the present when Thane says, "Ah... should she be kissing that?" He nudges his head to Lucy, who's holding a massive bullfrog an inch from her puckered lips.

"Don't—" My warning comes too late. Lucy kisses the frog.

"Now she's got warts too." Thane dumps his empty coffee mug into the dishwasher. "I'm one hundred percent out." He salutes me, noogies Lucy's head, then exits the kitchen via a door at the back of the room.

"Not a good kisser?" I ask Lucy when she lets the frog escape with her uncle.

"It was okay." I laugh when her face screws up as she licks her lips. "But he's no prince."

My heart clenches when she climbs onto the barstool beneath the island counter. She looks so tired. Little bags circle her eyes, and they're puffy and red.

I can't wait to end this nightmare for her. I am working on it every single day. We're close, so very, *very* close, but it will have to wait a couple more hours because my daughter needs me more right now.

"How about we cancel the rest of the interviews today, have a glass of warm milk, and then an afternoon catnap?"

I'm prepared for Lucy to rile me about day sleeping, so you can imagine my shock when a voice behind me prickles the hairs on the back of my neck. "Milk? I was once told a glass of warm water was the best cure for restlessness."

"Henley!" Lucy screams so loudly the window rattles.

She's off the barstool and racing across the kitchen before I can spin around.

When my body finally listens to the signals firing from my tired brain, my mind is overloaded for the second time this year. Long legs, a sweltering midsection, and shorts—*those goddamn fucking shorts*—that should be illegal confront me.

Henley's hair is back to its natural coloring, but the length remains the same as the last time I saw her. Excluding the faintest sliver of silver running across her delicate neck, she is without a single blemish.

Well, if you don't class freckles as blemishes.

I don't. Particularly when they belong to a woman as beautiful as Henley.

After bobbing down to remove the tears careening down Lucy's face, Henley balances her on her hip like she didn't turn the big six only weeks ago, before she slowly strolls my way.

The tension is still there.

The heat.

I just do a horrendously poor job of hiding it this time around.

My hand is so clammy, when Henley holds hers out in offering, it almost skids across her palm when I accept her friendly gesture.

After hiding her grimace, Henley greets, "Hi, I'm Henley Elsher. Your new nanny."

Over Lucy's ecstatic squeals, and while shaking Henley's hand, I reply, "Brodie Davis. The father promising you will be *way* more than that." Before I tug her in close and seal my lips over hers.

BONUS CHAPTER
HENLEY

Earlier...

I've never been one for stargazing, but today's sky is a peculiar blue. It is almost translucent, meaning even with it being only a little after noon, several stars are poking through the haze of pollution that forever clogs city skylines.

Or perhaps it's the wetness in my eyes that no number of "harden up" comments can dry.

I'm so sick of being trodden on and mistreated. It is an endless cycle of "do this" and "do that."

My thoughts and opinions don't matter.

Not even my mental stability does.

I'm just a prop to the people who brought me here.

A gimmick to be used and abused.

My father would roll in his grave if he saw how his colleagues have treated me. I'm tired of being puppeteered. I just want a minute to remember what it was like to attend a party without wondering if your so-called boyfriend is spiking your drinks or if you'll stumble onto the man who killed your mother when you wake up hungover after not touching a drop of alcohol.

I want to live so badly that I'd even go back to the shameful teenage years if it were all that was offered.

I was one of those awkward-legs-too-long-for-their-body girls at school. I had no idea how to control the natural kinks of my snow-white hair and no desire to learn a good skin routine. Why suffer through unjust protocols when my mother's teachings on self-worth assured me time and time again that even the ugliest duckling would eventually flourish into a beautiful swan?

Don't shred her to pieces just yet. Her wording will forever be more elegant than mine. She raised me with a backbone strong enough to render me unscathed through my gawky teen years, but regretfully, that steel rod crumbled like chalk on a poorly constructed driveway when I lost her.

My wavy locks are now under control, and my makeup is appealing despite its blandness, but I haven't known who I am for a long time. The shell is unchanged. It is as firm and presentable as the girl who stood on the front steps of a local police department, demanding to speak to someone in charge, like it wouldn't be the last nail in my family's coffin.

My insides are hollow.

There's no warmth about me.

No spark.

My eyes are dull and lifeless... much like hers.

As my eyes follow a little girl's trek across the courtyard reflecting the haze of a hot day, my heart rate kicks up a beat. Her nose is as cute as a button, her eyes as brown as the earth she should be terrorizing, but there's no fire in her engine, no true signs of life.

She looks a little lost, and I wonder how similar our predicaments are when the man racing her across the empty courtyard drops to his knees to tie up her loose shoelace.

He's doing everything right. The hair ruffle after securing her trip hazard, and the sneaky grin when she huffs about his overbearing nature, but he can't give her the one thing she wants more than anything.

A mother.

Her little pout announces this, much less what the man says when his focus shifts back to the cell phone attached to his ear. "I was meant to be here by ten, but Lucy's new nanny missed her train. Nancy said Ms. Seabourn won't arrive until four." He glances down at Lucy, who looked up when he said her name, before scanning the building of glass and steel several feet in front of her. "Grayson said I could bring her with me, but I don't know if that's a good idea."

"No, I'm here..." He spins away, making it hard to eavesdrop on the rest of his conversation. "I'm in the courtyard by the west entrance. Could you watch her for a little bit?" He stops and grinds his back molars. "You know I don't have anyone to watch her. If I did, I wouldn't have accepted a placement from the other side of the country." I can't see his face, but I picture his smirk when he murmurs, "Of course you'd think I overstepped the mark with my previous nannies." Another pause. "How? This is the first time we've left the house in months!"

He continues toward the main building, tugging a disgruntled Lucy with him.

They're only just out of earshot when I'm startled to within an inch of my grave. "He's a little old for you, isn't he?"

With a roll of my eyes, I twist my torso to the familiar voice. Agent Macy Machini smiles a blinding grin before angling her head to the side and twisting her lips. "Are you ready?" She gestures to the skyscraper on her right. "They're waiting for you."

"How long are they wanting me to go under this time?"

My nails dig into my palm when she answers with a sigh. "I don't know. But you can back out at any time. No one will hold it against you. You've given them more than enough."

"But?" I ask, aware there is always more.

I've been guilt-tripped into doing things I would have never done if my father were alive. The regularly used line is "Then he will go free." He—as in the man who killed my mother.

Macy rubs my arm but doesn't free me from the guilt enough for me not to follow her to a conference room most likely bursting at the seams with federal agents who'd rather see me dead than protect me.

The knowledge makes me desperate to mix things up, but I'm lost on how to end the cruel cycle that's been my life as of late.

That is until my eyes lock on a murky-brown pair at the end of the corridor.

Lucy is seated on a chair outside the FBI director's office, kicking her legs back and forth. She looks on the verge of tears. It is understandable when you spot the hideous finger puppets the director's secretary is trying to entertain her with. They're as old and ghastly as the wrinkles scoured in her face and dustier than the cobwebs I'm sure no one has cleaned out from between her legs in the past century.

I've seen many horrendous things in my short life. However, this one pains me more than I care to admit. Mrs. Boucher isn't doing anything to upset Lucy, but it takes everything I have not to rip the stupid finger puppets off her fingers and ram them down her throat.

The only reason I don't is because I have more pressing matters to deal with.

"I need to use the bathroom."

Macy's arched brow reveals her shock, but she hides it well. "Sure. They're down the end of the hallway and to the right." She removes her credentials from her neck. "You'll need these to get back in."

I snatch the lanyard out of her hand before hightailing it in the direction she gestured. To ensure my ruse doesn't get busted before it's fully implemented, I angle my head to the side to shield my face with my hair as I bypass Lucy.

My breath catches when my eyes lock on Lucy's father seated across from a plump man with a salt-and-pepper mustache. His shoulders are sitting as low as his daughter's, his face as sorrow filled. He is utterly miserable yet oddly endearing at the same time.

I'm so taken aback that I crash into the receptionist's desk instead of veering past it.

"Are you okay, dear?"

"Yes, I'm fine." My stern and snappy tone is the only thing stopping me from swearing.

When I peer down to inspect the damage caused to my thigh, my breath catches in my throat for the third time today. The director's appointment book is open. It is settled on today's date and exposes the name of the man currently sitting with the director.

Agent Brodie Davis.

"But do you need to sit in the middle of the walkway?" With my eyes locked on the lady I'm guessing is close to triple my age, I grip the open page of the planner, then push back on her desk. "You could really hurt someone."

The shredding of the page from the planner is hidden by the receptionist barking back with a bite sterner than I thought she'd have. "If you had been watching where you were going—"

I lose the rest of her reply when I jog to the end of the hall, scan Macy's credentials over the electronic lock next to the restroom, then sprint into the open space like twenty agents are hot on my tail.

"You are insane. I can't let you do this. Her father is a federal agent."

As I scan my eyes over the closest train station to the Davis resi-dence, I reply to my best friend's warning. "I'm not doing this for him. I am doing it for her." When she groans, I say, "She's so lost, Amelia. She doesn't know who she is." My last sentence gets her over the fence. "I don't know who I am either."

"Hen—"

"Please," I beg. "I'll never ask you for anything ever again if you will help me do this."

Her silence kills me.

It literally shreds me to pieces.

Then it is a godsend. "Okay. I'll help you." It wouldn't be Amelia if she didn't add on a list of demands for her services. "But since you're adamant our search must be reserved to the nanny agency, I'll be anticipating a ton of visual prompts to be coming my way. A girl can't be expected to work for free..."

She continues jabbering until Ms. Seabourn is identified and returned to the West Coast, and I've purchased a cell phone capable of taking ungrainy images.

The rest of our story is history.

If you enjoyed this story, please consider leaving a review.

Facebook: facebook.com/authorshandi

Instagram: instagram.com/authorshandi

Email: authorshandi@gmail.com

Reader's Group: bit.ly/ShandiBookBabes

Website: authorshandi.com

Newsletter: subscribepage.com/AuthorShandi

ALSO BY SHANDI BOYES

Denotes Standalone Books

Perception Series

Saving Noah *

Fighting Jacob *

Taming Nick *

Redeeming Slater *

Saving Emily

Wrapped Up with Rise Up

Enigma

Enigma

Unraveling an Enigma

Enigma The Mystery Unmasked

Enigma: The Final Chapter

Beneath The Secrets

Beneath The Sheets

Spy Thy Neighbor *

The Opposite Effect *

I Married a Mob Boss *

Second Shot *

The Way We Are

The Way We Were

Sugar and Spice *

Lady In Waiting

Man in Queue

Couple on Hold

Enigma: The Wedding

Silent Vigilante

Hushed Guardian

Quiet Protector

Enigma: An Isaac Retelling

Twisted Lies *

Bound Series

Chains

Links

Bound

Restrain

The Misfits *

Russian Mob Chronicles

Nikolai: A Mafia Prince Romance

Nikolai: Taking Back What's Mine

Nikolai: What's Left of Me

Nikolai: Mine to Protect

Asher: My Russian Revenge *

Nikolai: Through the Devil's Eyes

Trey *

The Italian Cartel

Dimitri

Roxanne

Reign

Mafia Ties (Novella)

Maddox

Demi

Ox

Rocco *

Clover *

Smith *

RomCom Standalones

Just Playin' *

Ain't Happenin' *

The Drop Zone *

Very Unlikely *

False Start *

Short Stories - Newsletter Downloads

Christmas Trio *

Falling For A Stranger *

One Night Only Series

Hotshot Boss *

Hotshot Neighbor *

The Bobrov Bratva Series

Wicked Intentions *

Sinful Intentions *

Devious Intentions *

Deadly Intentions *

Coming Soon

Nanny Dispute *

Protecting Nicole (November 23)